Losing Beauty

Johanna Garth

Copyright © 2011 Johanna Garth

All rights reserved. Except as permitted under the U.S. Copyright Act of 1976, no part of this publication may be reproduced, distributed or transmitted in any form or by any means, or stored in a database or retrieval system without the prior written permission of the publisher.

This is a work of fiction. Names, characters, places and incidents are products of the author's imagination or are used fictitiously and are not to be construed as real. Any resemblance to actual events, locales, organizations, or persons, living or deceased, is entirely coincidental

ISBN-13: 978-0-615-54612-4

(Fantasy Island Book Publishing)

ISBN-10: 0615546129

Credits:

Front Cover By Ceri Clark

Senior Editor: Pamela Brennan

Structural Design: J. Darroll Hall

Fantasy Island Book Publishing

Contact us at: **www.fantasyislandbookpublishing.com**

For Jared, who gave me the time and encouragement to write, Savannah, who was always certain I would get published and Sebastian, who still isn't quite old enough to read.

Prologue

"I've been to hell and back." Persey Campbell heard this all the time but she knew people didn't mean it the way she did. To the people who said it, it was just an expression, a more colorful way to express the pain and gravity of their suffering. They didn't know what hell was like and it wasn't her job to tell them.

Her job was to listen, and that's what she did. She accepted the outpouring of their deepest, darkest secrets wherever they chanced to find her; in coffee shops and bars, one time waiting in line at the grocery store. It was her beauty that caught their attention, drawing them in like the hypnotic sway of a cobra. Then the dark, uncomfortable part of her she never understood did the rest.

She inspired their confessions. They told her things and she listened. It was all part of the deal. Her beauty was the lure and what lay beneath was the trap. She wished she could warn them, tell them to run from her before it was too late, but she couldn't. That was the other part of the deal. She got to be beautiful but she never, ever got to tell the truth.

Chapter One

The first time Haden laid eyes on Persey she was sitting on top of a giant pumpkin at the annual Harvest Festival in Clear Lake, Iowa. Clear Lake was part of the great American Midwest that Haden sometimes passed through on his ventures away from home. Advance reconnaissance was how he thought of it.

In this modern age, few of them still believed in the kind of danger Haden presented. He was free. He could wander their world undetected. They remained unaware of his true nature until the cold fingers of death fell upon them. It was mesmerizing to watch. Understanding bloomed in their faces at the same moment as their most precious gift, the one thing that fascinated him, waned and flickered. Then it was gone, leaving behind nothing but a soul. Souls didn't fascinate Haden. Life, in all its excruciating brevity and heat, is what Haden preferred.

In the late afternoon sunshine of early October, the Clear Lake Harvest Festival was full of life. A jazz band played while a group of children shimmied their hips, whipping the plastic loop around and around, underneath a hand-lettered sign announcing the "Harvest Festival Hula Hoop Contest."

Further down the street, the flash of a camera caught Haden's eye. A photographer was snapping pictures of a pretty young girl while a small crowd of people watched. Haden joined the onlookers as the girl, on top of her oversized pumpkin, posed for the camera.

"Hold up the ribbon, sweetie," directed one of the photographers. The girl pushed her blonde curls out of her face as she reached down for the blue rosette pinned to the side of her pumpkin. "That's it. Now look this way," said the photographer.

The man standing next to Haden let out a chuckle. "Don't come much sweeter than that one," he said, glancing sideways at Haden. The man's lined face looked as though he'd spent many an

Iowa summer harvesting crops. His arms were crossed over the ample regions of his flannel covered stomach.

Haden nodded. "You know her?"

The man chuckled and rocked back a bit on the heels of his work boots. "I guess you must be new to town then," he said.

It was a statement not a question, the kind that invites explanation. It was on the tip of Haden's tongue to tell the man he was just passing through, on his way to visit his sister in California. This was the kind of thing he usually said in response to these types of questions. Except at that moment, the cameras stopped flashing, the photographers moved aside and the girl's deep blue eyes met his. Haden looked at her and for the first time in memory, he couldn't see anything at all.

The words he'd been planning to say died an instant death. All he wanted to do was stare at the girl. Instead he forced himself to say, in the folksy tones of small town Iowa, "Yep, I just got into town today."

"Well now," said the man with another chuckle. "I knew you couldn't be from around these parts, cause most everyone knows the Campbell family. That there's Persephone Campbell, everyone calls her Persey. Looks like she's going to be in the paper tomorrow, don't it? It's her second year winning the pumpkin contest. Won't tell a soul how she gets those things to grow so big but everyone knows it's her mother's doings. That woman could touch a graveyard and bring something to life."

An attractive woman with dark hair stood a few feet behind the girl. Although there was no particular resemblance between the two, something about the woman's expression seemed maternal. "Is that her mother?" asked Haden.

"Sure is," said the man. Then, as though something about the tone of Haden's questions struck him as suspicious, he asked, "You visiting family?"

"No," replied Haden. He quickly flipped through the eternal rolodex of death in his mind before he added, "I'm the new librarian."

The man's face brightened, reaching over and shaking Haden's hand, he said, "Pete Miller, mighty pleased to meet you. I'm down at the library couple times a week. Damn shame about Mrs. Powell. Not to say we aren't happy to get a new librarian."

He held up one hand as though Haden was about to argue with him. "But it's sad to see a good woman pass like that. She couldn't have been more than sixty."

"Sixty-two," Haden said automatically.

Pete nodded in agreement. "I do believe you're right. Sorry, I didn't catch your name."

"Haden Sarantos."

"Sarantos," said Pete, rolling the word through his mouth, "That Greek?"

"Something like that," said Haden, glancing back at Persey.

The photographers were finished and she had slid down off her pumpkin. She took her mother's hand and Haden watched as the top of her golden head bobbed away from him through the crowd.

"You a coffee drinker, Haden?" asked Pete, interrupting Haden's thoughts. Without waiting for a reply he added, "We got a brand new Starbucks just a couple blocks down. It'd be my pleasure to buy the new librarian a cup of coffee."

"Sounds good," said Haden with a smile.

He followed Pete down Main Avenue toward the lake, allowing the older man to usher him inside the coffee shop. The barista behind the counter grinned at Pete as they entered.

"Hey Mr. Miller, caramel macchiato today?" she said.

"That's right Susan, and whatever my friend Haden's drinking." Pete said, handing her a ten dollar bill.

They picked up their drinks and Pete steered Haden toward two unoccupied armchairs.

"It's a nice festival," said Haden as he sat down, "And a lucky little girl today."

Pete settled his bulk into the chair next to Haden. He took a long sip of his drink while he considered Haden over the rim of his cup. "Not as lucky as you might think," he said at last.

Haden feigned a look of concern, adding, "Why not?"

Pete paused and let out a long sigh. "Mind you, this isn't the kind of thing I'd normally tell a stranger, but seeing's how you're the new librarian and all, I imagine you'll hear it sooner or later. I reckon you'd be better off hearing the truth instead of someone else's cockamamie ideas."

Haden set his coffee cup down and waited for Pete to get on with the story.

"You see," said Pete in a somber voice. "I know all about it because I was the first one on the scene after Mike Campbell's accident. That's Persey's daddy, the little girl back there that won the pumpkin contest," he added, as though Haden was in need of a reminder. "I held his hand until the ambulance got there. He made me promise to look out for Demi, that's his wife. 'Look out for my girl.' Those were his exact words to me."

Pete swallowed hard and twisted the brown paper cup holder on his coffee cup several times before he continued. "You've never seen anybody half as much in love as Demi and Mike Campbell. After the accident, most of the town figured she was headed straight for the loony bin, that's how sick she was with missing him. She took it real hard, that's for sure." He shifted in his chair and twisted his cup holder several more times.

"I take it she didn't end up in the loony bin," said Haden.

"That's right," said Pete. "Nobody had a clue she was already in a family way. The Campbell family was all so torn up about losing that boy of theirs that they didn't pay no mind to his poor little wife. I don't believe they were ever too fond of her to begin with. The Campbells are a real proud bunch and they had a hard time getting over the way Mike up and married her so quick with no one knowing anything about her family. Can't imagine how hard it must have been for her after he passed. Anyway, a couple months after it happened, I says to Becky, that's my wife, I says, Becky, someone's got to check in on that girl. I don't believe anyone's seen her since the funeral."

"The next day, Becky drives out to the old farmhouse to look in on her, and finds her there—all alone, sick as a dog and half crazy with grief. Demi told Becky, then and there, she was expecting a baby but she begged her not to tell anyone. She said she was afraid her mother-in-law would make her come live with them and she said she couldn't imagine anything worse, poor girl." Pete punctuated this statement with a shake of his head.

"Now my Becky's got the softest heart you ever could want, she took it on herself to go out there a couple times a week after that. Mind you, she kept the girl's secret all right, but after the baby was born…it all came out. There was talk about whether Demi was stable enough to take care of herself, let alone a baby. Becky got real worried, so she sat Demi down and told her she'd better pull herself together, if she had any intention of raising that little girl herself. And sure enough, she did. Most people around these parts will tell you Persey gave her mother a reason to live. You can sure see why. She's so pretty it hurts your eyes a bit, don't it?"

Haden nodded and attempted to arrange his face into the proper expression of commiseration before asking, "So what happened to her father? How did he die?"

"Car accident," said Pete, setting his coffee cup down on the table. "Some kind a critter ran out in front of him and he swerved to miss it. Car hit the gravel and rolled a couple times. Doctors did everything they could, but in the end it didn't amount to much. God rest his soul."

Haden took a sip of his coffee, trying to recollect the soul of Mike Campbell, before dismissing it as unmemorable. What came to mind instead was the image of Persey's deep blue unknowable eyes.

Pete was now warmed to the sound of his own voice. Mistaking Haden's silence for rapt attention, he moved on to other topics of local interest. "Sure was a shame about Mrs. Powell. Her family's planning a nice little memorial service up at the Methodist church. I can put a word in if you'd like to come. Might mean a lot to them," he said, wagging his head once again. "Poor lady, but doggonit if she didn't go doing what she loved best. Her son told me she was rearranging the periodicals and they found her laying right there on the floor, looking real peaceful. God bless her, anyway, isn't that right?" He pulled out a handkerchief and blew his nose. His watery eyes looked over the top waiting for confirmation of his sentiments.

This second invocation of God reminded Haden he'd reached his limit for charades. He picked up his coffee cup and stood up. "Thanks for the coffee, Pete," he said.

"I guess you've got to get on your way then," said Pete with a disappointed smile.

"I do," said Haden. "But I'll look for you at the library."

"Well, good to meet you," said Pete giving Haden a mock salute. Haden returned the gesture then exited the coffee shop before Pete could dislodge himself from his chair. It was ironic, Haden thought as he made his way back towards the bustling center of town, how many of them lived exactly as they died.

'Doing what they loved,' was how Pete phrased it. It would certainly hold true for Pete. The heart attack would happen in two years' time. Haden whistled a jaunty tune as he walked along, thinking about Pete Miller's last moments. They would be spent in the chair he currently occupied. Susan, the barista, would admonish him for carelessly spilling his caramel macchiato on the floor, before she realized Pete Miller had passed out of this life and into the next.

Chapter Two

The job at the library wasn't hard to arrange. The library board of directors accepted his credentials, with only the barest suggestion on his part, that he was the perfect candidate for the position. It was all too easy. Not like long ago, when he'd been acknowledged, worshiped and called by the name Hades. In ancient times, they recognized him as the incarnation of all they feared. They trembled in his presence. Now they were beyond such superstitious fears. If this was evolution, Haden was all for it. It meant death could walk among them. Their fearlessness and reliance on a world ruled by medicine and technology set him free.

Haden settled into his office, in a room just off the main children's reading room. Busying himself with administrative chores, he waited.

The first time Persey came to the library, he felt her. Her presence was a dark space—a hole where knowledge should be. She entered the room and filled it up with nothingness. He found her sitting on the carpeted floor, between the stacks of older children's books. She looked up as though she was expecting him. He crouched down in front of her and she inched away.

"Hello, Persey," he said, smiling at her.

"You know my name." She said it without wonder or surprise. It was as though his knowledge of her name was just another thing she expected.

"I read it in the newspaper," he said. "It was right under the picture of you sitting on your marvelous pumpkin. I'm Mr. Sarantos, the new head librarian."

He held his hand out to her. She stared at it like it was something she didn't want to touch. Then good manners took over and she allowed her soft childish flesh to touch his. Reluctance and suspicion washed over him but that was all. Her end remained a mystery.

His first instinct was to sweep her into his arms and steal her away. It was an option. He'd done it before but it hadn't ended well. In fact, it had been a disaster. He suppressed the shudder that the memory provoked and gently released the small perfectly formed hand.

Until this moment, he had almost convinced himself she wasn't human. How could she be? It was unheard of that a human's end would refuse to make itself known to the ruler of death. But now, here she was in front of him and she was clearly flesh and blood. Her heart pounded at the pulse point of her wrist. Her faint blue veins carried her life force to her organs and supplied color to her red mouth with its pouting cupid's bow. Her beauty made him ache and the mystery of her end—well, that made him ache a little bit too. She could and would die. The question was how, and when. He stared into the dark abyss of her eyes and weighed the unfamiliar thrill of intrigue.

A throat cleared behind him and he quickly stood up.

"Five more minutes, Pers," said a tall woman with dark hair.

Haden recognized her from the Harvest Festival as Demi Campbell. She smiled at Haden like he was someone she knew and trusted.

"She'd be here all day if I let her," said Demi.

"I understand the impulse."

Before Haden could introduce himself, Persey jumped up from the floor. "It's all right mommy," she said. "I'm ready to go."

"It's a miracle," said Demi Campbell, feigning shock.

Haden arranged his face in a kind smile as he watched them go. He'd halfway expected not to be able to see the child's mother. But there she was, as clear as all the rest. It would be twelve more years before cancer would come to claim her as its own, brain cancer, to be exact. Not an easy way to go.

Chapter Three

Over the next year, Haden made it his mission to befriend Persey. He discovered she was inclined to dislike him. Her aversion to him wasn't bothersome. In fact he found her instincts—reminiscent of peoples from long dead civilizations—appealing. What bothered him was how everything else about her was unknowable. Haden noticed he wasn't the only one attracted to the girl. Her third grade class visited the library every week and he observed how the other children were drawn to her. They searched for her when she was alone and whispered their childish secrets to her. She peered out from beneath her tumultuous curls, listening to what they had to say.

Persey was a voracious reader. Under Haden's watchful eye, he noticed her patiently set her book to one side, again and again, to listen to her classmate's childish confidences. She was a kind child, and because of this, she gave no outward display of frustration at these repeated interruptions. If not for his immortal powers, Haden would never have been able to sense the frustration and impatience that emanated from Persey at each interruption.

One afternoon, he found her, deep in the adult stacks, hidden from prying eyes and interruptions. She was engrossed in her book and didn't hear him when he walked up behind her.

"Persey," he whispered, tapping her on the shoulder.

She glanced up and her hot flash of annoyance sliced through him. He smiled and said, "Sorry, I hate it when people bother me when I'm reading, too. I just wanted to let you know, you can use my office to read, if you prefer. It's down the hallway off the children's reading room. You know the one?"

She nodded but didn't respond.

"There's an old couch inside and the light's much better than it is back here. Most of the time I'm not even in there, but I promise," he held up his hand, as though taking a vow, "when you're reading, I won't talk to you and no one else will either. It'll be your private place."

She looked at him and he thought he saw the faintest hint of a smile on her lips. Instead of pressing his advantage, Haden stood up and left her to mull it over.

It wasn't long before she took the bait. The following week there was a light knock on his door. "Mr. Sarantos?" she said. Her voice was so quiet, he almost didn't hear it.

"Come in," he said

She came into his office, and without looking at him, set a book marked with a small red dot on his desk. "Mrs. Swain said I need your permission to check this one out."

Mrs. Swain was the children's librarian at the Clear Lake Library. She believed one of the most important aspects of her job was to avoid causing offense to anyone in the community. She was serious about her commission and spent much of work day combing through the volumes of children's books, pressing small red dots onto the spines of any books listed on banned book lists. Children wishing to check out the red dot books, as she called them, were referred to Haden.

"It's just a little system I put in place to make sure I'm doing my job," she explained on Haden's first day at the library. "I'm the check and you're the balance."

Haden knew Mrs. Swain would die when she refused to go to the hospital after being rear-ended at a stop light. "Oh, I'm probably just fine," she would insist, despite the fact that her head had bounced off the dashboard of her car like a basketball, and she had a pounding headache. That night, while she slept, her brain would hemorrhage blood. In the end, the most egregious offense of Mrs. Swain's life would be the one visited upon her neighbor, who would discover her body four days later, in an advanced state of decomposition. Haden knew all this and yet, on occasion, he was still tempted to take the matter of Mrs. Swain's death into his own hands. Persey's sudden appearance in his office made him grateful for his self discipline.

"Let's see what you have," he said.

Persey handed him a copy of *The Bridge to Terabithia*.

"Pretty racy stuff," he said.

Her blue eyes studied him. "What do you mean?" she asked.

He shook his head and motioned for her to have a seat. "It was a bad attempt at sarcasm. Do you know what sarcasm is?"

She nodded and he quickly stamped the library card in the back of the book for her. "I won't ruin it for you," he said, leaning toward her and lowering his voice to a whisper, "because it's magical, and of course, you can check it out."

At long last, he was rewarded with a wisp of a smile. "If you like it," he said, pushing it back across his desk to her, "let me know. I might be able to recommend some others you'd enjoy." He lowered his voice again and whispered, "Just between you and me, Mrs. Swain wouldn't know a good book if it hit her right between the eyes."

"No," said Persey and this time her smile was real. "No, she really wouldn't." She glanced wistfully at the couch underneath his office window.

"You know," he said. "I'm leaving for a meeting but my offer stands. If you want to read, the couch is all yours."

In the end, her trust was easier to gain than he'd expected. She was willing to ignore her better instincts for a few red dot books and a quiet place to read. She knocked at his door with increasing frequency to see if he'd put anything aside for her, and he supplied them to her with just as much cunning as a dealer of any other drug. Each time she came to see him, Haden filled up the space between them with a rush of words designed to intrigue her and to convince her to continue to ignore her instincts. His goal was to make sure she returned to him again and again. He needed to locate the crucial piece of information that he would use later when the time was right.

He purchased hot cocoa, the kind that came in its own individualized sterilized packets with powdered milk and dehydrated marshmallows. He stashed these packets in his desk for her frequent visits and it fast became part of their ritual. He would hand her a cocoa packet and a cup brimming with hot water. She would empty the contents of the packet into the steaming cup, and stir it until the marshmallows were reconstituted. He would chat, she would listen and then he would leave her alone. Leaving became the hard part. Now he understood the impulse of her classmates. When he spoke to her, he was overwhelmed by an inexplicable longing to reveal his true nature. She is a child, an innocent. He reminded himself of this again and again, but when he was with her, the impulse (almost irresistible in its strength) always returned. It was this impulse that led him to give her books covering darker subject matter.

One afternoon, she came into his office, in her usual quiet way, and set his most recent recommendation on his desk. The book was *The Giver,* a classic science fiction novel about life and death in a utopian society. He had seen her in the aisle several times, sitting on the floor, thumbing through it.

Instead of waiting for his usual onslaught of comfortable chatter, she said, "I know I'm not supposed to, but I liked it better when the people didn't have memories, when they believed in Elsewhere."

Elsewhere was the book's word for Haden's Underworld.

"Why do you think you're not supposed to like that part better?" he asked.

"Because it wasn't the truth. Most people think it's better to know the truth than to believe in things that aren't real. But I don't. If I had to pick, I think I'd much rather believe in something that's not real, than always have to know the truth about everything." She lowered her voice and whispered, "I think I'm not going to believe in Heaven and Hell anymore. I'm just going to believe in Elsewhere."

She looked up at him and her dark unknowable eyes locked on his. Descriptions of his dark kingdom surged unbidden to Haden's lips. He had an overwhelming desire to tell her everything. As though it was natural and right that she know all the secrets he held. He had to struggle with himself to prevent the words from spilling out. The sensation was so unexpected and intense, that for a moment, he experienced something like human fright. Then, with great effort he looked away from the deep pools of her eyes. After that, Haden was more cautious with his choice of books.

By the end of the school year, Persey felt at home in his office. The hot cocoa and book recommendations had worked their magic. Her guard was down. She trusted him. She provided Haden with more and more opportunities to study her. His long experience with humankind had taught him the key to each of their souls lay in discovering their weakness. If he could discover a small chink in her childhood armor, he could be assured it would grow with her. Later, it would give him the necessary foothold he could use to his advantage. Despite his vigilance and many opportunities, he was unsuccessful, until the late April afternoon when she came into his office hot, tear-stained and angry.

"I hate this book," she said, plunking it on his desk with more energy than necessary.

"*The Giving Tree*," said Haden, raising his eyebrows. "That's not one I gave you."

He picked it up and noticed a tag proclaiming property of Clear Lake Elementary on its spine.

"Mrs. McClain gave it to us," said Persey. "It's for Mother's Day, a present. We're supposed to write a paper about what it means to love. But I don't believe in love. Not that kind of love, anyway," she said, looking at Haden as though she was daring him to contradict her.

"Why not?" he asked.

Persey shrugged her shoulders and glared at the floor. Then, her blue eyes studied the wooden veneer of his desk. In her silence, Haden flipped through the pages of the offending book. Something occurred to him as his eyes slid over the illustrated pages. People needed her. Even he needed her. He shifted in his chair as he remembered his own impulse to confide his dark secrets. She must experience the need of everyone around her as a great crushing burden.

"Maybe you're saying love should be more than need and giving."

She looked up at him, her blue eyes colored with surprise.

"Or to put it another way, need and giving aren't necessary elements of love." He paused to let his words sink in. "If that's what you're saying, then I agree with you. Just because you give, doesn't mean you love. Sometimes, not giving can be more of a gift than giving."

She looked up at him as though an immense weight had been removed from her small frame. "Do you really think that?" she said.

"I really do," said Haden.

In the end, discovering her weakness was almost as simple as gaining her trust. She was desperate to be free from the immense unbearable need of everyone she encountered. Someday, Haden would be in the perfect position to offer her the very thing she most desired. Of course, it would come at a price. But by then, she would be an adult. She would have already discovered that nothing in life was free.

Chapter Four

It was the summer after eighth grade when Persey first discovered her mother's secret. She'd been hiding out in her room, hoping to escape her mother's notice. It was just after lunch and hot outside. To her mother, that was a sign Persey should go outside and enjoy the beautiful weather. To Persey, the beautiful weather was an invitation to open her bedroom window—the one overlooking the shady side of the old farmhouse—and let the smell of fresh mown hay waft over her as she sat on the window seat reading a book.

"It's beautiful outside," her mother would say, making the words sound more like an indictment than commentary on the weather. "Call a friend, ride your bike to the swimming pool, do something."

The problem was that Persey's preference was for solitude. On this particular summer day, she was thinking about her long lost Mr. Sarantos and attempting to work up the energy necessary to read *The Grapes of Wrath*. She'd found the book while she was dusting. It was tucked away, at the very top of the bookshelves lining the back wall of the living room. The title caught her attention because it was strange and memorable. She remembered seeing it somewhere before, probably on one of those lists of recommended reading they passed out at school. She'd left it where it was, returning to the living room after her mother went outside in order to carry the book upstairs in secret. The secrecy wasn't because her mother cared about her reading this book more than any other book. It was because Persey had a hunch the book had belonged to her father. The one thing her mother was predictably unpredictable about was anything having to do with her father. Because of this, Persey took care to avoid the subject whenever possible.

The book sat for two weeks hidden in plain sight on the bookshelf in her room. It was a dense book with a dark, undecorated cover. Not inviting, even to someone like Persey who would read almost anything. But on that hot summer afternoon, she'd been sitting on her window seat thinking of Mr. Sarantos. During his brief tenure in Clear Lake, he had supplied her with the right kind of books and the freedom to do nothing but read. He'd been at the library during her third grade year. Then he'd moved on. After all these years, she still remembered him. There was something different about him that set him apart from all the other grown-ups who had filled her life since the third grade. *The Grapes of Wrath* was the type of book she could imagine him giving to her, if he was still in Clear Lake. She jumped up and plucked the book from its spot on her shelf. She opened it to the first page where an envelope slid out onto her lap, as though it had been waiting there for her to find it.

The envelope was unsealed and inside it was a stiff piece of paper folded in thirds. Its weight and heft reminded her of the certificate she'd received at the ridiculous formal affair that was her eighth grade graduation. She unfolded it and discovered there was another piece of paper, folded inside the first one. The heavy piece of paper proclaimed itself, in all capital letters, to be a CERTIFICATE OF ADOPTION. Beneath the boldface heading, her full name, Persephone Mary Campbell, was typed on the blank line for the adoptee. Below her name, there was a line for the adopter. Underneath that line, her father's name was typed and signed in the no-nonsense handwriting she recognized, from the notes and love letters he'd written to her mother.

With shaking hands and a strange sense of foreboding in her stomach, she looked at the second piece of paper and saw it was her birth certificate. There was her name, the year of her birth and the signature of the presiding doctor at Finley Hospital in Dubuque. She took comfort in the reassuring familiarity of it all. It was information that wove the lore of her mother's stories about the time before Persey could remember. She scanned the document and her eyes were drawn to the line provided for the father's name. Instead of the name Michael Campbell, the space was blank. It gave the document the look of a test where someone had, by accident, overlooked a question.

Persey had never known her father. He died before she was born. Death notwithstanding, he still should have been listed on her birth certificate. He was still her father, wasn't he? Until this very moment, she'd never doubted she was the daughter of Michael Campbell. But now, glancing back and forth between her unfinished birth certificate and the stiff certificate of adoption she began to wonder. Why had he signed an adoption certificate before she was born? Her first instinct was to run clattering down the stairs and confront her mother with what she'd found. Possibly, very possibly, there was some legitimate reason that would explain the whole thing. She could already hear her mother laughing and saying, "Where on earth did you even find those old papers? They insisted I file the birth certificate before I left the hospital but I didn't have your father's death certificate on me. They wouldn't let me add his name. Well, you can't imagine the rigmarole I had to go through to have him legally listed as your father. Just between you and me, we had to have your Grandpa Campbell forge that signature on the certificate of adoption."

It would be an explanation typical of her mother. Demi Campbell had a unique ability to make even the oddest set of circumstances seem unremarkable. It was a quality Persey found both annoying and amusing. The thing that prevented her from asking her mother right then and there was that her mother's practical nature didn't encompass the subject of Persey's father. Too many questions about Mike Campbell caused her mother's voice to grow quiet and her face to go blank. When this happened, Persey knew she would be awoken in the middle of the night by the sound of her mother's gut-wrenching sobs. Even though thirteen years had passed, Demi Campbell still mourned her husband.

Persey glanced down at the document once more before refolding it and tucking it back in the book. No, she thought shaking her head. Her mother was not the route to the truth. Her thoughts were interrupted by the sound of her mother's voice, calling from the bottom of the stairs.

"Persey, are you up there? Someone's here to see you."

Persey tucked the book back in its hiding spot on her book shelf. She paused at the door, glancing back at it. There would be plenty of time to research the question later.

Chapter Five

Downstairs, Persey found her next door neighbor, Rudy, sitting at the dining room table, her mother standing in the doorway. "Hey," he said, shifting in his seat as she entered the room.

"Hi," she said, swiveling her head back to her mother with a questioning look.

Rudy was a year ahead of Persey in school, a fact belied by his small frame. He wore glasses and his hair was cropped close to his skull, revealing the frail contours of his neck. They'd been friends when they were younger, playing together off and on until around the end of fourth grade. It was at that time, Persey realized, close friendships with boys—or anyone else for that matter—were fraught with trouble.

Demi greeted Persey with her brightest smile. "Look who I ran into in town," she said. Without waiting for Persey to respond, she added, "Rudy's organizing a plant sale fundraiser for the high school. They're trying to raise money to upgrade some of the computers in the library. What did you say the name of your group is again, Rudy?"

"Sir Hacks-a-Lot," said Rudy, tracing a figure eight on the table.

"That's right," said Demi with delight. "Isn't that original? I thought it might be the kind of thing you'd be interested in Pers, so I told him I'd personally donate fifty dollars, if he'd stop by and convince you to join the campaign." As Demi spoke, the expression on Rudy's face went from glum to downright pained.

"Right," he said, making direct eye contact with the dining room table. "It's just what she said. We could use some help, if you're interested...but you don't have to, although we could use the fifty dollars."

It was evident, thought Persey, the Sir Hacks-a-Lots talents didn't lie in sales. She glanced back over at her mother. The sharp look on her face was impossible to misinterpret. "Sure, I'll help out," said Persey.

"Great," said Demi as she made out a check.

Persey knew her mother worried about her. She knew this, not because her mother confided in her, but because it was obvious to anyone with half a brain. Demi Campbell longed for her daughter to have a group of girlfriends, or even a best friend, with whom she could raid the kitchen and demand to be driven to the local mall. Persey understood that her mother's desire for her to have a normal childhood was the driving force behind most of her schemes. It was the reason Demi invited the entire fifth grade to Persey's eleventh birthday, enrolled her in after-school soccer, despite the complete lack of talent, and tried (here Persey had put her foot down) to sign her up for 4-H. Even though Persey was certain her mother knew the reason behind her reticence and preference for solitude, it was almost as if her mother believed a normal childhood would fix the problem.

The reason Persey didn't have a group of giggling girlfriends and a host of after school-activities was because she didn't want them. It wasn't the girlfriends and activities she didn't want. It was what went along with them. She knew, sooner rather than later, it all led to secrets. Not the kind of secrets middle school girls usually tell each other. Persey wouldn't mind hearing about who the other girls would make out with if they had to pick one boy out of the eighth grade class or what they thought about the girl that used to be their friend but wasn't anymore. Those secrets would have been just fine. The problem was those weren't the kinds of secrets people told her. The kind of secrets people told her were the sort of thing people never talked about.

She wished, for example, she didn't know Debbie Turner's father tickled her in bed whenever Debbie's mother was out for the evening. "His thing gets hard," Debbie told her, staring off into space as though Persey wasn't even in the room. "He lies on top of me and tickles me and I know if I move, his thing will get hard but I can't help it. It really tickles." Debbie told her this during a sleepover in the fourth grade. Persey didn't sleep over at Debbie's any more after that. Tracey Kidder told her that her mother bought her a candy bar every time she managed to steal a pack of cigarettes from the Hy-Vee. In fifth grade, Janet Morgan from the soccer team whispered into Persey's ear that she thought she might be one of "those" girls. "What girls?" asked Persey? "The kind that likes other girls," said Janet. They were sitting in Janet's room on her frilly white four poster bed surrounded by stuffed animals. She looked into Persey's eyes as though begging for absolution and said, "My dad says people like that burn in hell. Do you think he's right?"

It was as though she opened up a font inside anyone who got too close to her, and out poured their deepest, darkest, most terrible secrets. It wasn't just her friends either. It didn't take her long to learn grown-ups were just as quick to confide. And their secrets were worse than anything her friends told her. By the time she was in fifth grade, she knew that Mary Tretterino's father was sleeping with Terry Bass's mother and Karl Miller's father was sleeping with Mary's mother. She knew that Sharon Boje's mother thought the new high school football coach was dreamy, and she'd go down on her knees for that man in a quick minute, whatever that meant. She also knew that Denise Gentry's father always wore women's underwear. He confessed it one evening—choking back big sobs—as he drove her home. The worst, however, the absolute worst was when the secret was about her.

The first time it happened was last year. Mr. Scott was the young new science teacher. He was tall with dark hair that curled around his ears and an easy grin. Most of the seventh grade girls harbored secret crushes on him. Persey knew this, not because anyone had confided it in her, (by this time she'd become more adept at avoiding confidences) but because it was evident to anyone paying attention. When it came time to do their year-end group science projects, it was Persey's bad luck to be assigned to a group of girls that included Bethany Strauss. Bethany was known to have an ardent crush on Mr. Scott. It was Persey's further bad luck or bad judgment to go along with Bethany's scheme to work on their project after school, in the science lab.

To Bethany's fervent excitement, Mr. Scott was still correcting papers at his desk when they crowded into the lab, carrying their backpacks and notebooks.

"Do you mind if we work on our project in here?" asked Bethany with a flirtatious grin.

Mr. Scott, looking amused said, "No, of course not. Make yourselves at home."

He proceeded to ignore them for the next half hour until Bethany, apologetically but insistently, told him they needed 'his expert help.' Even when he put aside his papers to help them with their project, Persey didn't see any warning signs. There were almost always warning signs. People with secrets would circle her as they worked up their courage. At the very least, they would glance at her, as if daring her to make eye contact with them. But Mr. Scott displayed none of the usual signs of someone with a burning secret to tell.

She was completely unprepared for what happened next. As the girls filed out of the classroom, Mr. Scott put a hand on her shoulder and said, "Hold on Persey. You got an extra minute?"

Bethany shot her an envious glance but Persey was too focused on the alarm bells going off in her own head to notice. He'd caught her off guard and for once, she wasn't prepared with a quick excuse of needing to get to a doctor's appointment or her mother waiting in the car. He seemed to take her silence for acquiescence because he closed the door behind the other girls, sealing the two of them together in the science lab. She looked at him and noticed he was rolling a piece of paper into a funnel. Persey was filled with a strange sense of foreboding. This time was going to be worse than usual. She knew, without a doubt, she did not want to hear whatever it was Mr. Scott was getting ready to tell her.

"Persey," he said without prelude.

His eyes sought hers, entreating her to listen to him. He wanted her to accept his darkest secrets, just like everyone else. "Persey," he said again, looking at her with some emotion she couldn't place. "I think about you every night. I think about your hair and your skin. How it would feel to touch you." His voice took on a strangled quality. "You're so young. I know it's wrong," he continued. "I just," he paused for a moment, as though searching for a better way to say whatever was coming next.

By this time, Persey had recovered enough of her wits to resurrect a defense. "It's alright Mr. Scott. Really, it's okay. I understand." she said, speaking in a soothing tone and backing away from him as she might have done from a dangerous animal. "And don't worry," she added, her hand twisting open the doorknob behind her. "I won't tell anyone. I'll keep it a secret."

It was a reassurance she knew he would ask for. They always did.

Chapter Six

Persey sat next to Rudy, in his rusty Subaru Justy, as they bounced toward town. "What do the Sir Hacks-a-Lots do?" she asked to fill up the silence in the car. She tried to avoid this kind of situation. One-on-one time in a car was an almost guaranteed disaster. It was private without an escape route, but sometimes if she took control of the conversation, she could fill up the space with her own words. These were the kinds of tricks she had incorporated into her tool bag.

"It's like this club and we play games online. It's kinda cool. You can build your own world. It's kinda like Dungeons and Dragons, except on the computer. Do you ever play D&D?" he asked, glancing at her sidewise.

"Play what?" asked Persey.

Rudy let out the small sharp sound that was his laugh. "Why'd you agree to help us out anyway?"

Persey shrugged. "It was either that or listen to my mother complain about my lack of social skills for the rest of the afternoon."

Rudy gave her another one of his quick glances and then snorted. "Since when don't you have social skills? I can't imagine you're ever alone for long."

"That's the problem," said Persey, causing Rudy to shake his head. But before he could ask her what she meant she said, "So, tell me what we're raising money for again."

By the time they reached Shari's Diner, in the center of town where the Sir Hacks-a-Lots donations table was set up, Rudy had managed to give Persey a rudimentary understanding. They needed a new type of motherboard, necessary to support the Sir Hacks-a-Lot's computer gaming programs.

"Have you considered a different name?" Persey asked.

"Yeah, it makes us sound like we're hackers, right? That's what I told Justin, but he had the top score in Starcraft, so we had to go with it. He thinks it sounds edgy, the way it mixes the idea of a bad-ass hacker with an old school knight."

Persey nodded. She could have said a lot more on the subject but they were already pulling into the parking lot.

"Men, this is my neighbor Persey," said Rudy, introducing her to the two other boys waiting for them at the plant sale. Justin was tall and lanky with bad skin. Tim was overweight with chronic asthma. His asthma became apparent when he looked up at her and took a swig of Coke at the same time, sending it down the wrong pipe and causing him to cough for several minutes, necessitating the use of his inhaler.

"Are you a gamer?" asked Tim after his coughing fit subsided.

"What's a gamer?" said Persey.

Justin let out a nervous high-pitched giggle.

"She's just going to help us out today, okay," said Rudy, reaching under the table and slipping Demi's fifty dollar check into the change box. He inspected the table of plants while the other two boys stole glances at the newest addition to their group.

"Hey Persey," said Rudy, handing her two plastic pitchers. "Do you mind going inside Shari's and filling these up? They said it was fine to get water from the bathroom and some of these strawberries are starting to droop."

Persey took the pitchers and filled them in the Shari's bathroom. She carried them back through the lobby, pushed open the heavy outer door with one shoulder and heard someone call, "Yo, check it out, it's the geek squad."

Four boys wearing football jerseys were making their way through the parking lot toward the Sir Hacks-a-Lot's table. As she watched, the members of Sir Hacks-a-Lot seemed to shrink.

"Well, well, well, what do we have here?" said the largest boy in the group. He had a deep summer tan, dark shaggy hair and a smile almost broad enough to mask his evident sadistic streak. "A school fundraiser," now snorting as he read the carefully lettered sign taped to the edge of the table. "Isn't that thoughtful? Alright, little bitches, let's see how we did today. Cough it up." He gave the table a sharp shake which caused several of the smaller plants to slide off and hit the ground.

"Can't you read, Luke? Or maybe you don't have to read to be on the football team," said Rudy.

"I'm sorry fag boy, did you say something to me?" said Luke.

"The sign," said Rudy, his eyes glaring down at the table. "It says this is a fundraiser for the Sir Hacks-a-Lots, not the football team."

Luke grinned with delight. "The Sir Hacks-a-Lots," he crowed. "Is that what you call your little after-school fuck fest?"

"Shut up, Luke," said Rudy without looking up from the table.

"Oh look, I think he's mad. Watcha gonna do fag boy, hit me with your purse?"

The sensation of smoldering rage took Persey by surprise. There was no reason she should feel protective of the Sir Hacks-a-Lots. The only one in the group she'd known before today was Rudy. Still it was rage, combined with something that felt like anticipation, flooding through her body as she stalked across the parking lot.

"Excuse me," she said, causing the football players to move to one side. She banged her two pitchers of water down on the table, making the water slop over onto the ground. "We're not making donations," she said. She stared at them for a moment, allowing them to meet her eyes. "In fact," she continued, letting her eyes come to rest on the boy Rudy called Luke. "It's a sale—the kind where you buy something." She held Luke's gaze, letting him get lost in the deep blue of her eyes. The dark thing inside of her flexed like a muscle and, for once, she set it free.

She could feel the darkness inside of Luke. He was filled with coldness and fear. The thing inside of her called to it. It was hungry for it. Luke opened his mouth to tell her everything. He was hers to expose on the hot summer pavement of the parking lot. She could feel all his horrible secrets burbling inside, ready to spill out and the darkness inside her was gleeful, ready to pounce.

It was Tim's asthmatic cough (of all things) that brought her back to her senses. She reined herself in, forcing her eyes to disconnect from Luke's.

"Why don't you just take those that you knocked off the table," she said. Her heart was pounding in her chest and her legs felt weak. Luke blinked twice and then bent down to pick the plants up off the hot concrete.

"Here you go," he said, digging in his pocket to retrieve several crumpled bills.

"I'll take five," called a voice from somewhere behind Luke. Another boy was approaching the table. His sandy blonde hair was shower damp and his hazel eyes crinkled as he smiled.

"The A-man," said Luke, recovering himself enough to slap the newcomer on the shoulder. "What took you so long?"

"Personal hygiene, dude, ever hear of it?"

Luke laughed and gave the A-man a playful punch. "We gonna eat or what?"

"Yeah, you guys go on. I'll be there in a minute." He watched while the other boys trooped into the restaurant, then turned back to Persey. "Sorry about that. Luke doesn't mean to be an asshole. He just came out that way."

Persey laughed despite herself.

"I'm Aaron," he added.

"I'm Persey, Persey Campbell," she said, handing him a cardboard box with his plants.

"It's very nice to meet you Persey Campbell. Maybe I'll see you around soon?"

To her surprise, she heard herself saying, "Maybe you will."

The members of Sir Hacks-a-Lot evinced nothing short of worship for the rest of the afternoon. "That was awesome," Justin repeated over and over in tones of amazement.

"For a moment, I swear, he looked like he was gonna cry," Tim added after every few declarations of Persey's awesomeness.

By the end of the afternoon, the story had been retold often enough to make Persey wish it had never happened. She felt nothing but relief when Rudy looked at his watch and said, "Looks like a day."

As they bumped along in the Justy, the sound of Rudy's voice receded into the background and Persey stared out at the dusty, green corn fields. She didn't see corn. All she saw was Aaron's warm smile and brown curls just beginning to dry in the summer sun.

"Persey, is it okay if I tell you something?"

Rudy's voice was a comforting buzz in the background. By the time she remembered where she was it was already too late.

"Sometimes I masturbate," he whispered.

Persey groaned internally. She glanced over at Rudy, who was gripping the steering wheel, as he waited for her response. "It's okay," she said. "Most people do, even if they say they don't."

"I do it a lot," said Rudy. "Sometimes three times a day."

"Totally normal," Persey assured him, as she mentally calculated they were less than a mile from home.

"I'll probably think about you tonight when I do it," he said, squeezing his face up with self-contempt. "It's not that I think we would ever hook up. It's just that you're really beautiful. You know what I mean? It's like I'm some kind of sicko and I can't help myself. I mean, I think you're the coolest girl I know."

"It's okay," Persey repeated, suppressing a sigh. "But can we talk about something else?"

"Sure, totally," said Rudy.

They were always grateful when she changed the subject.

"Tell me about Aaron," she said.

"He's cool," said Rudy. "You know, he's on the football team but he's never a jerk. I could see him being your type," he said, glancing at her with a smile.

Persey smiled back. "Can I hang out with you guys, the Sir Hacks-a-Lots sometimes?"

Rudy looked surprised. "You want to be a gamer?"

"No," said Persey. She was sure, in fact, that she did not want to be a gamer. "You saw my mother today. She's always bugging me to get out of the house and have friends. I was thinking I could read while you guys play your games. I mean, if you don't mind me hanging around."

"No!" said Rudy, shaking his head and grinning. "We won't mind at all."

Chapter Seven

Daniel Hartnett was the first person to ever make partner at the New York offices of Goldman Parke before the age of thirty-five. He'd been thirty, to be exact. He started in the structured finance department right out of law school, and four years later he was a partner. Daniel understood the business, that much was clear. But it was his ability to work with clients that rocketed him through the usual hoops and solidified his position in the firm. He was known to be something of a client-whisperer. All it took was one lunch with Daniel and—all of a sudden—the business people at GECC or GMAC or AOL wanted, in fact, found they needed, Daniel's counsel. He "knew" them, they claimed. They'd never met anyone so intuitive. It was almost as if he could anticipate their goals before they did, and then bring those goals to fruition with startling speed. It was uncanny how, in a negotiation, he knew what to protect and what to give away; when to push harder and when to back down. It was as if he knew his clients and their partners better than they knew themselves. In fact, he did. It was the same trick he'd used all his life.

It wasn't that Daniel could read people's minds. All that business about having to shut out the voices and being driven crazy was a bunch of far-fetched nonsense; the kind of stuff used to sell half-baked books about fictitious monsters. For Daniel, it was simple. So much so, that he had gone through most of his childhood without realizing everyone didn't hear things the way he did. It was as though people's words were a bunch of blah-de-blah, obscuring what they wanted to say. It was amusing how often his clients tried to sell him the biggest line of bullshit. The words said one thing but the meaning behind the words, the piece that Daniel heard and understood, said something else.

"We believe in green energy and want to be at the forefront of the next technological boom," was a perfect example of the kind of bullshit a would-be client might tell him over lunch as they scarfed down their forty dollar entrée.

Daniel heard the message underlying the words, which was, "The CEO wants to have plausible deniability about the investments we've made in big oil, so we need to get something on the books that makes us look green with a twelve percent profit margin."

In the boardroom, a group of bankers would swear up and down another percentage off the strip rate, would tank the deal. He knew—as though they were screaming it at him—they had run numbers two percent lower and the deal was still viable, just not quite as fat as they'd hoped.

Daniel referred to his finely-tuned sense of hearing as his crap-o-meter. But it wasn't just his crap-o-meter that propelled him into the Goldman Parke stratosphere. He worked at it. He attended charity functions, worked late nights and kept up with all kinds of issues that had little to no bearing on structured finance. His crap-o-meter had taught him the value of being well informed. He took it upon himself to become hyper informed, with an almost religious zeal. He started each morning by reading the New York Times, cover to cover.

"What do you want with the Lifestyles section?" Linda, his secretary, teased him one morning when he bellowed out the door that it was missing.

"I want to be in the know," he said.

Linda put the pilfered section on his desk with a laugh. "I can see how it might be important for you to know khakis now have street cred," she said as she left his office.

Daniel knew that "being in the know", as he put it, was important. He was also intimately acquainted with its downside. Despite his rise to the pinnacle of Goldman Park, his life was still lacking. Every time he talked to his mother, she made it clear that despite Daniel's successes, he was still managing to disappoint her.

"Seeing anyone new?" she would say as though the question just happened to pop into her head.

"Nope," he'd respond and then launch into a monologue about his newest deal. The monologue was designed to get her off the phone as quickly as possible. Daniel knew nobody outside the legal field, not even his mother, had the patience to listen to him talk for more than five minutes about structured finance.

The last time she called, she didn't even bother with her usual show of casualness. "Daniel," she said, in a way that only a mother can.

He could hear the concern in her voice and cringed, waiting for the inevitable.

"Do you remember Paul? Diane and Ted's son? He's just a couple of years older than you and he's visiting from Los Angeles right now. I was thinking maybe you could show him around. You never know, the two of you might *hit* it off. It might be fun?" she said, her voice trailing off.

"Mom, I'm happy to show Paul around but I'm not gay," he said, surprised by this new approach.

"It's just that you're so handsome. Diane mentioned last week that Paul said you were far too good-looking to be straight."

He could hear her refusal to believe his denial. "Tell Paul, thanks for the vote of confidence but I promise you, I'm not gay."

"It's alright if you are. Your father and I just want you to be happy. You're thirty-nine you know, and you never even date anymore," she said with a sniffle.

His other line buzzed and he felt sincere relief. "I'm not gay. I just haven't met the right girl yet," he said. "Listen, I've got to pick up my other line. I'll talk to you soon."

It wasn't that Daniel had some singular desire to remain single or torture his mother. He knew she just wanted to see him happy. He also knew that she wanted to have pictures of grandchildren to show her friends when they had lunch. He knew this because she reminded him of it every time they talked. Even if she hadn't, he still would have known it in the same way he knew everything else. In some ways, it made it easier that there was very little hidden meaning to his mother's words. At least they could talk about what was on her mind. The truth of the matter was, he would have been happy to settle down into the same kind of life led by so many of his friends and colleagues. It was just that he seemed incapable of finding the right girl. It wasn't that he couldn't get a date. He was a good-looking guy, Paul was right about that. He was also a partner at a major New York City law firm, for chrissakes. It wasn't getting a date that was problematic. It was staying interested.

When he was younger, his crap-o-meter seemed like a God given gift. What sixteen year-old wouldn't give his left arm to know that the pretty new English teacher, Ms. Beckett, thought he was cute? Of course, she hadn't said that. What she'd said was, "Nice job on that paper, Mr. Hartnett." What he'd heard was, "That boy has the nicest ass I've ever seen." It was so clear he'd stopped and looked back at her, convinced she'd uttered the words aloud. But she was engrossed in a conversation with some other student. He came back after school and he and Ms. Beckett fully explored the contours of each other's asses in the supplies closet. That's the way it went through high school, college and law school. He was a source of inspiration to all his friends. It was so easy. They could say whatever they wanted but Daniel always knew what they meant.

For a long time, he just assumed everyone had a crap-o-meter. When the teacher put a problem on the board, he figured everyone else realized—heard the message—that the problem up there in front of them, in black and chalky white, would be on tomorrow's test. When your parents told you they were going to the Boardman's for dinner and asked you if you minded staying home by yourself, it was clear they were testing you. So clear, that the only thing it made sense to do was play video games and order the pizza they had recommended. That way when your mother came home halfway through the evening, ostensibly because she forgot her glasses, she would have every reason to give you a big smile, ruffle your hair and tell you not to stay up too late.

He never understood how anyone could be so careless as to get caught doing something they shouldn't. Or how they couldn't manage to come to school prepared. Were they not listening? Did they just not care? Why couldn't they toe the line and work the system when everything was so clear, so spelled out? It just didn't make sense. It continued to not make sense until he was fourteen.

Lorna Walker was one year his senior. She was a girl-next-door type, who to his pleasure, lived next door. He'd been outside shooting hoops when she came out to his driveway, dressed in cut-off shorts and a bikini top.

"God, Danny," she said, sounding annoyed. "You're making so much noise out here I can't even read."

Daniel's next shot was an air ball. It missed the basket and hit the garage door with a resounding bang. Lorna giggled and Daniel glanced over at her and said, "You want to come over tonight? I'm just going to be hanging out by myself."

"Sure, why not?" she said, giggling again.

It was unusual for him to ask her over. They hadn't played together since they were little kids. Even then, he hadn't particularly liked Lorna. She'd always been too bossy. But at that moment, in his fourteenth year, as she stood on the side of his cement garage patio simpering and giggling, it hit him. The words weren't just some stupid game of blah-de-blah. They meant something. Most people, he realized, heard only the words, not the meaning behind the words. What's more, he realized one epiphany piling on another; most people didn't even realize the hidden meanings and agendas behind their own words. These were the sudden realizations that caused him to throw an air ball, not as Lorna supposed, that her bikini clad presence made him nervous.

The knowledge, that Lorna couldn't or wouldn't acknowledge, even to herself, how much it bothered her to be the last virgin in her group of friends, shocked Daniel; but not for the traditional reasons. All this time, he'd never realized the information coming to him might not even be available to its source. It was like he was mining the collective id of everyone he met. He remembered a poster that had hung in his fourth grade classroom. It was a picture of gigantic fist with the slogan, "Knowledge is Power," printed underneath it in bold block letters. "It certainly is," thought Daniel, holding up his fist in imitation of the poster. Lorna had just broadcast her desire to lose her virginity with someone safe, someone nonthreatening; someone Daniel was happy to be for the evening.

Chapter Eight

After serving him well in school and business, and getting him laid many times over, Daniel's crap-o-meter started to present a problem as he edged his way into his third decade. It was part of growing up, he imagined. An irrevocable turning point, not all that different—when he stopped to think about it—from the point in life when you stopped envying your best friend's newest Lego Star Wars mini-figure. What was once cool now seemed juvenile. He was like his Uncle Charlie, who insisted on producing chocolate coins out of Daniel and his sister's ears at every family get together until Daniel was close to fifteen. The uncle stopped when Daniel, arrogant as hell—he knew that now—performed an excruciating parody of the same trick. Try as he might, Daniel couldn't stop doing his own trick, even though the current results were far from satisfactory.

The problem, the real problem when you got down to it, was he could never turn it off. As long as he could never turn it off, he could never have the normal life with the cute kids that his mother wanted for him. No two point five kids, no wife, no nothing for Daniel Hartnett. All because he was stuck knowing too damn much. And knowing too much rendered the girl, no matter who she was, uninteresting. A typical date went something like this. He would pick her up and they would attend a sporting event or dinner or performance or boat ride or a walk in the park. At some point during their time together, she would make conversation with him. The conversation might be about his career or lawyers or her career or his hobbies or her hobbies or family or friends or sports.

The point was it didn't matter where they went or what they talked about because he always knew how it would end. There were no surprises. He knew whether the girl was on a rebound date. He knew if she was into him or wasn't; if she was going through the motions or if she was looking for a long term relationship. It didn't matter what she said because the meaning behind her words was always clear. They convulsed inside

Daniel's skull with their insistence on being heard. In the end, every date became a variation on the theme of sameness, even when they wanted nothing to do with him.

The last time he'd gone on a date was six months ago. He'd agreed to be set up with a law school classmate's artsy younger sister. Over dinner at an uptown bistro, he asked if she wanted to pick out the wine.

"No, no, go right ahead," she said.

However, the message that imprinted itself on Daniel's brain was, "You arrogant fucking pig!"

"Maybe we should call it a night," he said, handing the wine list back to the sommelier.

She looked at him with surprise and laughed, adding, "Let's just go for a walk instead," as she slipped out of her chair.

By which he knew she meant, "That was unexpected. I wonder what he's like in bed."

He sighed, offered her his arm and found her a taxi.

That night signaled the end of his interest in the New York dating scene, which wasn't to say he didn't still sleep with women. He just shelved the idea of locating that perfect girl. The kind of girl that he could wake up next to every morning; feeling the rush that comes (he supposed) with having slept in the same bed with someone you would be happy to wake up next to every morning for the rest of your life. The ability to see through their words destroyed the mystery. It turned him into a reader who read the last chapter first. How could he ever feel the necessary sentiments of romance and infatuation, the prerequisites to love, when he was never certain if his feelings arose from somewhere within him, or were just an automatic response to whatever message was being broadcast?

Now, whenever he found himself horny at the end of a long day, he'd head to the bars and restaurants of Park Avenue South, home to junior editors and the men who wanted to fuck them. His good looks and Goldman Parke business card ensured a scene similar to what his father referred to as, "shooting fish in a barrel." He couldn't help but despise himself somewhat for taking advantage of their young bodies and upwardly mobile ambitions. Even the girls who declined to give him their phone number and tucked his card in their purse, while saying, "Sure, maybe I'll call." Even those girls were playing at a disadvantage because Daniel knew what they meant was, "I need to evaluate/assess/play hard to get with you. No chance in hell/after I Google you/absolutely."

To assuage his guilt, he always called them after he slept with them. It was the right thing to do, so he did it. He felt like it counted, even if he did make an effort to call at odd times in order to increase his odds of going straight to voice mail. His standard line was to tell them he was coming off a bad break-up, and despite the magic of the night before, realized he just wasn't ready to get back out there yet. Then he'd have Linda send them flowers. It was the least he could do but he wasn't inclined to do more. Not, at least, until he met Persey.

Chapter Nine

Ever since Aaron Strait bought a box full of wilting strawberry plants at a fundraiser for a group called the Sir Hacks-a-Lots, he'd been hooked. Even if she wasn't the most beautiful girl he'd ever seen, which she was, he still would have been hooked. He'd watched her from across the parking lot as she bulldozed her way through a group of linebackers, any one of them twice her size, and insisted they support an oddly named cause. Hell, looking the way she did, she could have been raising money to hogtie small children and he still would have fallen for her. They all would have. But it was more than that. There was something radiant about her that made you want to look but look away at the same time. It was like she managed to illuminate the part of them—well-hidden beneath layers of adolescent bravado—that throbbed with a suppressed desire to be better than they had been up to this point in their short lives.

Aaron felt her influence throughout their subdued meal at Shari's and afterwards, as they climbed into their cars and headed back to the football field for the second half of daily doubles. Nobody referred to her as a hottie or fresh meat. In fact, nobody said much of anything. It would have been easy to write off the change to the heat but Aaron knew it was more than that. It was as though the force of Persey's beauty and her something-elseness seeped inside of them for a little while. It made them recognize the limited nature of their normal conversations and left them without much to talk about. Whether or not the effect was lasting didn't matter. Aaron had seen it, felt it. It wasn't the kind of thing he would forget anytime soon.

By the time they were back at the practice field, Luke had regained his typical swagger. "Dude," he said to Aaron in a voice designed to be overheard by anyone within twenty feet. "I'm thinkin' I need to join the geek squad. What's their name, the Sir-Fucks-a-Lots?"

"Stay away from her," said Aaron with a ferocity that took them both by surprise.

"Bro, you barely know her, and I hate to play this card but I do believe I saw her first."

That was all it took. Aaron felt the rage as a burning sensation spreading up from the pit of his stomach. It propelled him in one long motion in the direction of his best linebacker. Several moments later, he was aware of arms pulling him off of Luke and restraining him. They were both bleeding, but Aaron noticed with satisfaction, he'd been able to land several good punches. The deep purple-y red marks around Luke's eye and cheek wouldn't fade anytime soon.

"What's goin' on here?" yelled Coach Peters as he came running over to survey the damage.

Aaron just glared but Luke said, eyes on his cleats, "Just some girl, Coach."

"Idiots!" Coach Peters spit a sunflower seed shell onto the ground at his feet to emphasize his point. "You know the rules. Bros before hos, and if I ever see you fighting on my field again, that's it. I don't care how fancy your footwork is," he said, glaring at Aaron. "You'll be benched for the season. Since you've got so much energy to expend, you can give me fifty forty's, right now. Get a move on." The two boys started out at the field. "I said move it," bellowed Coach Peters from behind them. "My six year old can run faster than that."

Nobody talked about it after that. They didn't need to. Aaron had staked out his territory. On the first day of school, he waited in the freshman hallway until he spotted her. "Hi," he said, leaning against the locker next to hers. "We meet again." She looked at him and the faintest suggestion of a smile passed across her face. "Where you headed?" he asked, trying to ignore the fact that he, Aaron Strait, a starting quarterback on the Clear Lake Varsity football team was being dissed by a freshman.

"I'm not sure," said Persey, scrutinizing the schedule in her hand.

He peered over her shoulder and the sensation of being "this close" to her made him a little giddy. "You've got Mr. Davies for Geometry. I'm headed that way, if you want me to walk with you."

Persey smiled at him, a real smile this time, making him certain that he was doing exactly what he needed to be doing. "Sure," she said. "That'd be great."

He left her in front of Mr. Davies room and then sprinted back in the direction he'd come, in order to avoid being tardy for his own class. When the bell rang at the end of the class, he reversed his sprint so he could be waiting near Mr. Davies room when she came out. "Hey," he called when he caught a glimpse of her blonde head. She waved and made her way through the crowded hallway until she was in front of him.

"You waited for me," she said.

"It's no big deal. My class is just down the hall," he said, gesturing in the direction he'd come. Then, trying to regain some of his usual swagger, he held out his hand for her schedule. "What do you have next?"

She looked at him and laughed. "Are you my self-appointed guardian angel?" As if sensing it was the wrong thing to say, she added, "Because I really need one. My sense of direction is terrible and all the halls look the same to me."

"Then I guess that's what I am," he said, giving her a ridiculous wink. What the hell, he thought. Why was it impossible for him to be in her presence for more than two minutes without acting like a complete dork?

After the first day it became their routine. Aaron deposited Persey in front of each of her classes and then sprinted off to his own before the bell rang. At lunchtime on the second day of school, he led her through the cafeteria to his usual table, crowded with football players and cheerleaders. "Persey, this is Angie, Jennifer, Michelle and Denise," gesturing at the four girls seated at one end of the table. They interrupted their conversation long enough to acknowledge her with quick hellos. He sat down motioning for her to do the same. She sat beside him with her eyes glued to her lunch tray. He noticed with concern that she was clutching her lunch tray and refusing to look at anyone.

"A-man," called his friend Brian from the other end of the table. "We're all headed to my house after practice tonight, you in?"

Aaron turned towards Brian, nodding his head, "Sure." By the time he glanced back at Persey, he relaxed. Angie had one arm threaded through Persey's, and the other cheerleaders were talking about their weekend plans.

"If your mom won't let you go, just ask if you can sleep at my house," he heard Angie say. "The party is going to be totally huge and your boyfriend's going to be there," she added. Aaron turned away before anyone could see him blush. He couldn't hear Persey's response but that was okay. He was just relieved she was having a good time and he wasn't sure he wanted to hear how she categorized their relationship.

That's why he didn't understand it when she told him she'd be eating lunch in the library. "But I thought you liked Angie. I heard you say you were going to spend the night at her house," Aaron protested.

"I do like Angie but I'd rather read. Besides, my mom doesn't like me to have sleepovers," she said.

"But you have to eat. You're not supposed to eat in the library."

"I'll be careful. Don't worry, I won't get caught," she said with a teasing smile.

Aaron had to admit defeat. He didn't know how to insist she eat lunch with him without seeming like some kind of weirdo stalker, so their routine was established. Every day at lunch time, he delivered her to the Switzerland of the high school lunch hour. It was the neutral zone of books and students seeking refuge from the social scene.

After two months of leaving her at the door of the library, curiosity got the better of him. What did she do in there every day? While the rest of the school happily rotated between the twin universes of the cafeteria and student union, what happened in the strange netherworld of the library? It didn't surprise him to find Rudy and the other boys who called themselves the Sir Hacks-a-Lots huddled around a computer at a table in the far corner. He loped toward them and eased himself down into a chair at their table.

"Hey," he said, as though he often hung out in the library during lunchtime.

"Hey," said Rudy.

"Ummm," said Aaron clearing his throat. "You guys are friends with Persey, right?" Rudy nodded.

"She hangs out here during lunch."

"Yeah, we noticed," said the smaller friend of Rudy's, the one Aaron thought was named Justin.

"Right, so I was wondering if you could just keep an eye on her. You know, in case she ever needs anything." Even as the words came out of his mouth, Aaron knew how ridiculous they were.

"You don't need to worry about Persey Campbell," said Rudy. "She can take care of herself." Then relenting a little he added, "But yeah, we'll watch out for her."

"Cool, great," said Aaron, holding up his hand for a high-five.

Rudy raised his eyebrows and looked at him for a moment over the edge of his computer.

Aaron lowered his arm without the high-five and muttered, "Thanks."

Aaron knew he was being compulsive about Persey. What he didn't understand was why. Why did he feel this deep and burning need to keep her safe, to be as she'd put it, her self-appointed guardian angel? It was stupid and he knew it. It was almost as if there was something inside her that called to him. Like everything else about Persey, it was impossible to ignore. Another thing that had become hard to ignore was the uncomfortable matter of their relationship. The entire school assumed they were a couple which made Aaron experience equal parts satisfaction and dismay.

"People think you're my girlfriend," he said one afternoon while he was driving her home. The minute the words left his lips he felt ridiculous and needy. Why did he always make such a fool out of himself around her? Holy crap, those uncomfortable fluttering sensations in his stomach meant he was desperate for her to confirm what everyone else took for granted.

"They do?" said Persey, glancing at him from her seat on the passenger's side of his car.

"Yeah," he said, shaking his head as though he couldn't understand it. He felt a blush beginning to burn on his cheeks. "I should tell them we're not together... right?"

"No," said Persey. "Don't tell them that. You don't need to tell them anything. Neither of us do. We don't owe anyone an explanation."

"Okay," said Aaron, nodding as though they'd come to an agreement even though she hadn't answered his question. "So, are we a couple?" The words floated between them in the car. Already, he hated himself for asking. He was such an idiot. Despite his best intentions, it was like he had no control over the things that came out of his mouth when he was around her.

She glanced at him with a strange expression on her face and said, "You're my best friend, Aaron. I know that's not want you want but, please believe me, when I tell you that's the best thing I have to give."

"Persey," Aaron heard his own voice thick with emotion as the gravel of her driveway crunched beneath his tires. "You're in my prayers every night. I pray that nothing bad will ever happen to you."

She smiled at him and leaned over to kiss him on the cheek. "Aaron," she whispered, "that's the nicest secret anyone's ever told me." Then she opened the car door and was gone before Aaron, still blushing at the horror of his confession, could respond.

Chapter Ten

Coach Breen of the Clear Lake High School swim team was a hard ass. That's how the kids referred to him, "a hard ass." Haden liked the term because it described him perfectly—although his ass, in this current incarnation as Coach Breen, was far from hard. It was more of the sagging middle-aged man variety. He didn't, however, have the rotund gut that so many of the other men in Clear Lake bore before them. The gut would have made him look ridiculous. While he wanted to be authentic, he didn't want to be ridiculous in his authenticity. He knew he wasn't going to gain the respect of a bunch of high school students if he looked like someone's idea of a punch line.

On his first day at Clear Lake High School, he'd set the tone. "I'm not gonna say much about Coach Phelps. He was a good coach. He was a good man and I know he'll be missed. My name's Bob Breen, Coach Breen to you folks, and I'll be doing my damndest to whip this team into shape for the State Championship meet this year. We're gonna do Coach Phelps proud." The team was subdued. Haden wondered if he was overdoing the gruff coach bit. Then he remembered most of the team was present when the good Coach Phelps dropped dead from sudden heart failure on the pool deck, two weeks earlier.

Six years, thought Haden with something like disbelief. He surveyed the faces assembled before him, careful to keep his eyes from resting on the only face on the team that interested him. She was a sophomore in high school now. Her limbs had stretched out and the endearing chubbiness of her childhood cheeks had melted away. She wore the same unadorned black practice suit as the rest of the team which only served to emphasize her modest curves and nascent fertility. Despite all the changes, she was still his same Persey. Hair the color of butterscotch, mixed with honey and dark blue pools where her eyes should have been. And she was still, as always, a mystery.

He'd hated leaving. He'd been aware of every moment of their separation during the last six years. For the first time in his existence, he'd been forced to measure the passage of time in human terms. It had dragged and plodded.

He'd left her on her own to fend for herself for six whole years. Every day of his absence, he'd been plagued with the anxiety of the unknown. Would this be the day she died? If not today, then maybe tomorrow or the day after tomorrow, next month, next year...? When would it happen? Would he be too late? It had gone on like that for six years but he'd had no choice. He knew she had to grow. She had to be capable of making the choice that would ensure her position at his side. She needed time, and for once, Haden didn't know how much time she had. It was almost worse to be close to her. He tortured himself by counting her life in minutes and seconds. He lived in constant fear that her rogue death, which refused to reveal itself to him, would stake its claim before he was ready. Then she would be gone and there would be nothing he could do about it. The very thought was enough to push him to the brink of insanity.

When the strength of the body he inhabited during his time at the library began to wane, he made the decision to return to his kingdom. There at least, he could lose himself in the endless business of ruling over souls. After all, he'd found what he needed. He knew her weakness and now there was nothing to do but wait. Waiting might be better accomplished in the land of the dead.

He announced his intent to depart the library and his staff planned a good-bye party, complete with cake, punch and a Hallmark card signed by library workers and patrons alike. Persey arrived wearing a new sundress and holding a bouquet of flowers.

"They're just wildflowers," she said, handing him the wilted little bouquet. The touch of her small hand against his took his breath away. "You should put them in water soon. I don't know how much longer they'll last." She stared at him without a trace of her customary slight smile.

"Come on. Let's do that right now," he said, leading her back to his office. He found a coffee cup in a cupboard, filled it with water and placed the flowers inside.

"I wish you weren't going," she said.

He was immensely gratified to see the tears swimming in her eyes. He crouched down so he could look at her, eye-to-eye. "I wish I didn't have to go too, but my mother is very ill," he said, repeating the story he'd concocted.

"Will you come back and see me?" she whispered.

"Yes," he said. Seized with sudden inspiration he took her into his arms. "I will come back again and again until you are old enough for me to love you the way you should be loved. You will always know me because I will never ask for anything in return. I'll never make you feel like the Giving Tree. Can you remember that Persey?"

She nodded as she returned his gaze.

Haden was on the verge of telling her more, telling her everything when Mrs. Swain interrupted them with a timid knock on the door.

"There you are," she said in her wavering voice. "Are you ready for cake?"

He left Persephone Campbell and the Town of Clear Lake behind. He returned to the place (across an ocean), where the man—whose name really was Sarantos—was destined to meet his end. Fourteen months earlier, Haden had met Sarantos in a little bar overlooking the Red Sea. After three drinks, Sarantos believed Haden to be his friend.

"This man who calls himself my friend, I have seen him staring at my wife!" he told Haden. He looked out at the white caps forming on the water. "Friend—? Bah! I would like to cut out his eyes. She is MY wife. You understand? She is mine."

The deal wasn't hard to arrange. In exchange for a year of the man's life, his neighbor was to be blinded in a welding accident. Sarantos didn't bother to ask what would happen to his body while it was in Haden's care. He also didn't know the year he was bargaining with was destined to be his last. Haden would have told him if he'd thought to ask, but he hadn't. No—Sarantos was greedy for what Haden had to offer and he accepted Haden's terms without question.

Haden steered the body in his care back to the small village where he'd first located it. Sarantos's sudden return was hailed by several small children and a pack of mangy dogs. Haden vacated the body of Sarantos and watched as the man found his way home. Haden knew Sarantos would open the door to his modest home and be greeted by the sight of his wife being tended to by the—now blind—neighbor. In a fury, Sarantos would rush at the couple with the intention of beating them both to a pulp. Instead, the pull string of his son's wooden dog would tangle around his ankle and cause him to stumble. Sarantos's head would bounce off the grate of the fireplace. In the moment before his life force exited his body, he would realize he had made a very bad bargain. Haden agreed with his assessment. What Sarantos didn't know, is it could have been worse. Sarantos had only bargained away a year of his life. In the end, he had fared far better than the ones who surrendered their afterlife. After all, a year or two was a blink of an eye, but the afterlife was forever.

Chapter Eleven

Coaches at Clear Lake High School were also expected to teach classes. Haden didn't mind teaching high school math. In fact, he couldn't help but enjoy the stress and frustration that radiated through the room each time he explained a new concept. However, when Persey entered Haden's classroom each morning at 10:35, all thoughts of other human life left his head. After his first day at Clear Lake High School, it was clear to Haden that Aaron Strait was a constant shadow at Persey's side. He understood, as he always understood, about their base emotions and that the boy hadn't slept with her. Haden knew from long experience that emotions were the most reliable barometer of a soul. Haden also understood, and here it didn't take any special understanding of humankind, that the boy was desperate to sleep with her. He wanted to ravish her with the energy and depravity found only in a teenage boy but something was holding him back. Haden wondered if it was the boy's own sense of Iowan morality or Persey's. Whatever the reason, he was pleased at the result. Like any immortal, he didn't like the idea of sharing.

Six years earlier, Haden had noticed the way children were drawn to Persey. Time had only served to increase the gravitational pull of her orbit. When she spoke in class—which she only did when she was called upon—the room went silent. The other students watched her with a mixture of lust and something else, something undefined. Haden knew what they wanted. It was the same thing he wanted. They wanted to know the secret contained in her bottomless eyes. It called to them, filling their bellies with the fire of endless need which her beauty served to flame. Haden smiled. They could desire her all they wanted but he alone knew her secret. He knew what she was waiting for, and someday, he would give her what she craved. He would free her from their need and in so doing, she would become his.

It was Haden's second week of coaching the swim team before he realized how wise he'd been to return to this particular moment in her life. "Warm-up with ten laps and meet me back here," he shouted at the swim team.

Persey finished her warm-ups laps and climbed out of the deep end. Water ran down her body in rivulets. She accepted a towel from Aaron, who made no effort to avert his appreciative gaze. Haden's eyes lingered on Aaron as the boy followed the towel-wrapped Persey back to the bleachers that lined the side of the pool. Haden had never given the boy much thought past his immediate emotions, which were transparent. But, as he stared at him, there it was. He saw the end of Aaron Strait and it was, pure and simple, the best gift he could have ever hoped to receive. The simplicity of it, combined with his absurd failure to discover what had been in plain sight ever since he returned to Clear Lake, almost made him laugh out loud.

"Aaron Strait," Haden called out, pacing back and forth in front of the assembled swim team.

"Coach Breen," Aaron called back from the bleachers.

"You're times are consistently the best on the team."

"Thanks Coach," Aaron replied.

"Don't thank me. You're the one putting in the hard work," said Haden, before he moved on to a standard pep talk for the team. Later, after practice, Haden lingered in the entryway of the swimming pool until Aaron came out. "Nice work today," he said, clapping the boy on the shoulder.

"I don't know," said Aaron with a laugh. "I probably could do better."

"Yeah? Then bring it. I want to see everything you've got at the next practice."

"Hey Aaron," said Persey, exiting the girl's locker room. Her hair was still wet, lying heavy on her shoulders.

"Do you two have a second?" Haden asked as though something had just occurred to him. "Come on, I've got something in my office I want to show you."

They followed him down the hall and sat down in the chairs he motioned towards. Haden rummaged around on his desk until he found the sheet of paper he'd located earlier. "Here it is," he said, handing the paper to Aaron. "These were the top times from last year's championship meet."

"Thanks," said Aaron.

"Nope, that's yours to keep," Haden said when Aaron tried to hand the paper back to him. "I think you've got it in you to beat those times."

"Thanks," said Aaron again.

"I was just going to make myself a cup of cocoa. Want one?" he asked. He tore open the little packet and dumped its contents into a Styrofoam cup. Persey looked at him and he saw something flash in her eyes. Did she remember their old ritual? Did she recognize him or was it only his imagination?

"I haven't had that kind of cocoa in years," she said, staring at the package in his hand like a long-lost totem.

"I'll take that as a yes." he said, tapping the package to dislodge any errant grains of powder from the top before he ripped it open.

He handed each of them a cup and their own packet of cocoa and watched them prepare it. Persey finished stirring then glanced at him again. She was nervous. He could feel it filling up the room. Haden remembered how he'd had to overcome her childhood instincts about him. He was gratified both her instincts and virginity remained intact. "Well, cheers," he said, holding his cocoa cup aloft. "Here's to the nicest couple on my swim team."

Aaron blushed and averted his eyes. Haden felt Persey's eyes on him and averted his own gaze. "What?" he said. "Am I embarrassing you? Listen; take it from an old man who's been around the block. Every now and then, you see two people together and you know they're right for each other. I'd be lying if I didn't say that doesn't describe the two of you."

Persey stood up. Her chair scraped against the floor and she set her cup back down on Haden's desk with more force than necessary. "We should get going," she said, glancing at her watch. Then she added, "Aaron's driving me home and my mom worries if I'm late."

"I understand," said Haden in a tone of voice that implied he too would worry about his daughter, if she were to arrive home later than expected.

"Thanks for the cocoa," said Aaron, following Persey out the door. He held up the time sheets in his hand and said, "And these too, it gives me something to work on."

Haden lifted his hand in a salute and watched them go. He'd made his move and now he had to wait. One thing was certain, this time the waiting wouldn't be so torturous. He had an insurance policy and it was called Aaron Strait. He'd seen the boys end and it had given him all the reassurance he needed. The boy's dogged devotion to Persey was all part of the plan. They were destined to be part of each other's futures. He understood that now. Persey would be there at Aaron's end, alive and well. He'd seen it just like he saw all the rest of humanity. For the first time, in the seven years since he'd laid eyes on Persey Campbell, he could stop worrying. He would have the time he needed to make her his. Death would not claim her before he did.

Chapter Twelve

In the beginning, after he'd first been sucked into Persey's orbit, he'd wondered if she was a portent of things to come. Was this the next step in the ever-evolving dance of humanity? But she remained an anomaly. Throughout the land of the living, he could see their deaths. He saw them all except for her. He saw each human end and was as powerless to change it as they were to stop it. Oh, to have the powers given to immortals in human myths. Gods—they were called—but Haden had no illusions about the truth. He was as bound by the limitations of his immortal existence as humans were by their mortal one.

The business of being immortal was exactly that; a business. Things happened on time in an orderly fashion. There were rules to follow and responsibilities to be upheld. Every moment of every day brought a new slew of souls passing from this life to the next. And each soul, like its human precedent, was unique. They were all different and in desperate need of guidance and tending. If Haden took a firm line with them it was because he believed himself to be a ruler committed to justice. They entered, were judged and escorted to their place in eternity. And there was a place for each of them. He made sure of it. Part of being a just and wise ruler entailed knowing how to mete out punishment. He dealt harshly with any who tried to escape, cheat or avoid their designation.

He passed judgment on them, yes. But not as the human myths and legends foretold. There was no careful consideration of their misdeeds weighed against their kindnesses. It wasn't necessary. More than that, they were so numerous that individual consideration was impossible. Each soul shone with its own individual color. The color provided a clear translation of the type of life the soul had led. The worst souls—the kind of humans who tortured or killed their own kind, preyed on children and other defenseless creatures—were swirling masses of muddy gray and brown with throbbing red centers. These were easy. They went straight to the darkest regions of the Underworld. The children, and there were many of them, were white shot through with streaks of pale yellow. They were just as easy as the evildoers. They were accorded the bliss of the Elysium. Almost everyone else was somewhere in between. It was Haden's job to interpret the swirling masses of colorful souls that thronged into his kingdom and shepherd them to their rightful resting place. He never knew the details of the lives that colored the souls swirling before him. Their sins and transgressions related to their humanness, and even in death, their humanity was not for him to know.

He'd had six years to ponder his distance from Persey and the rest of humanity. At some point during that time, Haden realized he was lonely. He alone, among the other immortals, could pass through eternity without ever coming into contact with life. He spent his days alone with no company other than that offered by dry swirling souls. Haden understood this was the reason he—again alone among the immortals—appreciated the full bloom of human life with the enthusiasm of a connoisseur. Souls varied between the two poles of good and evil but that was it. They were not, and could never be, passionate, full of heat, life and breath. They were vessels, emptied of their most precious gift. Their emptiness called to the emptiness inside of him, making him long to assuage it. For so many years, he'd relied upon the voyeuristic thrills of human acts of violence, passion or debauchery to appease his pangs. This was the only kind of remedy he'd ever expected the land of the living to provide, until he met Persey. Then with a flash of self-realization, he understood that all his earthly wanderings amounted to a search for something more.

Now that his goal was defined, in the form of this strange young human, he knew he must proceed with caution. The natural law that governed and protected them, mortals and immortals alike, could only be altered by human consent. Even with their consent, Haden was still unable to change their ending. A human end was sacred and untouchable by all immortals save one, and the consequences for failure to follow the natural law were severe. Haden had learned this the hard way. His first and only transgression of the natural law dated back to the time of initial human civilization. It was another girl, one also possessed of an entrancing, almost inhuman grace and beauty. She was young, maybe eleven or twelve when he first discovered her. He'd been unable to approach her. It had been impossible in that time, long, long ago because they still recognized him by instinct and feared his presence. Instead, he'd been forced to return again and again to the small village where she lived and watch her from the shadows.

Her end was clear to him and as the day grew closer, he became desperate to thwart it. The thought of her death tore at him until he made his decision. He would subvert natural law. He would steal her from the mouth of destiny. He could keep her safe in his kingdom of the dead. He was almost certain of it. So his dread of her final day turned to excitement as he waited for the moment when he would be able to reveal himself as her savior. The man who was destined to take her life was a beggar who slept in the forest by day and stole from the village people at night. On the appointed day, Haden watched from his place in the shadows as the girl's mother sent her to the farthest meadow to harvest the late summer fruit. Where the villager's meadow touched the forest, thickets of berries grew. It was to this place, at the edge of the forest, that his obedient, beautiful obsession headed to complete her task.

The beggar was awakened from a drunken stupor by a radiant vision of youth and beauty. He stalked her, as an animal stalks it prey. Haden knew her end. He had already seen the knobby, dirt-darkened fingers of the beggar's hand close around the white flesh of the girl's neck while the other hand ripped the dress from her body. He knew the beggar would take his fill of the girl. When he was finished, he would choke the air from her until every last trace of radiance disappeared from her luminous eyes. Then he would leave her body behind, disgraced and rotting among the sun-ripened blackberries. But no, she wouldn't end this way. He wouldn't allow it. He swept her into his arms, stealing her from her fate. It was a simple act, done in an instant and forever regretted. He had begun to believe the woven tapestry of human mythology. Haden thought he was a God, able to act without repercussion.

Chapter Thirteen

Kronos, the immortal keeper of time, ruler of immortals, father of both the world and Haden, was merciless in his punishment for Haden's transgression.

"By your actions, this human has escaped her destiny," Kronos said.

His cold smile made something inside Haden constrict. Many years had passed since he'd last seen his father, but the passing of time had done nothing to erase memories of his father's tendency towards hungry violence and capriciousness. Kronos enjoyed inflicting pain on both mortals and immortals alike.

"If it is your will that she live, then she shall live," continued his father. "However, she can no longer live as a human. She has come to the end of her time in this realm and I shall not grant her the gift of immortality. She will live as you have desired but her life will be unnatural. Watch, my son, behold the gift you have bestowed upon this human," his father said.

And Haden watched, unable to turn away, as his father made the years fall away. The girl's beautiful flesh and hair withered and faded but she didn't die. Death would have been a gift but Haden wasn't watching death. He more than anyone recognized death and this girl was suffering a fate far worse. As Kronos manipulated time, her life was stripped away. She became the frail old woman she was never destined to be. Then before his eyes, her skin decayed and rotted leaving behind bright exposed bones. Her internal organs swelled then exploded while the skeleton surrounding them began to disintegrate into fine powder, it blew away into nothingness with the wind. Even after she was nothing more than dust, Haden could still feel the fear and pain of her soul; and the reverberating echo of her screams, as she suffered underneath his father's cruel manipulations of time.

"I will claim her soul as mine in the Underworld," Haden cried.

Kronos shook his head and for an instant Haden thought he saw something like compassion cross the older immortal's haughty features. "No one will claim her. She is gone, as though she never existed. Only her suffering remains behind to haunt the world. You are lord over only those who find their way to your kingdom as ordained. You see their fate and you judge them in the Underworld. That is your dominion. Follow the natural law my son. Do not bring its wrath down upon the souls of your kingdom or it will unleash its wrath upon you."

Since that time, Haden had heeded his father's warning. His conscripts were clear. In life, he could manipulate them, bend them to his will and grant their petty wishes in return for the use of their body or the sale of their soul. Once they agreed to alter their destiny, they belonged, once and for all, to Haden. Even so, he was required to wait until their end came to pass, as proscribed by natural law, before he could collect on his bargain. He kept them in the grey gloomy forgetfulness of Erebus where they retained no memory of their former lives. In that dim place, they were unable to experience the joy or misery allotted to other souls of the Underworld. They belonged to Haden alone, to use as he saw fit.

But what about the one he didn't see? His fortunate glimpse of Aaron's end had brought him comfort from the first piece of that question. Now, it was the second piece of the question that haunted him. Did the natural law apply to one whose fate was unknowable to the lord of death? How could he be accused of subverting the laws of fate when it appeared as though she had no fate? Despite the appealing logic to that argument, he still felt he must proceed with caution. He had no desire to incur his father's wrath again. He would not risk an offense of the natural law which would demand Persey's life and soul in return. The best course was patience. She must come to him of her own accord. Once she was his, he could keep her safe in his dark kingdom while he searched for a way to subvert her inevitable death and bind her to him forever.

Chapter Fourteen

Persey Campbell-Strait started at Goldman Parke, fresh out of law school. She wasn't hired through the summer associate program which was unusual. Although that wasn't the reason Daniel remembered her. Her resume was plucked from a pile of similar resumes sent from middle-tier law schools. He knew what her resume contained because he'd been one of the partners in her initial series of interviews. The recruiters at Goldman Parke often asked Daniel to interview because he, no surprises here, had the ability to suss out information about prospective candidates that other interviewers missed. He glanced at Persey's unremarkable resume, five minutes before she walked in the door, and prepared himself to arrange his face into a genial expression designed to hide his annoyance at having to postpone his lunch plans.

The firm's custom was to set up a series of interviews for each potential new hire. Someone from the recruiting department would walk the candidate to the first lawyer's office. That lawyer would walk the prospective candidate to the next office on the list, make the necessary introductions and then leave. It was an elaborate charade designed to camouflage the inner fiefdoms and rivalries of the firm by painting everything with the broad brush of chummy collegiality. Oddly enough, the first thing that struck Daniel about her was not her physical appearance. It was the way her previous interviewer was talking to her. George Rosenberg was a senior partner in the trusts and estates department. He was well-respected at the firm despite, or maybe because of, his reticence to weigh in on most matters. On the rare occasion he saw fit to make his opinion known, people leaned in to hear him speak as though his words carried the wisdom of ages.

Daniel heard them coming down the hall to his office before he saw them. George's voice boomed out, "That's right Persey. I've been saying that for years." A second later, George knocked twice on Daniel's open door. The two walked in but George seemed inclined to linger. He made the necessary introductions but did nothing to detach himself from the conversation. George had already stretched the interview past the boundaries of conventionality when he took the girl's hand between his own and said, "I don't know when I've enjoyed talking to a candidate more. You've got my card, right?" Persey nodded. "Don't hesitate to call me if this one gives you any trouble." he said, nodding towards Daniel.

Daniel was struck by the way she didn't giggle or falter under the elderly man's excessive attention.

"She's a keeper, Daniel," he said in open disregard of Goldman Parke hiring policy. Then, with one last look at Persey, he relinquished her hand and closed Daniel's office door behind him.

"Umm," said Daniel, clearing his throat.

"It's alright," said Persey. "I understand it's probably all done by committee. I know he can't promise me a job, and this firm is a little out of my league. Maybe I'll learn something just by going through the interview process, right?" She said all this as though she was trying to put him at ease instead of the other way around.

It was then he noticed her blonde hair, curling around her face and felt the sudden impact in his stomach that her deep blue eyes made. She smiled at him from the other side of his desk, as though he was in need of encouragement and that was all it took.

Later—he was certain only a few minutes had passed—his phone rang. He ignored it. A second later, Linda rapped on his office door before poking her head in.

"Mr. Hartnett, I've got your 1:00 on hold and Ms. Campbell is way behind schedule. Ms. Abrams is waiting for her."

"Right," said Daniel, jumping up out of his chair.

Linda raised her eyebrows at him. He had the absurd sensation of feeling like he'd been caught whacking off instead of losing track of time for a few minutes. "Can I see your schedule?" he asked Persey, hating the way his voice sounded pompous and somehow ingratiating.

"Sure." She pushed her interview sheet across the desk to him.

"Ellen's the last interview on her list," he said to Linda who was still standing in his door. He glanced at his watch and then at Persey. "I'm hungry. Are you hungry?"

"I could eat," she said with a small smile.

Daniel looked back at Linda. "Call Ellen and tell her I'm taking Ms. Campbell to lunch."

"What about the call?" asked Linda.

"Reschedule it. Tell them something came up."

Linda gave Daniel a grim nod that he almost didn't notice. He was too happy to be taking Persey Campbell out to lunch to care about anything else.

What did they talk about over their lunch? Afterwards, he could only remember bits and pieces. All he knew is that he was overcome with the strongest urge to tell her things he had never needed or wanted to tell anyone else. He found himself divulging the most private details of his relationship with his mother. "She thinks I'm gay," he said shaking his head. He was struck by the way she listened to him, no judgments or laughter. He was also struck by her complete oblivion to her own beauty. By now, her deep blue eyes were radiating through Daniel's consciousness like a strobe light. Either she didn't notice or didn't care about the way heads—both male and female—turned on the crowded midtown sidewalk to watch as she passed by. She took no pleasure in the solicitude of their waiter or the hovering busboy who refilled her water glass after every sip. Nor did she use Daniel's candor as an excuse to flirt or giggle her way into a job. Instead, she just listened. Daniel was entranced.

"But you're not? Gay, I mean." she asked.

"No, not even bi-curious," he stressed. His unexpected use of this trendy word elicited a smile. "Tell me about Iowa," he said when he realized he'd monopolized most of their conversation.

"Okay," she said, then bit the side of her bottom lip, drawing his attention to the fullness of her mouth.

He could tell it wasn't premeditated but its effect on him was as though someone had grabbed hold of his lower intestines and squeezed. His palms grew clammy at the thought of what he'd like to do to her lips. He rubbed them on his pants and tried to quell his improbable need to tell her what he was thinking.

"It's the only state that starts with two vowels, but you probably already know that," she said, giving him a mischievous look that made him laugh. "And, it's the home of the world's largest strawberry."

"And here I was expecting you to tell me about corn," said Daniel.

"There's that too," said Persey. "But I was trying to think of things you didn't already know."

After lunch, he said a regretful good bye and returned to his office to recover from the complete intoxication of her presence. It wasn't until he was back at his office staring at his computer screen that the full impact of her words hit him. She'd come right out and said it, he thought shaking his head in amazement. She was trying to think of things he didn't already know. And she had. When she told him Iowa was home to the world's largest strawberry that was all he heard, nothing else. It was all he thought about for the rest of the afternoon even as he pretended to participate in meetings and respond to email. Was it possible this girl, alone among all the other girls he had met in his thirty-nine years, possessed no hidden messages burbling up in her subconscious trying to communicate with Daniel? He didn't think so. There was something about Persey that was different than anyone else he had met, male or female. She left him wanting more. She made him feel off-kilter and uncertain. In fact, the only thing he was certain of, was that all the time she'd been talking about vowels and fruit, all he could think about was kissing her. He had no idea if she wanted to kiss him back or if she even found him attractive. He didn't know anything about her and he was desperate to see her again.

She was hired. There was no question about it in anyone's mind. Daniel made a call to Bill Weiss, the hiring partner himself.

"I'm looking forward to meeting this girl." said Bill. "You're not the only one who thought she'd be an asset. George called me as soon as he finished her interview. I've already sent a memo down to the recruiting department with directions to extend the offer."

The problem with a law firm the size of Goldman Parke was that it had a certain amount of inner bureaucracy. There were hiring protocols to be followed, training to be negotiated and time-off extended as a courtesy for all first year lawyers to study for and take the New York state bar exam. Daniel never recognized how problematic Goldman Parke's slow-moving bureaucracy was until three months after his fateful lunch with Persey. On that anticipated day, Persey walked in the front doors of Goldman Parke as a full-fledged employee. Except she was no longer Persey Campbell, now she was Persey Campbell-Strait looking tanned, fresh and untouchable.

"Congratulations," said Daniel, poking his head into her office on her first day. "I didn't even know you were engaged and now I hear you're married?"

Persey smiled up at him and Daniel felt the shock of those serious blue eyes meeting his own. "It was a whirlwind," she confessed. "We've known each other since high school. We kind of fell out of touch but then we ran into each other this summer.

When he asked me, I said yes. He wanted to do it right away so we did. It just felt right," she explained, saving him the need to ask any questions.

Daniel could feel Persey's secretary hovering just behind him. The woman's presence saved him from the ridiculous and inappropriate speech that almost emerged from his lips. Persey was now, right there in front of him. Except she was married and all the fervent workings of his imagination would never come to pass.

"Well, I just stopped by to congratulate you," he said again. Then he walked back down the hall to his office feeling as though she had inserted a knife into the depths of his heart.

Chapter Fifteen

On the morning of her twenty-eighth birthday, Aaron gave Persey a Hermes Birkin bag. "This is a ten thousand dollar purse," she said, gasping at the supple luxury of it underneath her fingers.

Aaron grinned. "Do you like it?"

"It's so fancy," she said. Then she added, "Of course I do. I love it."

"Check inside. There might be something else." She slid the bag open without taking her eyes off of Aaron. If you didn't know him the way Persey did, you'd never guess his true nature—his elemental goodness. He inhabited the role of Wall Street investment banker with the same ease he'd inhabited the role of starting quarterback at Clear Lake High School. Beneath all his apparent brio and ruler of the universeness, he was the same high school boy who had always protected and loved her, without ever demanding anything in return.

Her fingers touched an envelope and she pulled it out of the purse. It was imprinted with a red logo for a place called "Studio H". "What's this?" she said without opening it.

"A gift certificate," said Aaron. He sat down next to her on the bed and smoothed her hair away from her face. "For a yoga studio."

"A yoga studio?" she said.

"Yeah, you keep saying you want to do yoga," he reminded her.

"I have been saying that, haven't I?" She leaned into him and kissed him on his nose.

"I researched this place," he said, tapping the certificate. "It's near here and supposed to be great. At least that's what all the reviews said."

He was so enthusiastic she couldn't help but smile.

"I knew you'd never get around to doing the research on your own so now you have a year's membership for unlimited classes."

"Thank you. Best present ever," she said, sliding onto his lap. She wrapped her legs around his waist and kissed him. "You weren't planning on going to work before I said thank you, were you?" she whispered, loosening his tie.

Persey loved Aaron. If she was sure of anything in this life, it was that. How could she not love him? He'd discovered her (rediscovered her) in the reading room of the Schwarzman Building; that grand branch of the New York Public Library best known for its stone lions and cameo appearances in Ghostbusters. She'd been sitting at a long table surrounded by New York Bar study guides. A homeless man had been sitting across from her all morning and she had been avoiding his gaze. She knew even the tiniest glance in his direction would result in the man unburdening himself upon her. She really, really didn't want to know his secrets.

She was so intent on not looking up that she didn't notice Aaron until he said her name.

"Persey Campbell?" he said it as though it was one word, like an incantation.

She looked up and his face lit up with disbelief and joy. He was wearing a suit. She'd never seen him in a suit before and for some reason it struck her as funny. He looked like a little boy, playing at being a grown up. Before she could say anything, two other men in suits appeared at his side and Persey was reminded of the way Aaron was always surrounded by football players in high school.

"You coming?" asked one of the suits, with a curious glance at Persey.

Aaron waved them off. "Go on. I'll catch up with you," he said.

"I heard you were in New York," she said. She had, in fact, heard this more than once. All at once, she felt guilty about not having made any effort to track him down.

"I'm sorry about your mother," he replied.

Persey looked down at the floor tracing a pattern with her foot for a moment before she answered. "Thank you for the flowers," she said without looking up. She swallowed hard trying to get rid of the lump in her throat. "They were beautiful. She would have loved them. She used to spend so much time in her garden. Do you remember?" She blinked back the tears that were already welling up in her eyes.

"God, I'm an asshole," Aaron said, coming to her rescue. "I don't know why I said that. I just wanted you to know......" He broke off shaking his head. "I don't see you for nine years and the first thing I do is make you cry."

He loosened his tie as he spoke and Persey caught a glimpse of the man he'd become.

"Are you thirsty? I'm thirsty," he said.

He was respected. She could tell by the way he spoke and by the way the other two suits had disappeared at his direction. Of course, how was that any different from high school? Nothing had changed. He was still the same person she'd known all those years ago, except now he was grown up.

"Come on," he said with the smile she remembered so well, "let me buy you something to drink."

"Okay," she said, stacking up her study materials. He scooped them up as she'd known he would and maneuvered her out of the library and into a café across the street. He was Aaron, just as she remembered him and he still wanted to keep her safe.

Over the years, Persey had developed a well-honed sixth sense about people. She knew who she could trust (which was not to say the ones she trusted still didn't tell her things) and who she needed to be careful around. Everyone told her things. Persey knew it was just a matter of degrees. The kinds of things good people told her weren't so bad, she could handle it. But the bad secrets were terrible. The worse the secret, the more desperate its holder was to confess. This meant she couldn't rely on her sixth sense alone. Evasive maneuvers were often necessary. She was proficient at sidetracking people, interrupting, making excuses to leave the room, and most important of all, never being alone with someone. Secrets, she knew, preferred to be told in private. But with Aaron it didn't matter. She could be herself and let him talk because she knew there was nothing dark hiding inside Aaron Strait.

"I can't believe I'm sitting here with you," he said, grinning at her across the table like a little boy. "I mean I think about you all the time but I haven't seen you in so long. I'm seeing this girl right now and even when I'm 'with her', you know, I'm not with her," he said with an emphatic raise of his eyebrows that left no confusion as to what he meant. "It's like all I can see is your face." He broke off, blushing. "God, it's all coming back to me. What is it about you that turns me into a complete idiot? Remember all the crazy stuff I was always telling you in high school? It's almost like I can't help myself."

"I don't mind," said Persey, smiling at him.

"Yeah, why would you?" said Aaron shaking his head. "I'm the crazy guy who tells you everything. It must give you a lot to laugh about."

"No, it's not like that at all," she said, even though she was laughing. Then, because she was happier then she'd been in a long time and she knew it was what he wanted, what he'd always wanted, she leaned across the table and kissed him.

Despite all the time they'd spent together in high school it was the first time their lips had touched. They'd only had the two years together. By the time she started her junior year and he was off at college a pattern was set. Nobody bothered her because it was a known and accepted fact that Persey Campbell and Aaron Strait were together.

This was true, just not in the way people assumed. They spent a lot of time together. Aside from her mother, Persey had spent more one-on-one time with Aaron than anyone else in her life. There was ample time for Aaron to divulge all of his secrets to Persey. It was no mystery to Persey he wished the rumors were true. His inability to prevent himself from divulging all his thoughts to her made him resolute about waiting for her to take the lead. "I don't know why I tell you all this stuff," he would say over and over. "But I don't ever want you to feel pressured. If you ever want to take it to the next level, then you need to make the first move."

Afterwards, when she became more aware of what it meant to be a teenage boy, Persey realized how much it must have taken for Aaron to never even attempt to kiss her. Each time he told her—and there were many occasions—of his need to touch her, sink himself inside her and crush her with his body, he was thoroughly mortified. Persey was less so. If anything, she liked hearing his secrets because they never came with the unanticipated new spin on horrible that other people's secrets contained.

Even though she knew what Aaron was waiting for, she never made that first move. It wasn't that she didn't want to. If anything, she wanted to feel him against her body as much as he did but something held her back. Maybe it was the fear that mixing physical contact with all the secrets swirling around in her head would overwhelm her. Or maybe it was some vague notion that the perfect boyfriend wouldn't need to tell her his secrets. She often sat alone in her window seat and stared out over the trees wondering if it would ever be her turn to talk while someone else listened.

Then he'd gone away to college and she'd released him.

"You need to find a girlfriend," she whispered to him on her porch in the heat and waning sun of a late August evening.

"I don't want anyone else," he said, squeezing her hand. "I just want you. You know how much I want you. I love you, Persey."

They were sitting on the wicker loveseat and she could feel the heat emanating off his body, making its need felt as something distinct from the warmth of the muggy night.

"I can't," she said, not daring to look at him. "Not yet and Aaron," she continued, rushing the words together so she didn't have to think too much about their meaning. "I can't make you wait for me anymore because I don't know if I can ever give you what you need."

"Do you love me?" he asked, releasing her hand from his death hold and tracing her fingertips. "All I need to know is that you love me."

"I do love you, like family, like a brother," she said. She hated the words but she knew they were necessary to ensure his escape. "Like the best brother in the world."

He put her hand back in her lap and looked out into the darkness. When he turned his face back to her, she could see the tears in his eyes. "I don't think I can see you for awhile," he said, not meeting her gaze.

"I know," she said. She sat on the porch and waited for him to get into his car and drive away before she succumbed to tears of her own.

Nine years later, their first kiss at a sidewalk café in New York City lasted only a moment. But when Persey pulled away, she knew she'd done something irreversible.

"Let's go for a walk," Aaron said. He picked up her heavy bag of study guides, as though they were still in high school. They walked downtown, escaping the push and rush of Fifth Avenue, until they came to a park on lower Madison Avenue. They walked like old friends or a long-married couple comfortable with silence. He led her past the small fenced playground with its Caribbean nannies cluttering the narrow paths with their strollers. On the other side of the playground was a fountain, Aaron led her to a bench, where together they watched the rushing water together.

"You kissed me," he said at last.

When he turned towards her, Persey saw the same expression of disbelief he'd worn when he first discovered her not more than two hours ago.

"Yes," she said. "I'm sorry. I know you're seeing someone. I just thought…." her voice trailed off because she didn't want to give words to what she'd thought.

"Persey," he said. "Don't you understand there's never been anyone but you? I've been waiting for you to kiss me since high school." Then he kissed her again and she could feel the hunger in his lips and the safety in the way he held her in his arms. He was her protection against the rest of the world and she knew he'd never allow anything to hurt her.

They walked further downtown, towards the village. He told her everything, the worst of his everything as he always had. His worst secrets only confirmed his kindness, reliability and essential goodness. Every few blocks, every few moments Aaron stopped and pulled her to him again, kissing her. He looked at her with a strange look of disbelief and wonder.

"I never thought I'd be doing this," he said, running his hand along the softness at the base of her skull. "I dreamed about it but even my dreams weren't half as good as the reality."

Persey leaned into his waiting mouth and kissed him again, enjoying the press of his lips against hers. Then she said, "I'm starving."

They found a restaurant. It was an old-fashioned Italian one, the kind with banquettes and red-checkered tablecloths. They sat together side-by-side. Persey told him about law school and the job waiting for her at Goldman Parke, as he traced patterns on the backs of her hands. He looked at her, rapt and starry-eyed. She had the feeling he was so overcome by her physical presence that he was unable to process the words coming out of her mouth.

After the waiter left them alone with their dessert, Aaron whispered to her, "Marry me."

"Aaron, it's only been a few hours," she said. She started to laugh but then she realized he was serious.

"No one knows me better than you do," he said. "I've been waiting for you all my life, ever since high school, and now you're here again. I don't want to lose you. I understand if you need to think about it, but I don't need any time because I know this is what I want. It's what I've always wanted more than anything. Will you marry me?"

"Yes.......yes I will," said Persey because she knew how much he loved her. Because she knew his worst secrets and still wanted to be with him and because she was so tired of being all alone.

Chapter Sixteen

Daniel knew his reasons for monopolizing most of Persey's time weren't entirely professional. Screw that, his reasons were as good as anyone else's. She was damn good at what she did. She never complained. She knew her shit. She never acted like the work was beneath her and she got things done on time. What more could he ask for? He wasn't alone in wanting to work with her. He'd already had a couple of power plays with some other partners at Goldman Parke who'd also discovered Persey's talent-set. He'd been stupid to ever let anyone else get wind of her. He should have monopolized her time right from the beginning. He would have done just that, if a heretofore unrecognized sensitive side hadn't reared its ugly head. He'd avoided her during her first months at Goldman Parke. He'd needed that time to mourn her marriage.

Persey's first two months at Goldman Parke inspired something like clinical depression in Daniel Hartnett. She was an open wound that became re-infected every time he walked by her office. If he heard someone mention her or chanced to ride up in the elevator with her it hurt, physically hurt! It sucked. He spent two months being pissed off about how much it sucked. How could she get married? He took it personally, as if she had entered into her marriage for the sole purpose of torturing him. It had only been three months between the time he first interviewed her and her first day at Goldman Parke. Who goes from being unengaged to married in three months?

The first two months after she started at the firm, Daniel spent a lot of time moping in his office with the door shut. One day Linda came in, closed his office door behind her, and said, "We're all a little worried about you, Mr. Hartnett. Is everything all right?"

By which he understood her to say, "Bill Weiss's secretary, Miriam, overheard Bill say he was concerned about you." Linda liked him. He knew that. He also knew that she wasn't here just because of the kindness of her heart. It was good to be the secretary of an influential partner and she wasn't going to let his ship sink if she could help it. Still, he appreciated the gesture. It told him he'd wallowed in his misery long enough and it was time to pull his shit together.

So he did. Before Bill Weiss could so much as get his panties in a bunch, Daniel sealed up all his (now ridiculous) hopes and thoughts about Persey and got back to the business of law. Despite what anyone else might say, Daniel understood that the business of law was also the business of making money. "That's what a law degree is after all," one of his law school professors liked to say, "Just a license to print money." His legal license, combined with Daniel's own special license, allowed him to sign two new clients by the end of the week.

"Looking forward to working with you," said Intelicorp's head of business development over dinner on Thursday. By which Daniel knew he meant, "Bring this deal in on-time without any major fuck ups and I'll put Goldman Parke on everything I've got going on in the Asian market."

"Absolutely," said Daniel, shaking the man's hand. Even though it was close to ten o'clock when they left the restaurant, Daniel decided to head back to the office and draft up the Intelicorp contract for representation. His new client would be pleased at the efficiency of receiving the contract first thing in the morning, not to mention the other partners at Goldman Parke would get their second reminder this week about his status as rainmaker extraordinaire.

The office was dark when he stepped off the elevator. He headed down the hall that led to his corner office. In the months since Persey had started, he'd taken to circumventing this most direct route to his office because it passed by Persey's office. Ever since she'd disclosed her happy news and ripped his heart into shreds, he'd regretted telling the office manager to put her on his floor. It made avoiding her more difficult than it should have been in a firm that took up six floors and had over a hundred attorneys. During the day, he avoided passing by her office by using the farther hallway. But tonight, with the lights turned out and everything quiet, he headed to his office by the normal route—the one that led right past Persey's open door.

She was working by soft lamplight which was why he hadn't seen the light when he turned down the hallway.

"Hey," he said, surprised to see her still at her desk. She was bent over some kind of form, pen in hand, her hair pulled back into a late-night pony tail except for the few escaped curls that framed her face.

At the sound of his voice, she started and then laughed, "You scared me."

"Whatcha got there?" he asked, trying to push the thought of kissing her (and more alarmingly, the desire to tell her he wanted to kiss her) into his internal lockbox.

"Commercial lease," she said, "WITH about a million comments. Who signs these things anyway?"

"Lazy people who don't read the form or poor people who can't afford an attorney," said Daniel, leaning up against the doorway. "You're here pretty late," he said glancing at his watch.

"Yeah," she said. "You too, what are you working on?"

It was the way she looked at him, Daniel thought, as he sat down uninvited in one of the chairs facing her desk. Resistance would have been futile so he didn't even try. Instead, he told her all about his new client and what it meant for Daniel. He would have told her—in fact, could feel himself warming to the subject and getting ready to tell her—how he'd been able to know what the man had meant.

Daniel didn't think of his crap-o-meter as a secret. It just wasn't something he talked about. It wasn't like it ever came up in conversation. But he was on the verge of telling her all about it.

At that moment, Persey's phone rang.

Even though Daniel couldn't hear the meaning behind her words when she held up one finger and said, "I should really take this," he was astute enough to notice the look of relief on her face that he'd been brought up short.

The phone conversation was a murmured series of "Yeses," and "Not much longer." Then she hung up. "It was my husband," she said. "He worries about me."

Daniel glanced at his watch. "Shit," he said with surprise. "I didn't realize what time it was."

Persey nodded.

He stood up to leave then on an impulse, he added, "I want you to work on this deal."

"Sounds great," she said.

"Great," he said, even though he knew she didn't have much choice about whether or not she worked on his deal. He also knew she was just being polite by listening to him babble about it for almost a half an hour. But still, he left her office feeling light-hearted and optimistic. It was the best he'd felt in three months. Maybe... he thought as he headed down the hallway to his office, just maybe it would be enough to just talk with her. And maybe he didn't need to feel the touch of her skin on his and know the contours of her mouth.

He had a sudden overwhelming urge to rush back to her and give voice to all his thoughts. He could hear the words in his head as though he'd already uttered them. "I'm sorry I was such a prick when you first started but it's because—and I know this sounds crazy—but I think I fell in love with you that first time I met you. Do you remember our lunch together... because it was all I thought about this summer. But now I'm thinking it might be okay if we just work together, you know, hang out. I'd like to get to know you better."

He glanced back down the hallway but Persey's light was turned off and her door was shut. He drew a sudden sigh of relief. What was wrong with him, he wondered as he fired up his computer? What on earth would possess him to even contemplate the notion of such an excruciating conversation?

Chapter Seventeen

Their late night conversation was a milestone of sorts. Daniel was able to withdraw the knife, so to speak. He put his crush into perspective. True, Persey was married, but that didn't mean he couldn't work with her. Aside from all the obvious stuff you saw when you looked at her, she was also hard-working, efficient and smart. She was still a little distant with him, but he had hopes she would let down her guard as they got to know each other better. Their friendship was a work-in-progress. That's what he told himself.

In fact, he'd never met anyone so adept at avoiding situations that might lead to any kind of intimacy. As the months passed, he realized what a rare moment he'd experienced when he stumbled on her working alone. It made him feel better that her cool reserve wasn't just for him. Daniel wasn't the only one in the office who was drawn to her. She fended off clerical workers, fellow first year associates at the firm and other enamored partners alike. What was the message behind her words, he wondered for what felt like the millionth time? Could it be something as simple as 'leave me alone'? Whatever it was, Daniel still couldn't hear it.

He often invited her to grab lunch with him.

She always turned him down with some variation on the same theme. "Thanks, but I have a lot of work to catch up on," or "I would but I brought my lunch today."

That's why he was so surprised the first time she said yes.

"I'm meeting Bob McCleary for lunch," he said to Linda when he walked in that morning. Persey was passing by and before she moved out of earshot he called, "Hey Persey, want to meet one of the titans of the airline industry? We're having lunch today."

She paused without turning around and said, "Okay."

"Okay?" he said, unable to keep the note of surprise out of his voice.

"What time?" she asked, looking back at him over one shoulder.

"Twelve-thirty, I'll stop by your office," he said and then retreated to his own office, hoping Linda hadn't noticed how flustered he was.

He briefed Persey on Bob McCleary as they walked to the restaurant. "He's huge. He's just been made CEO and he's looking to upgrade his airline's fleet. The financing for that kind of project is easily going to be billions of dollars. We want to convince him that Goldman Parke can negotiate his projects and bring them in, on time and on budget."

Halfway through lunch, Daniel's phone rang. He pulled it out of his pocket and saw it was Linda calling for the fourth time. "Excuse me for a minute. I'm really sorry but I have to take this," he said, sliding out from behind the table and headed toward the lobby. He couldn't have been gone more than five minutes but when he returned Persey was staring at heavy set, flush-faced Bob McCleary, the CEO of a national airline, with undisguised contempt.

"It's all settled then," said Bob, glancing at Daniel. He swiped at the sudden beads of sweat that had popped out on his forehead with a handkerchief. "We're looking forward to using Goldman Parke. I'll...I'll have my secretary send the documents over this afternoon," Bob stammered, pushing his chair back.

"Is everything alright?" Daniel asked, glancing from Bob to Persey.

Persey was staring at the table refusing to meet Daniel's eyes.

"Fine, fine," said Bob, shaking Daniel's hand. "Sorry to run out on you like this, but I've got to get back to the office, things blowing up all over. You know the drill. Looking forward to working with you."

He gave Daniel a strained grin as he backed away from the table and headed towards the front of the restaurant. Daniel watched him go with confusion, because underneath all of Bob's words, Daniel heard him say, "God, don't let her tell anyone. Please God, don't let her tell."

"What just happened?" Daniel asked, sitting down across from Persey.

"I don't know," said Persey with a shrug. She was studying the tablecloth.

To Daniel's immense frustration, all he could hear was her words. "Did he hit on you?" he asked.

"No," said Persey and her shoulders started to shake.

For a moment Daniel thought she was crying but then he realized she was trying to suppress her laughter.

"What happened?" asked Daniel again. He felt like a child begging to be let in on a private joke.

"I think," said Persey after taking a deep breath and dabbing at the corners of her eyes with a napkin. "I think he might have been embarrassed about the pictures he showed me."

"What?" asked Daniel. "What kind of pictures did he show you?" That was the problem with private jokes. They always needed to be explained.

"It seems... I can't believe I'm telling you this," said Persey, staring hard at her plate and trying to keep a straight face. "Our new client enjoys wearing diapers. He prefers the cloth kind, less chafing he says. He has this woman who changes him. She spanks him if it's wet or," and here she paused and made a little face. "Or dirty."

Daniel stared at her in amazement. "Why would he tell you that?" he asked, shaking his head in disbelief.

Persey shrugged her shoulders. "I don't know, but he did. Does the reason matter why?"

"No," said Daniel as he thought of his own urge to tell Persey the untellable. "No, I guess it doesn't."

Chapter Eighteen

After that day, Daniel made it a point to observe Persey. He was methodical about it. After all, he prided himself on being in the know. Ever since his lunch with Persey and Bob McCleary, it was obvious that there was something about Persey he didn't understand.

Observation of this sort was a new experience for him. So much of what he needed to know in life had always come to him through people's words. Daniel noticed, for example, when she went out for lunch with the other associates it was always in a group. She kept her office door open, the better, he realized, to avoid one-on-one conversations. When she was on client calls, she kept them on speaker phone. "Just so you know," he overheard her say again and again as he walked by. "I have you on speaker phone."

The only time she held the phone to her ear, cradled it lovingly up against her cheek was when she was on the phone with her husband. "It's Aaron," she would mouth to Daniel if he happened to be in her office.

Daniel would nod and slink out of her office, knowing full well if it had been any other junior associate in the firm, he would not have allowed himself to be dismissed. No, with anyone else, he would wait until they brought their conversation to a speedy conclusion.

Aaron, the man was a constant thorn in Daniel's side. What was so special about him? How had he managed to swoop in and convince Persey to get married so quickly? As far as Daniel could tell, Aaron was nothing more than your typical Wall Street fraternity boy.

He hated the way Aaron came to pick Persey up from the office on Friday nights. He was jealous—all right he was a big-boy, he could admit it—that Aaron and Aaron alone was given the privilege of sitting in Persey's office with the door closed.

The man was her husband. Daniel knew this. Even so, every time he walked by her closed door on a Friday night he was overwhelmed with childish resentment.

"Glad to hear you're taking care of my girl," Aaron would say whenever he saw Daniel.

Then he'd shake Daniel's hand and give him that stupid midwestern grin. What was even worse is Daniel could hear the real meaning behind Aaron's words. He knew Aaron was sincere. He was glad to have Daniel looking out for Persey. What Persey had said was true. Aaron worried about her.

"So you and Aaron were high school sweethearts?" Daniel asked one night when they were working late in his office.

He'd worked hard for the privilege of this kind of intimacy. It didn't take a genius to realize she didn't like to be alone with people. What had been real work is to figure out the source of her aversion.

He'd been slow on the uptake given the strange client luncheon with Bob McCleary—maybe he wasn't half as smart as he thought he was. In the end, it was the smallest thing that pulled it all together for him. They were at one of the monthly departmental luncheons held in the firm conference rooms. He was standing behind her in line when she reached for a sandwich from the lunch buffet.

"How's the tuna salad?" Persey asked the caterer.

Before she could pick it up, the caterer stopped her. "Not that one," the woman whispered, searching for a better specimen. "I sneezed on it."

He stood without moving for a moment as the pieces clicked into place. People told her things, things that they wouldn't tell anyone else. God, Bob McCleary and his weird fetish, it all clicked. Daniel remembered his own desire to tell her things and swallowed hard. All of a sudden, he had a lot more insight into Persey Campbell-Strait.

The first thing he worked on was conquering his own urges. The next day he pulled the door shut behind him as he went into her office. He caught the glimpse of resignation flit across her face as he sat down across from her. She'd been here before. That's what that look said. She was steeling herself for whatever was coming. He had the bad fortune to make eye contact with her and the need to bare his soul to her became an almost unbearable physical pressure. He had to confide or he would be crushed by his need. Instead he faked a coughing fit.

"Be right back," he said as he ran out of her office.

The next time he returned to her office, he was prepared with a pen and paper. Again he shut the door and again she gave him that same look. It was almost expectant. This time he was more careful. He didn't meet her eyes. He didn't look up from his legal pad. Instead, he forced himself to ask her the questions he'd already scrawled on the paper.

"Great, you're doing great work Persey," he said, braving a glance in her direction before he stood up.

"Thanks Daniel," she said.

That was all it took, that one look. He could feel his innermost thoughts desperate to spill out. He rushed out of her office before they could.

The next time was easier. And the next time easier still. He learned little tricks. It was easier if he jacked-off first. He wasn't proud of it and he had to fight back the constant need to tell her he'd just jacked-off but it made the whole process less painful. He shuddered to think how many horny teenage boys had confessed to her that she was the vision they saw each night in their lonely beds while they stroked themselves. He didn't want to be part of that club.

He also learned it was easier if he didn't make eye contact. Losing yourself in those deep blue eyes was a little like swallowing truth serum. Little-by-little, day-by-day, he worked up his resistance to her. He felt like Mithridates, the King of Pontus, who swallowed a tiny amount of poison every day so as to make himself immune to a large dose. In Daniel's case, the poison he was swallowing was of his own making.

She began to trust him. He could see it in the way she stopped bracing herself every time they were alone. He wished he could reassure her that she was safe with him. He would never burden her with the dregs of his humanity. But he knew this was just another kind of confession and so he kept it to himself. He was afraid one confession might lead to another. Like water pouring through a broken dam, everything he'd been holding in might come spilling out of him. Instead, he bided his time and enjoyed the sweetness of small victories, like the one at present. It was very sweet to be alone with her late in the night when the quiet of the office gave the overwhelming impression of intimacy.

Unsure whether she was ignoring him or hadn't heard him the first time, he repeated himself, "So you and Aaron were high school sweethearts?"

"Sort of," she said, glancing up from the documents spread out in front of her.

"I have this vision of you two as king and queen of the Prom."

"I didn't go to my Prom with Aaron. Actually, I didn't go at all," she said softly.

Daniel listened. He was afraid any interruption in her train of thought would make her stop talking.

"Aaron's two years older than I am so he was in college my senior year. When he went away, I told him I wanted him to date other people." She paused for a long time staring out the window of Daniel's corner office.

He knew she wasn't looking down at the glittering line of traffic making its way up Park Avenue. She was back in Iowa. Clear Lake, Iowa, if he remembered correctly. "But you didn't date anyone else?" Daniel prompted.

Persey looked at him and smiled sadly. "I'm not even sure I really dated Aaron. We never even kissed," she stopped talking and shook her head as if to banish the conversation.

"You cared for him, though," he said.

"I trusted him," she said without taking her eyes off the traffic far below. "I knew he was a good person and he wouldn't hurt me. He came between me and everyone else and that's what I needed. That's also why I told him to date other people. I felt so guilty that he spent all his time as my self-appointed protector and I couldn't give him anything in return. I couldn't be a real girlfriend to him."

'Why not?' The question burned unuttered in Daniel's throat but he couldn't bring himself to ask it. Not when he had the unshakable sense that the reason she still had her back to him was so he wouldn't see the tears in her eyes.

"Daniel," she said, turning away from the sinuous stream of light outside.

Her eyes met his and he felt himself being pulled inside, unable to speak, almost unable to think. All he wanted to do was press his lips against her warm flesh, bury his hands in her hair and turn himself inside out so she could know every infinitesimal piece that made up Daniel Hartnett.

"Sometimes I feel the same way with you," she said with a hint of a smile. "I feel like I can talk to you and I don't ever have to worry," she stopped and laughed, looking away for a moment. When she looked back in his direction the moment was over. Her mask was back in place. "I guess I'm just saying I like working with you," she finished.

It took every ounce of self-control but somehow Daniel pushed back his need, desire and confessions and said in what he hoped was a steady voice, "I like working with you too, Persey."

Chapter Nineteen

Aaron had to work all weekend. "I'll try to be home before five," he whispered early Saturday morning. He kissed her gently on the forehead before tiptoeing out of their bedroom. She heard the solid thunk the front door made when it closed and the sound of his key turning, locking her safely inside. She turned over underneath the covers and would have gone back to sleep, if a car alarm hadn't started shrieking out on the street ten floors below. Their apartment, like most New York City apartments, was a trade-off. In exchange for the solidity of prewar architecture, large open space and three exposures they traded location. Not to say their location downtown was bad, it was just noisier than Persey would have liked on the rare weekend when she had the time and inclination to sleep in.

She slid out of bed with a sigh and walked into the kitchen, clad only in one of Aaron's old t-shirts. Ignoring the bar that separated the kitchen from the living area, she stood in front of the refrigerator spooning cereal into her mouth while she toyed with the idea of going into her own office and finishing up a few loose ends. The bulletin board next to the fridge was cluttered with take-out menus from their favorite restaurants. It was the contrast of the stark white envelope in their midst that caught her eye; or more accurately the Studio H insignia did. Seized with inspiration, Persey pulled up the studio's schedule on-line and found a 9:00 class optimistically entitled "SERENITY".

She put her empty bowl of cereal into the sink, tossed on some clothes and descended the elevator in search of Studio H. It was several blocks away in an old warehouse building that had somehow escaped conversion into an art gallery or hipster boutique. Checking the address on the gift certificate, Persey mounted the six flights of stairs and let herself into a cramped anterior room.

"First time here?" asked a thin woman with long gray braids seated at a desk in the corner.

"Yes," said Persey, nodding and fishing the envelope back out of her purse. "My husband gave me a gift certificate," she said, handing her the envelope.

"What a thoughtful husband," said the woman, taking the envelope and setting it down on the desk without bothering to look inside. "Come with me," she said, standing up and walking gracefully over to another door. "I'm Joy, by the way," she said smiling over her shoulder. "Let's get you all set up."

"I've never taken yoga before," Persey said as she followed Joy down a narrow hall.

"Don't worry," said Joy with a laugh. "Everyone is somewhere on their journey. This is an auspicious day for you to begin. Haden has an opening in one of his classes.

"Who's Haden?" asked Persey.

"The founder of the studio," said Joy, glancing back at Persey as though the question was surprising. "Usually his classes fill up, but like I said, you're in luck." They reached the end of the hall and Joy opened the door ushering Persey into a cathedral-like room with windows stretching up to a high ceiling where lazy fans circulated the air. People sat on yoga mats soaking in the light that streamed through the windows. Joy noiselessly wove her way to the front of the room where she spread out a yoga mat and gestured for Persey to sit down.

"He'll be here in a minute," Joy whispered, pressing her palms together in front of her chest and bowing before she slid back out of the room.

Taking her cue from the other students, Persey sat down on her mat, crossed her legs and gazed out the window. The room, with its bank of floor to ceiling windows, gave her the sensation of lightness. She felt like she was floating—clean and removed from the grime and confusion of the city. Despite being surrounded by other people, she felt the same sense of peace that she felt when she was alone. It was as though they were all enmeshed in a web of silent contemplation that held them so tightly there was no room for desire, need or confessions. The instructor, when he arrived, was tall with bushy, dark hair and fierce eyes.

His eyes rested upon Persey for a moment and she felt a shiver course down her spine. Something about his eyes dredged up forgotten memories of childhood. For an instant, she felt as though she'd seen those eyes before in some ancient nightmare. She was seized with the impulse to run out of the studio, back down the six flights of stairs to the safety of home and Aaron. Instead she took a deep cleansing breath. "Don't be ridiculous," she thought. "It's just yoga."

The instructor guided them with his voice. He walked among them inspecting their poses. He lingered over crinkled fingers and smoothed out furrowed brows. "Breathe," he whispered, coming up behind Persey. He didn't touch her, not that first time. Even so, she couldn't shake the sensation that something emanated from him; a kind of warmth that felt dangerous and, yet, familiar. His voice in her ear was seductive; demanding nothing, knowing everything. At the end of the class, after they'd said their Namaste's and were rolling up their mats, he squatted down beside her.

"I'm Haden," he said meeting her eyes. "This is your first time doing yoga."

She nodded, even though it was clear he was making a statement, not asking a question.

"Did you enjoy the class?"

"Yes," she said. She took a deep breath in order to quell the unreasonable feeling of panic that welled up inside of her.

"You're nervous," he said. His voice was gentle as he reached out and smoothed her shoulders down away from her ears. "Why are you nervous?"

"I...I don't know?"

He held her gaze until she looked back down at her mat. "I'd like to see you here again....?" His voice trailed off in an unmistakable question.

"Persephone," she said. Then she added quickly, "But everyone calls me Persey."

"Persephone," he repeated as though he was savoring the word in his mouth. "I'd like you to come again. I'm teaching Monday."

"I work." She said it as though she were apologizing for something.

"My class is in the evening, eight-thirty. Tell Joy I'd like her to save you a spot," he said as though she hadn't just told him she was unavailable.

Persey did not deliver Haden's message to Joy. Even so, when she arrived five minutes late for the Monday evening class, Joy greeted her with a warm smile and led her to the same spot in the window-filled studio.

Throughout the months of May and June, Persey attended Haden's class regularly. Aaron was working on another big deal that kept him late at the office most evenings. Even when Persey opted to go home early, he was almost never there. His long hours didn't matter so much, she told herself, because leaving Goldman Parke at a reasonable hour was a rare option.

Daniel continued to put her on deal after deal. She worked long hours. Not that she was complaining. She didn't mind the long hours. Not even when she had to work late into the night with Daniel as her only company. Even though Persey was beginning to suspect Daniel's devotion to her wasn't based solely on her work product, he was unfailingly appropriate. Not once had he burdened her with uncomfortable confessions.

It might have been his very appropriateness that left Persey wondering, on occasion, what path her life might have taken if she hadn't impulsively accepted Aaron's marriage proposal. What would have happened if she had returned to Goldman Parke as a single woman? It was a question that bubbled up out of nowhere, leaving her feeling guilty for having thought it.

These were the kind of thoughts that led her again and again back to the yoga studio. In yoga she was free. In yoga she was just another girl. Haden's studio felt safe. She could drop her defenses there. Studio H provided her an escape from the scrutiny of others and the thoughts she didn't want to examine.

The studio worked its spell on all of them. She could sit on her mat in a crowded room without worrying whether the person next to her was stalking her with their darkest secrets. All she had to do was close her eyes and move her body in time to the rhythm of Haden's voice. There was no time or place for unwanted small talk or revelations. The movement pushed it all aside.

She wrote off her initial feelings of panic at the studio to anxiety, reluctance to try something new. Haden's presence was magnetic. It no longer filled her with dread. Something about him felt comfortable, almost familiar. He pushed her, literally pushed her body into positions that made her muscles tremble with effort. His hands moved without reservation along the contours of her back, neck or thighs.

"Breathe, Persephone," he would say, whispering the word into her ear like a magical incantation as the heat from his hands spread through her body. "Tap into what's inside of you."

For ninety minutes, Persey could be free, un-hunted and un-needed. She drank up every second of it that spring and on into the late, hot, sticky days of summer when the city turned fetid, like a glass of milk left out overnight.

It was on one of those late summer nights when Aaron crawled in bed next to her and rested his hand possessively on her stomach. "Let's have a baby," he whispered into the darkness of their bedroom.

Even though she'd always known he wanted a family, his words caught her off guard, causing her to gasp a little. Instead of saying anything, she pulled Aaron close, kissing him deeply. Aaron wanted children. It shouldn't have surprised her any more than the Hermes purse for her birthday. Aaron was determined she want for nothing, not even a family.

Chapter Twenty

Persey had been expecting to get her period since the middle of fourth grade. That was the year the early onset of Denise Miller's menses briefly became Denise's most deeply-held secret. Of course, it was a secret she shared with Persey.

In the space of a year, Denise's early introduction into puberty went from shameful confession to shared experience. "I'm totally on the rag today. God, there is no way I'm going to P.E. with these cramps. Does anyone have a tampon I can borrow? She must be PMS'ing."

The girls at Clear Lake Middle School were obsessed by their own metamorphosis. The changes to their bodies gave them their own version of locker room talk based on their mutual sisterhood of monthly visitation and discomfort. Persey assumed it would only be a matter of time before she too was included in the rites of womanhood.

By the time she was sixteen, her mother took her to see Dr. Coughlin. He was the same pediatrician who had checked Persey's reflexes throughout her childhood with his red rubber hammer and allowed her to listen to his heartbeat through his stethoscope. After performing a cursory gynecological exam, he told her she could put her clothes back on.

"Everything points to normal," he told Persey and her mother back in his office. "Without running a bunch of tests, I'd say she's in the range of typical late onset menses. If she still hasn't started by next year, you can make another appointment and we'll do some more thorough testing. But I really wouldn't worry about it too much."

Persey's seventeenth birthday present was late. Three weeks late to be exact. On that morning, she was visited with such terrible stomach pains all she could do was lie in bed and moan.

"Maybe you're coming down with a bug," her mother said, laying a cool hand on her forehead. "Why don't you stay home from school today?"

After several hours of attempted, but unsuccessful sleep, Persey managed to crawl out of bed and down the hall to the bathroom. It was then she discovered she wasn't sick. Even though she'd been expecting it for years, the sight of blood in her underwear was momentarily confusing and unexpected. Late that afternoon when her mother came home from work, she discovered her daughter wrapped in a nest of blankets watching Oprah.

"Mom," called Persey weakly from the couch. "I got my period." That night they celebrated with hot fudge sundaes. "I think I was craving chocolate," said Persey, licking the last bit of hot fudge from her spoon.

"Of course you were, honey," said her mother, smiling at her.

Persey had finally become part of the sisterhood.

It didn't occur to her that the long absence of her period was abnormal until sometime during her senior year. She'd known it was supposed to come monthly but she also knew, due to her mother's exhaustive research on the subject, sometimes it took a while for your body to settle into a routine. She had no inclination to discuss her body's failure to fall into a routine. She'd had enough of her mother's worried looks and awkward medical appointments.

Instead, she decided to fake it. Every four or five weeks she emptied a box of tampons, one-by-one, into the garbage can. Magically, without any need for discussion or reminders, a full box would appear when the old one was almost empty. She continued her fake periods until she moved out of the old farmhouse and away from the watchful eyes of her mother.

During her college years, Persey was thankful to be spared monthly visitations of cramps, moodiness and bloating. Her classmates were still obsessed by their bodies but their obsessions had taken on different forms. It was easy enough to forget about the whole thing, which is what Persey did, until her third year of law school.

In her last year of formal schooling, one of her older classmates gave birth to a baby girl. The new mother brought the infant to class, watching hawk-eyed, as the tiny bundle was passed from arm to arm. When it was Persey's turn, the baby looked up at her and opened her mouth in a perfect miniature yawn.

"She's beautiful," Persey said as she handed the baby on to the next set of waiting arms.

It was at that moment she had her first inkling of worry. Cramps and discomfort weren't something to be avoided. They were the dues you paid to create a tiny perfect life. She'd been stupid to let it go this long. She resolved to make an appointment with a doctor as soon as finals were over. It was odd, she thought in retrospect, how many doctor's appointments she ended up making in the five months that followed.

After her last exam, she flew home for Christmas break. Her mother was waiting for her when she got off the plane in Des Moines. "You okay Mom? You look tired," Persey said giving her a hug. Underneath her coat, her mother felt frail in a way Persey didn't remember.

She didn't argue when Persey offered to drive the hour back to Clear Lake.

"You want to get dinner in town?" asked Demi as they exited the highway.

"Sure," said Persey, pulling into the Shari's parking lot. It was where they always ate when she visited. "Do you remember Aaron Strait?"

"Of course I do," said her mother.

"This is where we first met," Persey said as she brought the car to a stop.

"I always liked him," her mother said. "Do you ever hear from him anymore?"

"No, not in a long time," she said.

They ordered cheeseburgers and milkshakes. "I never eat like this anymore," said Demi, pushing a french fry around on her plate.

"I'm not sure you can call what you're doing eating," said Persey, eyeing her mother's untouched food.

Demi looked down at her plate for a long moment and then back at her daughter. "I have cancer," she said in a voice hoarse with the strain of unshed tears.

The dean at her law school was extremely sympathetic. His mother had died of cancer three years earlier. He had no problem, under the circumstances, granting Persey an academic exception. She would be allowed to attend her classes remotely.

"I want you to see you graduate from law school," her mother insisted.

So Persey scheduled her mother's chemotherapy sessions and doctor's appointments around her courses in Corporations and Criminal Procedure. She drove her mother back and forth between the hospital and doctor's offices. She studied in the hospital cafeteria and waiting rooms. The cancer was advanced and the treatment was aggressive.

"We have to be as aggressive as possible if we're to achieve any success," Dr. Worth told Persey at one of her mother's first appointments.

Dr. Worth was Persey's favorite on her mother's team of doctors. She was younger than the others and the most sympathetic to a young girl who was losing her mother. One afternoon in late April, Dr. Worth came looking for Persey in the hospital cafeteria. "Persey," she said, as she set her tray down on the long cafeteria table. "Do you have a moment?"

Persey looked up. Even though Dr. Worth was awkwardly studying her chicken salad, Persey knew what she'd come to say.

"I haven't had my period in years," Persey blurted out. It was an effort to avoid the inevitable. She felt certain she knew what Dr. Worth had come to tell her and she wanted to put it off for just one more moment. Dr Worth was professional enough not to bat so much as an eye.

She looked at Persey for a moment as she thought, then she said, "Best guess, keeping in mind this isn't my area of expertise, would be stress. You're in your third year of law school and doing all the care for your mother, right?"

Persey nodded.

"What I remember from med school is most cases of amenorrhea occur as symptoms of something else. Typically you wouldn't get to twenty-four without some other symptom that your body isn't functioning correctly. After you've had a chance to grieve, things will probably return to normal..." Dr. Worth's voice tapered off, realizing what she had just said.

"How long does she have?" Persey whispered.

"Not long, a month at most," said Dr Worth.

Her mother lived three weeks longer than predicted. Just long enough to see her daughter graduate from law school. Persey organized the funeral, closed up the house and flew to New York for job interviews. She was numb. She was alone. She accepted the position at Goldman Parke because it was the biggest firm to give her an offer. There was safety in numbers, right? That had always been her mantra.

That summer, while she studied for the bar exam, Aaron had come to her rescue just the way he had in high school. Only this time, he'd saved her from herself. It felt right to marry him, like the natural arc in her life's storyline. It all happened so fast. It hadn't occurred to her to tell him she might not be able to have children. Later, after she'd seen him frolicking with other people's children, she realized the magnitude of her omission. But by then, it was too late. They were married. She hadn't told him. The link between her missing period and the very real possibility she might not be able to give Aaron a family was another thing she didn't want to think about—another reason to go to yoga.

Chapter Twenty-One

Persey lay on the floor of Studio H. It was the end of class and she was calm. She was peaceful. If only she could stay this way forever. By the time she pulled on her shoes and rolled her mat into a tight cylinder, the room was almost empty. She ran down the stairs and let herself out onto the darkened street, pausing to glance at her cell phone.

"Good work tonight, Persephone," said a voice behind her.

She jumped at the sound of his voice.

"Did I startle you?" asked Haden.

"No," she said attempting to sound casual. "You know, everyone calls me Persey." She hitched her yoga bag over her shoulder and headed off down the street.

"You mentioned that before," he said, falling into step beside her. "But I prefer Persephone. It suits you. Tell me, where do you go to, Persephone, when you're not in my class?"

"I'm a lawyer," she said.

He chuckled under his breath. "Of course you are, but I was wondering about your mind. Where does it go when it's not paying attention?"

"Oh," said Persey. "I'm sorry. I'm just," she paused for a moment, "distracted. I guess I've been feeling distracted lately."

"You have a lot to think about?" he said. His voice contained the unmistakable invitation for her to say more.

They were at the street corner waiting for the light to turn. The words came to her lips before she could stop them. "My husband wants to have a baby."

"And you don't?" he asked.

"No, it's not that. I just don't know."

"It's natural isn't it," said Haden.

"What do you mean?"

"Husbands need wives to reproduce, to carry on their lives. It's a natural consequence of marriage. I can see how it might be overwhelming. Children, with their frailty and unending need—they're a constant reminder of our own humanity.

"That's not what I meant," she protested.

He reached out and traced an invisible line underneath her eye and down her cheek. "Didn't you?" he said. "It's normal to be frightened as one chapter of your life comes to a close. But I imagine you'll be duly compensated for your loss of youth and freedom by what grows inside your heart."

She jerked away from his hand with a hot flash of anger. "That wasn't what I was saying at all. I want to have children who need me. I'm not worried about getting old. It hadn't even occurred to me."

Haden looked amused at her outburst. "Is that what you think I'm saying? You are the only person who knows what you need. I'm merely telling you to trust yourself." He leaned closer to her, his lips almost brushing her hair and whispered, "Remember my beautiful Persephone, alone no human is immortal, but you have the ability to live on through each other forever."

Her anger melted away leaving behind a rush of heat that flooded through her body. The dark thing inside of her, twisted as though Haden's presence called to it. It was awake and it wanted Persey to feed it but she wouldn't do it. She squeezed her eyes shut, as though mere lack of sight could eradicate the unpredictable emotions welling up inside of her.

"Good night, my dear Persephone," she heard Haden say. "Go home. Aaron is waiting. He needs you."

A moment later, she opened her eyes to find herself alone on the hot, dark street. Save for the noise of traffic, the only thing she could hear was her own heart pounding in her ears. "It wasn't what I meant," she whispered to herself again. She wasn't afraid of death and aging. She wanted a child of her own. She wanted a family as much as Aaron wanted to give her one.

Why then, asked a tiny argumentative voice in her head, had she allowed her symptoms of infertility to go unchecked? Why had she been unable to do something as simple as make a doctor's appointment? And why, oh why did her heart pound in response to the heat and touch of Haden's hand on her arm? "I didn't mean to," she whimpered as tears sprung to her eyes.

It wasn't until the next morning that another question occurred to her. How had Haden known her husband's name?

Chapter Twenty-Two

Every month Aaron waited eagerly for news, any kind of news. It was up to her to manipulate the lack of information. Her body refused to give any symptom of its ability to sustain a life other than its own.

Some months, she would wait until he reached for her underneath the covers, then whisper, "Not tonight. I just got my period."

Other months, she would exit the bathroom despondently and without saying anything hand him the little plastic stick with its sad single blue line. Through it all he remained upbeat.

"Don't worry. It took my boss and his wife two years," he said after the last negative pregnancy test.

That Thursday night in bed, Aaron moved his hand up under her t-shirt and whispered in her ear, "Aren't you glad we didn't hit the jackpot yet? It's so much more fun this way."

"God Aaron," she said, pushing him away without bothering to hide her annoyance.

"What's wrong?" he asked.

"Did you ever think it might be upsetting for me?" she said with more conviction than she felt.

In truth, Aaron's voice in her ear had pulled her back to the street outside of Studio H. It reminded her of the heat and hunger that surged through her body in response to Haden's proximity. It wasn't Aaron's fault that he'd summoned Haden into their bedroom. Still, it was clear to Persey she needed to take action. She was no longer an innocent bystander.

The next day at work, Persey Googled fertility specialists near her office. She spent the rest of the afternoon attempting to work up the nerve to make an appointment.

"You seem preoccupied today," said Daniel, poking his head into her office. "What's up?"

"Nothing," she said shaking her head.

Daniel stood framed in the doorway of her office. He didn't seem to buy her quick denial. The way he stood there, ready to listen gave her a small unexpected pang. Would Aaron have noticed if she was preoccupied? Would he have offered to listen? Aaron was so preoccupied with disgorging his own thoughts and feelings that it left little time for Persey's.

"I'm okay," she said, smiling up at him and for a second their eyes locked.

"I..." said Daniel. Without finishing his sentence he backed out of her office. "I think I hear my phone," he called from the hallway.

Persey glanced back at the telephone numbers she'd scribbled on a notepad, and then at the contract sitting on her desk waiting for her comments. With a sigh, she ripped off the sheet of paper, folded it in half and tucked it in the top drawer of her desk. Small steps she told herself as she picked up the contract.

At ten to two, she put down her pen and headed to Daniel's office for a conference call. They liked to spend the minutes prior to a conference call going over major deal points to make sure there would be no surprises. She heard the tinny sounds of a voice magnified by the speaker phone as she walked down the hallway. At first she thought she was late but as she approached Daniel's office door she overheard her own name.

She glanced over at the secretary station to make sure she wasn't being observed then she paused—just out of sight—to listen.

"That girl you've got over there. Got a name like a boy, what's her name again?" said the disembodied voice.

"Persey?" said Daniel.

"Yeah, that's it. Come on man, you gotta tell me if you're gettin' some of that?"

Persey heard Daniel pick up the receiver to disengage the speaker phone.

"She's married," he said. Then he laughed and added, "Right, then it'd be a different story."

Persey was surprised. It wasn't the sudden confirmation of his sentiments that surprised her. What was surprising was how he'd managed never to confess those sentiments. He'd had plenty of opportunity. They'd spent many nights working together, just the two of them. Despite all those evenings, just the two of them alone in a conference room, he'd remained unfailingly professional.

She knocked on the door as she walked in to Daniel's office.

He looked up at her with a grin. "Ready?" he asked.

She nodded, trying to ignore the way her stomach turned a flip-flop in his presence. The call dragged on for several hours. Afterwards, Daniel pushed back from the small table in his office and propped his feet up on it. "Take-out tonight?" he asked, crossing his arms behind his head.

"I was thinking of working at home," she said. Straightening her documents into a pile, she added, "I haven't seen Aaron all week."

"Oh, yeah, then you should do that," said Daniel. He spun his chair around to face his computer before she had time to look at his face.

Persey felt guilty all the way home. Not because she'd lied. But because for a moment, she'd wanted to stay at the office and eat take-out with Daniel almost as much as he wanted her to be there. She knew he'd been disappointed but he'd kept it to himself. Why? Why didn't he tell her things? From the sidewalk, she could see the dark windows of her apartment above. For a moment, she toyed with the idea of going back to the office. Daniel would still be there. They could order take-out. They could work and they could talk. She thought about it a minute longer before discarding the idea as a bad one.

Still, the one thing she didn't want to do tonight was go home to an empty apartment. She didn't want to be alone with her thoughts. With a sigh, she crossed the street and headed toward Studio H. All she wanted to do was breathe.

She climbed the stairs and headed to her familiar spot on the floor. She sat down, crossed her legs and waited for the moment Haden's voice would fill the studio and resonate through her body. When the class began she moved her body and let her thoughts go. Afterwards, she sat on her mat soaking in the peace of the room. Around her, the other students rustled as they rolled up their mats but Persey ignored them. She wasn't ready to leave yet. She didn't want to give up her calm.

All of a sudden she was aware of his presence behind her, radiating heat.

"Persephone," he said, placing his hands on her shoulders. He eased her back until she was lying against him. "You're worried." He moved his hands in small circular motions down the length of her arms.

"It's just..." she started to say but he shushed her like a small child.

"Let me support the weight of your body. All you need to do is breathe." His hands were on the sides of her neck pushing and massaging her skull. "Close your eyes," he said as his hands smoothed her furrowed brow. He maneuvered his other hand beneath the waistband of her yoga pants until it was positioned directly over her stomach. "Let go," he said. "Breathe into my hand. Fill yourself with air."

She did. Ignoring the spreading heat from his hand placed so intimately on the bare skin of her belly, she followed his instructions.

"You're the object of so much desire," he said. As though he could anticipate her reaction his hands tightened, increased their pressure against her skin. "Let it fill you up."

"Let what fill me up?" she asked.

"Freedom," Haden whispered. "When you leave this place, everything out there will be waiting for you. All the needs and desires that circle and stalk you will still be there but right now, in this moment, you can be free."

"Free from need," whispered Persey.

"Yes," he said.

His hands seemed to expand and sink into her body, filling her with a strange pang of desire. Her eyes opened and met his.

"Pure perfection," he said smiling down at her.

"But it won't last forever," she whispered.

"No," agreed Haden as he removed his hands from her body and helped her back to an upright position. "Almost nothing does."

Chapter Twenty-Three

It was uncanny the way she kept running into him. That was the word that came to mind whenever she thought about it, uncanny. He kept popping up where she least expected him. Every time it happened she felt oddly compromised. It was like she was having an illicit affair instead of making small talk with her yoga instructor. She ran into him at the Duane Reade. It wasn't so strange given its location between Studio H and her apartment but still, it was unexpected.

"Persephone," he called in his deep unmistakable voice.

She was mindlessly wandering the aisles looking for something else to add to her basket; something cheerful and lighthearted, like a new formula of Cover Girl mascara or a package of Nutter Butters. "Haden," she said turning around quickly. It was already too late to whisk her shopping basket, loaded with one box each of Stayfree Ultra Thins and Tampax Tampons, behind her back. Until now the pill had "stopped" her periods. But now that she and Aaron were "trying", she was back to her old tricks.

To her immediate mortification, he made no effort to avert his eyes from the contents of her basket. "No progress on the baby-making front, I see," he said.

"No," she said shaking her head. Then because she didn't know what else to say she added cheerfully, "It's a process."

"Yes," said Haden, "usually an enjoyable one. Are you coming to class tomorrow?" he asked, ignoring the bright color that Persey could feel flooding to her face.

She nodded, grateful for the change of subject but her relief was short-lived.

"I'll incorporate some poses to increase circulation to the hips and pelvis. They're wonderful for fertility. Most people have a lot of tension that builds up there," he said. He cupped his hand around the top of her thigh, pushing his thumb into the crease that was uncomfortably close to her groin and held it there.

Her intense mortification melted away underneath the pressure of his hand.

"It feels good to let go, doesn't it?" he whispered and she was startled to realize she had closed her eyes.

The next time she ran into him was at a summer associate lunch. Every summer, the law firm used its summer associate program to recruit the most promising group of second year law students from a handful of top tier schools. The students were given nominal work and paid obscene amounts of money. Then they were wined and dined throughout their ten week summer tenure.

The head of the firm recruiting department had cornered Persey early that morning in the elevator. "Are you free to take a group of summers to lunch today?" he asked. Before she could reply, he added, "They come back from lunch with you and you're all they can talk about. I think the entire summer class has a little crush. Honestly, if I weren't gay I'd have a crush on you too. Actually, I do have a little crush, you're my girl crush, you don't mind do you?" Somehow he'd extracted a promise from her before the elevator doors had opened.

She took the summers to a trendy Chinese fusion restaurant not far from the office. In the center of the cavernous dining area, a Buddha, two stories tall and covered with flickering candles, presided over the diners. At the table, Persey let her mind wander as the group chattered to each other.

She was studying the Buddha when she felt someone watching her. She looked across the room and her eyes met Haden's. He was watching her with a contemplative smile. Persey smiled in his direction even as a nervous quiver clutched at her insides. What was he doing here? It seemed somehow out of character for a yoga instructor to eat lunch at a midtown hot spot. Someone else was seated at his table. From her angle, Persey couldn't make out the other person without craning her neck or standing up. Haden leaned closer to his dining companion and Persey felt an unexpected stab of something that felt a lot like jealousy.

The woman—it was a woman seated next to him—slid out of the booth and away from Haden. She was the most beautiful person Persey had ever seen, almost radiant. Her long dark hair fell in waves to her waist and her ivory complexion seemed to be lit from within. But it was more than that. Something about her compelled you to gaze upon her. Looking away from the exquisite lines of her face felt painful, like a miniature death. The woman moved across the restaurant causing conversation to cease and mouths to stop chewing. Motion was temporarily arrested in her wake.

She appeared in front of their table and Persey's dining companions fell silent.

"Would you join us for a moment, Persephone?" the woman asked. If possible, her voice was more compelling than her beauty. The strange music contained in her words made Persey desperate to hear her speak again. The voice was a drug and the desire for it to continue—once it had stopped—felt like the pull of a long-held addiction.

Persey slid out of the banquette and to the woman's side as though in a dream. One moment she was surrounded by summer associates, and the next moment she was gliding across the restaurant. The woman led her to Haden's table and then reseated herself at his side, gazing up at Persey with undisguised fascination.

"Hello," Persey said. Her voice sounded meager and awkward in the presence of the other more lyrical one.

They both studied her for a moment before Haden spoke. "It's an interesting concept. Don't you think?" he said, flicking his eyes towards the Buddha. Persey followed his gaze.

"He's a symbol of peace," she said. It wasn't what she intended to say but as soon as the words came out she felt their essential truth.

Haden chuckled. "Yes, that's correct," he said. He guided her down to the seat next to him. "I haven't made proper introductions. This is my dear friend Leucy. She's very loyal. Good friends should be loyal to each other, don't you think, Persephone?"

Leucy smiled at her and reached across Haden, grasping both of Persey's hands tightly in her own.

Some instinct from deep within, long denied and ignored, urged Persey to pull her hands away from this creature, to run. Escape, it urged. Escape while you can.

"Tell me," Leucy whispered. Her golden, liquid voice entered Persey's head driving out every thought except desire. Persey wanted to touch her, feel the sensation of Leucy's skin sliding against her own. Leucy's eyes locked on Persey's. Instead of spouting her darkest secrets, it was almost as though Leucy entered into her, feeding on the darkness that caused others to disclose their souls. "Tell me about your darling husband," she purred.

The absence of Leucy's magical voice felt like a cold blade of steel plunged deep into Persey's stomach. She would tell her anything, both the things she thought and the feelings she refused to think about if only she could hear her voice again. As if from very far away, she heard Haden calling to her. "Come, Persephone," he commanded. His steadying hand was on her shoulder pulling her back from the abyss.

"Until we meet again then my darling," said Leucy, reluctantly allowing Persey's hands to slide out from between her own.

Haden's hand was at the small of her back. The warmth of his touch radiated through her body, awaking her from the dream. She glanced back, for one last glimpse of Leucy, as Haden guided her back through the crowded dining room. "Who is she?" she said, turning to look at him.

"A loyal friend," he said, smiling but something in his eyes remained cold. "Just as I am a loyal friend to you," he whispered as they approached the table.

Persey slid back into her spot at the summer associate's table. They were still chattering to each other as though they hadn't just witnessed a flawless vision of beauty.

"Perfect timing," said Haden. Two waiters appeared with food-laden trays. He stepped back to allow the waiters to unload the contents of their trays onto the table.

After the waiters were gone, Persey looked back across the room to where she had just been. Haden and Leucy were gone. Somehow it didn't surprise her.

Chapter Twenty-Four

Aaron finished washing his hands in the bathroom sink, straightened his tie and took a deep breath. The deep breath was more of a ritual than a sign of actual nerves. Most people headed to the USB boardroom to make a presentation to the CEO and Board of Directors needed that deep breath. They would be nervous, sweating rancidly by the time they made it to the long hallway, lined with museum quality artwork that led to the boardroom.

Presenting an unexpected hiccup, in the most complicated double merger and hostile takeover of the decade, wasn't for the faint of heart. Aaron Strait was a lot of things but one thing he could not be described as was faint hearted. He was a good guy, a straight shooter. Everyone knew that. But that didn't mean he didn't like a challenge. He thrived on challenge, it fueled him. That's why he'd always played sports. It didn't matter whether it was football, swimming or spring baseball; as long as there was a game to win or a score to beat, he was happy. For an adrenaline junkie, he couldn't have had a more perfect job. It was moments like these that provided the exhilarating rush of adrenaline Aaron used to experience when he was running a ball into the end zone.

John Bairns, the CEO of USB's asset management and investment banking division, recognized Aaron's potential right away. After his first meeting with Aaron, Bairns requested he be assigned to work—not under but with—the senior bankers in the New York office. Although Bairn's request caused many raised eyebrows at USB, it didn't take long for Aaron to prove Bairn's instinct was correct.

Now Aaron was proving himself to a whole new echelon of investors with this merger/takeover. Until two weeks ago it had been a cake walk. After the numbers glitched, he'd worked late nights and straight through the last two weekends until he figured out the fix. He'd been working so much that he felt like the only time he saw Persey was when she was asleep. That part sucked, it was true. But as soon as this deal closed he would take a little time off. Maybe he'd take her to St. Thomas or something. They could relax, chill out and focus on each other. Nine times out of ten, women got pregnant as soon as they stopped trying. That's what his secretary told him.

He shook his head in order to clear his thoughts. He needed to be focused. He was headed down the hallway to the boardroom...almost game time. This deal was going to make his career. He could already feel the anticipatory rush of adrenaline. He paused for a moment in front of the double walnut doors which opened into the USB executive boardroom, glancing at the oil painting gracing the wall on the left—just another piece in Bairns' renowned art collection. If he remembered correctly, it was a Waterhouse. He was almost sure that's what John told him the first time they'd toured the building.

The painting depicted a man tied to the mast of a boat surrounded by creatures, half-women, half-bird. He glanced at the small gold plaque on the bottom of the frame to confirm his knowledge. "Ulysses and the Sirens; J.W. Waterhouse," it read. He'd been right. It was a good omen, he thought as he confidently pushed open the conference room doors.

"Gentleman," he said in the same commanding baritone he'd used to call out football plays. "I've got good news."

Lunch included copious amounts of steak, back-slapping and hand-shaking.

"You got a minute?" asked Bairns.

"Anytime," Aaron said with a grin.

They said their goodbye's and left the others, making their way past the sea of blue-suited traders who were smoking and eating on the steps of the stock exchange.

"My wife's putting together a little dinner party. She was hoping I'd ask you—you and your wife that is."

"Sounds great," said Aaron. "I mean, I'll have to check with Persey first but I'm sure she'd love to."

"Ironic, isn't it," said Bairns with a shake of his head as they stepped into the elevator. Aaron raised one eyebrow and waited for Bairns to explain what he meant. "Even Masters of the Universe have to bow down before the social whims of our wives," Bairns said with a chuckle. "And I mean that as a compliment because that's where you're headed."

"Thanks," said Aaron shaking his head. "But I couldn't have done it on my own. My team deserves most of the credit."

John gave him a knowing smile. "Sure it does. I'll have my secretary get your wife's contact information from your secretary. We'll turn it over to the women."

Back in his office, Aaron was still too high on adrenaline to focus on the pile of messages waiting for him. It had gone well today, really well. He wanted to tell someone. He wanted to tell Persey. He quickly flipped through his messages to see if she'd called. She hadn't. He tried not to be disappointed. She was busy too. He was a modern man. He wasn't like John Bairns, making references to "the women".

He picked up the newest spreadsheets, recalculated based on the findings of his last two weeks of round-the-clock work. He flipped through them but he couldn't focus. He needed to talk to Persey. He'd never understood his need to tell her everything. It didn't matter what happened to him. Nothing ever seemed real until he'd poured out every last detail to her. Today was no exception.

He reached for the phone and dialed her number.

"I'm sorry sir but she's in a meeting," her secretary told him.

"Okay, can you just tell her Aaron called," he said.

He hung up and tried not to be frustrated. That was the thing about Persey. Even though they were married and she'd taken a vow to be his and his alone, somehow she was still elusive. Maybe it was because every time he looked at her it made him feel fifteen all over again, awkward and stumbling over his words. He mentioned it to Rudy one time. Rudy was one of the few people who had known Persey longer than Aaron. It was crazy how three people from small town Iowa had all ended up in New York City. For Rudy, the computer games had been his ticket out.

Aaron could still remember the way some of the guys on the football team tortured Rudy and his computer club friends. They called them computer geeks and bumped into them in the hallways. "Don't let them do that," Persey would say. He'd tried but maybe not hard enough. In the end, it was Rudy who had the last laugh. Now he was some kind of computer engineer working hours almost as crazy as Aaron's in Silicon Alley.

Every few months, they met for drinks at a shady little Korean place in the East thirties not far from Rudy's office. Even though he didn't understand the ins and outs of Rudy's work, Aaron had a sneaking suspicion he would hit it big someday. It was another reason to meet for drinks on a semi-regular basis. If Rudy ended up creating the next Google, Aaron wanted to be the guy he called to set up the deal. Of course, if Aaron was really being honest with himself, he knew there was more to it than that. Rudy knew Persey and besides himself, few others could claim knowing her at all. He had his own special insights into her. And in the end, didn't pretty much everything in his life come back to Persey?

Chapter Twenty-Five

Aaron picked up the phone and dialed a different number. Rudy answered on the first ring.

"Meet me for a drink?" asked Aaron.

"Man, it can't be more than....oh yeah, it's four o'clock."

"You in?" asked Aaron. "I'll come to you."

"Alright, sure," said Rudy. "I could use a break anyway."

Aaron tucked the spreadsheets he'd been pretending to look at in his briefcase and then picked up the phone again. This time when her secretary picked up he asked for voicemail. "Hey beautiful," he said after the beep. "I'm meeting Rudy for a drink and then I'm headed home. Sorry I've been working so much but I'm hoping dinner by candlelight will make up for it a little bit? Any chance you can sneak out before six? Call me. Love you." He put the phone down and headed back outside to catch a cab.

Rudy was already at the bar when Aaron walked in. It was the kind of place hipsters hung out—the kind of people who looked more like Rudy in his jeans and hoodie than Aaron in his Wall Street suit. Aaron slid into the seat across the table from him and ordered a beer from the Korean guy behind the bar.

"Dude," said Rudy. "You look like you got hit by a truck."

Aaron laughed. "No man, that's just the way I look."

"Seriously, what's up?"

"It's been a long two weeks," said Aaron, stretching his arms up over his head.

They were on their second drink before the conversation took its inevitable turn to Persey. "Sometimes I think I'm going to wake up and she'll be gone," Aaron confessed.

"What are you talking about man?" said Rudy. "You're the one she married for chrissakes. You hit the fuckin' jackpot. Every single guy in Clear Lake wanted to be you in high school... just because you got to drive her home every day. Now she's yours for the rest of your life. I'm thirty-four and I still want to be you," said Rudy.

"Yeah?" Aaron shook his head sheepishly. "It's not just about the way she looks," he added, making a half-hearted attempt to play down his good fortune.

"You mean it's NOT about how fuckin' gorgeous she is?" Rudy interrupted.

"Watch it, that's my wife you're talking about," said Aaron.

"Yeah, tell me something I don't know," Rudy muttered.

"What is this we're drinking?" asked Aaron, picking up the glass in front of him.

"Cheongju," said Rudy. "Kind of like Sake. Go easy there big guy, it hits you all at once."

Aaron downed what was left in his glass. He paused for a moment letting the alcohol burn its way into his system. "You know," Aaron said shaking his head. "Sometimes I feel like my beautiful wife could have this whole other life and I would never know anything about it."

"What do you mean?" asked Rudy.

There was something wary in Rudy's expression, like he was in on some secret. Aaron shook his head as though to push the thought out of his mind and said, "I don't know. Do you know she's never even told me about what she went through when her mom died?"

"Must have been a majorly shitty time for her," said Rudy.

"Yeah," said Aaron. "I'm always so worried about her. I always have been. It's like I feel like something is waiting out there to swoop in and take her away from me. Then I'll never see her again. It's stupid, I know," he said shaking his head. Before Rudy could say anything he added, "I'm an idiot and I'm a little drunk. You don't need to listen to his." He pushed himself to his feet. "Thanks man, I gotta get going, promised the wife I'd be home by six."

Aaron threw some money on the table and turned to go but before he could leave Rudy said, "Hey Aaron, you shouldn't worry so much. She can take care of herself you know."

There it was again, just a flicker of expression across Rudy's face. Aaron couldn't shake the feeling that Rudy understood something essential about Persey; something Aaron had yet to figure out.

"It's part of the package," Rudy added. "Part of why we were all, hell......still are in love with her."

"Yeah?" said Aaron, allowing Rudy's words to erase the information his face had so briefly conveyed.

"Yeah," said Rudy nodding. He picked up Aaron's cash and handed it back to him. "This one's on me," he said, ignoring Aaron's protests.

Aaron decided to walk home. The fresh air would clear his head. There was something about the way Rudy looked at him that he couldn't shake. He'd said he was still in love with her. Aaron knew everyone in Clear Lake had been in love with Persey. Everyone she met still seemed to fixate on her. It was one of the things he loved about her but maybe it was also the crux of the problem. It wasn't easy to be married to a woman who inspired raw desire in everyone she met. Over and over, he saw his own lust and sheer need reflected back at him in the eyes of the people around her. In fact, that was the reason (well, one of the reasons) he'd spent his junior and senior year of high school pretending to be her boyfriend. What kind of teenage boy agrees to pretend to be a girl's boyfriend for two years? It had been torture. The truth of it was, the way people acted around Persey frightened him. She made them irrational and he was no exception.

He stopped at Dean & Deluca just below Union Square and filled a bag with expensive take-out. He wanted tonight to be romantic. He tried to remember if they had candles in the apartment. Just to be on the safe side, he stuck a couple of tapers into his basket. He glanced at his watch. It was a quarter to six. He wondered if she was home yet.

Sometimes he wished Persey would quit her job. He liked the idea of her being more available. If she wasn't working she could come down to his office for lunch. If he wanted to take her on vacation they could just go. They would only have one work schedule to manage.

"Wait until after you have a family," his mother cautioned when he'd casually mentioned the idea to her. "These things have a way of working themselves out for the best."

His mother gave good advice, for the most part, and he was doing his best to follow it. But sometimes it was hard to wait and be patient. It wasn't the only thing that was hard, he thought to himself as he grimly readjusted his briefcase in front of his pants. Geez, could he be more of a fifteen year old? Hopefully, the doorman hadn't noticed, he prayed as the elevator carried him upstairs.

Chapter Twenty-Six

Aaron opened the door to his apartment. He could hear water running in the bathroom. At the sound of it, his stomach muscles tightened in a familiar way. It was the way he always felt when he saw her. "You must've got my message," he called in the direction of the bathroom, quickly shucking off his coat and setting down his briefcase and groceries.

When he looked up, a woman was coming out of the bathroom but it wasn't Persey. The woman had dark hair that cascaded over her shoulders. Her red lips were impossibly full and tempting against the backdrop of her pale skin. She was wearing a dark silk bathrobe which only served to emphasize the delicate fairness of her skin. She gleamed like polished marble in the shadow of the hallway.

"Did you leave me a message?" she asked with a throaty laugh.

He felt her voice deep in the pit of his stomach, pulling him irresistibly toward her. The questions, all the questions he normally would have asked anyone appearing in his home without explanation were pushed aside by a strange frenzied desire.

"I'm Leucy," she said, advancing slowly toward him. "I'm a friend of Persey's." Here she uttered that delicious laugh again and added, "Or more accurately, a friend of a friend."

As she moved, the bathrobe moved around her, exposing a long expanse of marble thigh. Aaron stood transfixed, unable to formulate any thought beyond acute desire.

"Come to me, Aaron," she said and her voice melted into his ears.

He complied, desperate for her, unable to resist. Her voice surrounded him. It pushed everything else away leaving only the two of them, only the moment. His body—already primed—throbbed and ached with desire. He was in front of her. The warmth of her body radiated against his. He was aware she was speaking but he couldn't understand what she was saying. He didn't care about the words. The words weren't important. What was important was the magic call of her voice. It urged him on and he obeyed it without question. He pressed his body against her magnificent warmth, allowing his hungry hands to tear at the fabric which covered her. The person that had been Aaron was gone. What was left behind was raw animal need and desire. Her words in his ear were soft and exquisite. He was so close to having her, to exposing the perfectly white skin that filled his hands with its strange heat.

She moved away from him. Somehow she was already halfway down the hall. It was as though she was teasing him, floating away from him and out of his reach. A horrible groan filled the air and Aaron realized the noise was coming from his own throat. Her departure felt like a wound. His hands, his lips, his dick, every part of him ached to be near her again. He moved after her without question, without thought. She was lying on the bed. She had discarded the robe and her white skin glistened against her dark hair. She began to sing and the sound of her voice was so exquisite it rendered him immobile.

Her deep red lips curved into a smile and she whispered, "Take off your clothes."

He did as she commanded. He was hers to do her bidding.

"Come to me," she said and he mounted her alabaster form.

In one motion, he plunged himself inside, becoming one with the almost unbearable beauty of her voice and body. He thrust himself deeper and deeper inside of her. Sweat trickled down his back and wet his hair. Still he continued, as if there could be no end to his mad frenzy of pleasure.

Then everything went quiet. It was like waking up from a dream. Those hands groping her smooth white breasts, did they belong to him? How had they gotten there? Her skin was so hot, sickeningly hot. He snatched his hands away like a criminal caught in the act. But the realizations kept coming. Just like a childhood nightmare where you think you've found safety only to discover another more frightening demon. He was inside of her. He was physically inside of this woman. He started to pull away in horror but froze at the sound of footsteps in the hallway.

"Aaron, I'm home," called Persey and with sudden clarity he could hear the sound of her briefcase being placed next to his. He only had a moment before she would come into their bedroom and discover him.

His heart started to race but before he could move Leucy whispered in his ear, "Our darling Persey is home."

At the sound of her exquisite voice, his traitorous member moved inside her, as though it had declared independence from the rest of his body.

"How shall we greet her?" whispered Leucy. She threw back her head and let out a terrible, hungry noise—half-shriek, half-song.

In that moment, Aaron knew this thing, that called herself Leucy, wasn't quite human. But it didn't matter because Aaron was gone again and all that was left behind was hungry, greedy desire for the creature beneath him. The last notes of Leucy's cry faded away and Aaron exploded inside of her with shudders of unwanted delight just as Persey opened their bedroom door.

There was nothing but silence; stunned silence. He pushed himself off the bed, wrapping a blanket around himself to hide the insult of his still erect penis. Persey backed away from him, away from the tableau in front of her. He followed. As it always happened with Persey, words spilled out of him as though they somehow belonged to her. "Persey, Oh my God. I'm so sorry. I don't know how it happened. I really don't. She was here when I got home and….," his voice tapered off.

"And what?" said Persey. Her voice was quiet.

"She said she was your friend. I didn't mean for this to happen. You have to believe me."

"I do," said Persey but she sounded far away, out of his reach. "I know you wouldn't lie to me."

"That's right," he said as he tightened the blanket around his waist. "I would never lie to you. I've always told you everything."

She studied him with her deep blue eyes. He had the sudden irrational hope that she could see into him and somehow make sense of what had just happened.

Instead, she said in that same quiet voice, "And I've always listened." Then she eased out the front door, shutting it firmly behind her.

Aaron stood staring at the front door for a moment before he realized what he needed to do. He had to go after her. He would have gone after her that moment except for the fact that he was wearing a blanket. Back in the bedroom, the sight of the empty rumpled bed stopped him, threw him off course. He felt the mixture of steak and Cheongju lurch in his stomach and he ran for the toilet. As he emptied out the contents of his stomach, he realized Leucy must still be in the apartment. She had to be. There was only one door out of the apartment and she hadn't passed through it. He viciously wiped his mouth on the back of his hand without bothering to rinse out the rancid taste of regurgitation and banged out of the bathroom.

"Leucy," he called. His voice echoed in the stillness that had settled over the apartment. The front door was still closed. She hadn't used it. It was an old door with cranky hardware. He would have heard the knob's complaints, the complicated click of the latch's mechanisms settling back against the door jamb. He searched the entire apartment, looking in closets and under the sink, as though he and Leucy were engaged in some adult version of hide-and-go-seek. The apartment was empty, like an abandoned crime scene.

He walked back to the bedroom and noticed the window. Its screen was off and it gaped open. He peered out, half expecting to see the outline of her body on the sidewalk ten stories below. There was nothing. Everywhere he looked there was nothing to see. A silky white feather danced on the windowsill in front of him and, on impulse, he reached out to catch it.

It wasn't until he turned away from the window that he noticed the other feathers, identical to the one he held in his hand. There was a trail of them leading from the bed to where he stood by the window. As he watched, a gust of wind stirred the feathers again, pulling them aloft and sucking them outside where they floated out of Aaron's sight.

Chapter Twenty-Seven

Persey moved through the city and it moved with her, pushing her along. Winter was coming and the windows along Fifth Avenue were decorated for the holidays. The sidewalks were choked with tourists. She embraced it, all of it. The sound of taxis honking, buses accelerating up the avenues, the press of other pedestrians as they jockeyed for position at a red light—these were all welcome distractions. Anything was welcome as long as it prevented her from thinking about what she'd seen. It was one thing to hear people's darkest secrets. It was another thing altogether—she now realized—to walk in on them. The only way not to think about it was to keep moving and allow the relentless sound and motion of the city to obscure everything else. Her phone was ringing. She dug into the recesses of her purse and turned off the ringer. Then it started to buzz, insistent in its refusal to be ignored. She set it down on an empty bus bench and kept walking without looking back.

It wasn't until she came to the reservoir in Central Park that hunger set in. She walked halfway around the hard-packed jogging trail enjoying the gnawing pain in her stomach and the lightheadedness that accompanied it. Hunger was basic. It didn't leave room for anything else. That was exactly what she wanted. The only problem with hunger was her body was too weak to sustain it for long. Her body was human and it demanded food.

She cut through the park towards the upper west side and found a table at the first restaurant she passed. She rarely came to this neighborhood and she was struck with the sudden feeling of being a tourist far from home. The restaurant was a bistro—the kind that opens its wide French doors and overflows onto the sidewalk during the warmer months. It was cold outside so patrons were crowded inside around small marble-topped tables while indifferent servers moved through the din.

The hostess appeared before Persey. She was dressed in black and chewing gum. "How many?" she asked sounding bored.

"Just me," said Persey.

The hostess nodded and led her to a table for two by the window.

"Thanks," said Persey.

The girl handed her a menu. "No problem," she said. The hostess returned a moment later with a glass of water and a dish of olives. "Make sure you don't leave cash for your waitress," she whispered. "Whenever I can, I steal it."

"Good to know," said Persey as she reached for an olive.

The hostess turned to go but then she paused. "You might not want to eat those because I just went to the bathroom and I didn't wash my hands."

Persey dropped the olive and sighed. She glanced at her watch, saw it was almost eight o'clock. In the space of two hours, her life had become unrecognizable. Aaron was supposed to be her safe place, her point of refuge. But no, she couldn't think about it like that yet. She couldn't think about it at all.

Her stomach growled, reminding her of the business at hand. She looked around for an available waiter to take her order, but what she saw almost made her heart stop. It was Haden. For a moment, she was convinced that this was just another chance meeting. Then the thieving, non-handwashing hostess glanced in her direction and motioned for Haden to follow her.

Persey watched as they threaded their way toward her.

"Here you go," said the hostess, plunking down another menu on the table.

"Hello Persephone," said Haden. He pulled out the chair across from her and sat down.

She fought off the inexplicable urge to hide or to run, the same panicky feeling that had almost overtaken her the first time she'd been in his studio.

He reached across the table and took her cold unyielding hand in his own. "Are you all right?"

She removed her hand from his grasp and looked out the window without speaking. To acknowledge him would be to admit what had happened.

"Look at me, Persephone," he said.

The presumption of him coming here and sitting across the table from her filled her with sudden rage. It coursed through her body making her feel light-headed. "She was your friend," she said, glaring at him. They were only four words, but somehow she made them convey all her bottled-up contempt and anger.

The waiter chose this unfortunate moment to arrive at the table. Before he could recite the specials, Persey turned her furious blue-black eyes on him. "Just bring me whatever's good," she snapped. "I'm starving."

"A-a-a-actually," the waiter stammered. "The food's not very good here."

"I don't care," she said, her eyes still boring into the waiter. "Just bring me something to eat."

"Alright," he said, rubbing one hand against his tight black jeans. "I won't bring you the soup. They put all the vegetables that are beginning to rot into it."

"Good," said Persey. "Don't bring me the soup."

She watched the waiter as headed back toward the kitchen. Then she turned back to Haden. The way he was staring at her, coolly assessing the situation, only fanned her fury. She glared at him, burning into him with the full force of her gaze. "This is your fault," she said. The instant the words were spoken they framed her anger. "You told her about him. Why did you do it?" She felt the dark thing hidden inside of her convulse, as though it was angry too. She gave into it, letting her eyes sear into his, calling to all of his inner darkness. If she'd expected him to wilt and babble his secrets and darkest confessions like a small child, she was disappointed.

Instead, he unflinchingly met her gaze. "What you don't understand, couldn't possibly know, is that Leucosia is not well." He enunciated each syllable as though he were explaining something to a small child. "Unfortunately, you've become her favorite obsession. Ever since she made your acquaintance, she's been unable to understand my fondness for you. In the end, it seems she is determined to make you suffer. She wants you to suffer as she feels she has suffered," he said. "You are right to blame me. It's why I've come. Blame me, blame Leucy but do not blame yourself or your husband."

"I saw him with her," Persey said. The words were hoarse in her throat.

"I know you did," said Haden. "I'm sorry you had to see him that way. I know how difficult this must be for you, but some part of you must understand. After all, you've met Leucy, felt the pull of her attraction. He was alone with her. Few men would be able to resist her."

"Then Aaron should be one of the few," Persey interjected. "Aaron loves me. I've known him ever since I was thirteen and he's always loved me. He is kind. He would never, ever hurt me. He's always told me everything. I know, better than anyone else, there is nothing bad hidden inside of him."

"Then what I'm telling you must make sense," said Haden. "You must go to him. He loves you. He always has."

"No," said Persey shaking her head at his suggestion. "I can't go back. I saw them together. Somehow she made him forget about me. I know that's what he'll say and I can't bear to hear him say that."

"Persey," Haden said. He picked up her hands in his own. "I know this is hard for you, but we both know that sometimes the hardest course is also the correct one."

A tear rolled down her cheek. "Don't you understand?" she said. Her throat tightened so that the words came out in a whisper. "Aaron keeps me safe. His secrets aren't supposed to hurt."

"Here we go," said the waiter. He placed a hamburger and thin, limp French fries in front of Persey. Her stomach turned at the sight of the food and for an uncomfortable moment she thought she was going to be sick. "You didn't tell me whether you wanted anything to drink so I brought you lemonade," the waiter said as he set it next to her plate.

"Thanks," Persey whispered, picking up the glass and taking a sip of the cool liquid. She set the glass back down and looked out the window.

"My poor Persephone," said Haden. He moved into the seat next to her and placed his hands on her shoulders. He squeezed methodically causing warmth to radiate through her arms and into her body.

Her anger drained from her, leaving her limp and tired.

"You're so sad," he said.

He was right. She felt her body slump against his.

"It's all right," he whispered. "It's all right to be sad." He smoothed her hair as her mother had done when she was a child. Her whole body began to shake with sobs. "You're going to be okay. I promise you're going to be okay," he whispered, wiping away her tears.

Chapter Twenty-Eight

She cried until there was nothing left; no pain, no sorrow, just empty exhaustion. Her hamburger and French fries sat untouched on the table, cold and congealed.

When the tears were gone, she was left with nothing but an empty ache in the pit of her stomach. "I understand why he did it," she said, looking up at Haden with her swollen eyes.

"There are few, very few, who are immune to Leucy's presence," he said.

Persey's moments with Leucy came to her again. "It was like I was drawn to her, like she was irresistible. He must have felt the same thing. It felt like the rest of the world wouldn't matter if I could be near her. That's how he must have felt." She was silent for a moment, staring out at the sidewalk. Then she turned and looked at him. "There's only one thing I don't understand. What about you? Why don't you find her irresistible?"

Haden shook his head as though she had asked him something ridiculous. "There is only one person I find irresistible and I can assure you, it is not the creature Leucosia."

Another question occurred to her—one that displaced her need to know what Haden meant by "the creature Leucosia." "How did you find me tonight?" she asked. "I didn't tell anyone where I was. How did you know I was here?"

Her eyes searched deep inside of his and this time they hit their mark. His words came slowly, as though they were being torn from him against his will. "It doesn't matter where you are, Persephone," he said. "I can always find you." It was the real answer. She could tell from his face that his honesty surprised him almost as much as the answer surprised her.

As if to forestall any more questions, Haden turned and signaled to the waiter to bring the bill. Then he looked back at Persey and tucked a lock of hair behind her ear. "I should take you home," he said.

"No," she said. Her voice sounded panicked and hoarse. She still had so many questions. She needed more time. If for no other reason than to wipe away the images she'd seen earlier that day. "I'm not ready to go home yet," she said.

He looked at her with sad eyes. "I wish there was something I could do to take your pain away."

"I just wish……" she said, breaking off her thought.

"What," Haden prompted. "What do you wish?"

"Nothing," she said shaking her head. "It was stupid, childish."

"Persephone," he said. "Don't negate your feelings. Whatever it is, you can tell me."

Something in his voice made her heart beat hard, like a warning. But then he placed his hand on her thigh and squeezed rhythmically. Her body felt soft and quivery, as though her muscles were trained to respond to his slightest touch.

"Don't be afraid. You can tell me anything," he said again. "You don't need to keep it to yourself anymore."

His warmth spread through her like a stiff drink. Jealousy was a natural emotion under the circumstances. It made sense that she felt the way she did. She heard her own voice, barely audible, say, "I wish I could make Aaron feel that way. I wish I could make him forget everything else in the world so there would be nothing else for him but me."

"Of course you do," said Haden winding an arm around her. The sudden warmth enveloped her like a stiff drink. He reached into his pocket and threw some money on the table. Then he said in a voice that only she could hear, "It's time to go."

Wordlessly—almost as if she were in a trance—she let him lead her through the tables and out onto the sidewalk. As they walked by on the dark sidewalk, she had one last glimpse of her untouched food and the avaricious hostess heading straight for their abandoned table.

It was late. The traffic was quieter and there were fewer pedestrians. They walked down the street. Even though it was cold, Persey couldn't feel it. Haden's arm around her was almost like a warm blanket warding off the chilly December winds. She wondered if Aaron was thinking about her. She'd been gone a long time. Was he worried about her or had Leucy returned to give him solace? They turned up a side street then crossed the avenue. On the other side was Central Park. It was only when she realized where they were heading that she stopped, suddenly filled with caution.

"Haden, where are we going?"

"You said you weren't ready to go home yet," he said, leaving her question unanswered.

"It's not safe to go in the park after dark," she protested. The words sounded ridiculous, as though she were warning him not to take candy from strangers.

He paused looking down at her with a bemused expression. "Don't worry, Persephone," he said, running his finger down the side of her face and under her chin. "I'll keep you safe."

Chapter Twenty-Nine

Central Park on a dark December night was cold and abandoned. The lamps cast little pools of light onto the brick pathway. In between the lamp light, they were bathed in darkness. Persey could hear branches sighing in the wind and the occasional sound of brush breaking, as though something was stalking them from the shadows. Haden led her deeper and deeper into the park.

Little by little, the noises of the city became muffled. They were in the urban wilderness, far from the reassuring world of honking traffic and city lights. If the darkness or the sounds from the underbrush bothered Haden, he didn't show it. He pressed on, unafraid or oblivious to the dangers Persey felt certain were lurking just out of sight.

The sight of Belvedere Castle, rising out of the gloom, caused Persey to draw a sudden sigh of relief. It was the kind of relief—she realized with sudden trepidation—that comes from seeing something familiar when you think you are lost. A fog had swept through the park while they were walking. Its damp fingers seeped through Persey's coat and boots, causing her to shiver. Haden took off his coat and wrapped it around her shoulders.

"It's beautiful isn't it?" he said staring up at the castle. "Have you ever seen it at night before?"

"No."

"Good," he said. He led her to a bench in a small garden across from the castle. "It inspires me when I'm feeling lost. I was hoping you might be able to draw similar inspiration."

He sat down next to her. They were in the darkest shadows of the immense grey building with its turrets and parapets. She could feel the heat emanating from his body, warming her even more than the coat he'd wrapped around her.

"Maybe it was a dream," she said. "Maybe this is a dream. Do you think I might wake up and find out this entire day was a dream?"

He laughed and then was quiet for a moment. There was no sound save the wind and a distant siren. "Tell me again, Persephone," he whispered, breaking the silence. She looked up at him, still not fully convinced she wasn't dreaming. "Tell me what you desire," he repeated. His voice was insistent.

Her heart beat faster as if she was in danger. Haden looked at her. He was waiting to hear her words instead of breathlessly filling up the silence with words of his own. If it was all a dream then it didn't matter what she said.

"I want Aaron to love me that way," she whispered.

"What way?" asked Haden, cupping her chin in his hand and tilting her head up. "Tell me."

Her eyes met his and with icy certainty she knew this was real. She recognized those eyes. She'd seen them before, but where? She looked deep into them, searching, calling to their secrets.

"I want to be more beautiful than Leucy. I want Aaron to look at me and forget everything else." She said the words slowly, enunciating each one.

Haden held her chin tightly, almost cruelly with one hand. He leaned close to her, so close she could feel his breath upon her lips. Their eyes were still locked. As he moved closer, she could feel something wild and urgent inside of her struggling to be set free.

She had already accepted the inevitability of their kiss. It was as strange and unexpected as everything else that had happened on this day. His lips were almost upon hers. Then he stopped. He brushed his thumb down the side of her face creating a ripple of tiny goose bumps up and down her spine.

"I can make it happen," he said. His grip on her was so tight it was almost painful. "I can give you what you wish. But if I do so…" He paused. His breath swirled around her like silk, waiting, withholding.

Suddenly she understood. It was a negotiation. "It's impossible." she said.

"Nothing is impossible," he said in a voice that sounded deeper than it should have. "Give me what I desire and nothing will be impossible." His shape seemed to flicker and she could feel the heat of his body, so hot it almost burned.

"Who are you?" she asked and a pained expression passed over his face.

"The desire must come from within."

His voice sounded strange but simultaneously familiar—like a long forgotten childhood memory. "Who are you?" she asked again. Her eyes searched his, willing him to answer her question.

"What does it matter," he said in that strange rough voice, "if I can give you your heart's desire? And I promise I can."

Her heart pounded, warning her, admonishing her not to do it. It was too late to run away. Something deep inside of her awoke and whispered the words it knew he was waiting for, "Take me. Take whatever you need." She felt a warm wetness trickle down her cheeks as she pressed her lips against his. Was she crying? The next moment, the heat of his lips burned through her and all other thoughts were gone.

A chasm opened up inside her. The darkness and hunger she'd denied for so long rushed in, consuming her. His tongue probed hers, stealing far into her inner recesses and claiming her as his own. The heat of his body threatened to suffocate her with its intensity. It was more than heat. It was devastation, sorrow, musty odors from rooms where people sobbed lonely tears. His secrets were inside of her, consuming her. She could feel their darkness and the horror. Each one was more devastating than the next, and yet, something in her called to them. They were part of her, their pain and suffering belonged to her. Then as quickly as it had begun it was over. She gasped turning away from his lips, tongue and terrible heat. He was behind her, uttering soothing words, but it was too late for that now. There was no going back. She'd felt his darkest secrets—and they were death.

Chapter Thirty

A black Lincoln Town Car screeched to a stop the moment it spied them exiting the park. It was late and they were a fare. Haden held the door open for Persey, allowing her to climb in first.

"Are you ready to go home, my darling, mysterious Persephone?" he asked.

She nodded without looking at him.

He knew she was frightened. But he didn't mind. How could he mind when the plan, that which he'd been waiting to set in motion for years, was now afoot? It had taken an unexpected turn in the park but he still believed he would be successful. Already, he could taste his victory. "Head down Fifth," he instructed the driver. "I'll tell you when to pull over." They rode in silence. Persey gazed out the window as Haden scrutinized her across the vanilla air-freshener scented backseat.

She continued to surprise him. In fact, stunned was a better way to describe it. Not once in an eternity of dealing with humans could he remember being surprised by one of them. That wasn't the way things worked. He granted their trifling requests and they gave him what he sought in return. He'd been so sure of himself with his lips hovering over hers. But then her skin had touched his and things hadn't gone according to plan, not according to plan at all.

She'd given herself to him, allowed him to invade her soul just like all the others. Except this time, his best efforts had been insufficient. The secrets of her soul were stubborn. They refused to reveal themselves. The more he thought about it, he knew no more about her future now than he ever had. Her end was still a blank—a nothingness with no clues. Despite the warning signs, he'd allowed himself to believe she would be no different than any other human. He'd been foolish. He could see that now.

He'd ignored the way she managed to spot inconsistencies when he spoke to her. His suggestions alone would have rendered any other human mute. In the face of his immortal power, she still managed to press him for answers. He'd entered her soul expecting to read it, to see some version of the form that would appear before him in the Underworld. Instead, he'd felt her invade his own.

Haden didn't have a soul. No immortal creature did. Still, as he attempted to probe her depths, he became aware of something strange and unexpected. His plan had gone awry. Persey could see inside of him. She could feel his darkness and death as surely as he could feel her fear and desire. His immortal body vibrated with urgency under the strain of her scrutiny. It took all his strength to break the lock between them in order to preserve the human body in which he currently resided. Even in a situation such as this, he was bound by the natural law. No death before it's time.

He had miscalculated, misjudged her in more ways than one. He hadn't expected her to invade him. Why would he? Nothing like this had ever happened before. He'd been caught off guard and needed to rally all his efforts in order to escape her penetrating kiss. It all happened before he'd given her the thing she most desired. She should have belonged to him, but now—uncomfortably—she didn't.

What she'd asked for—without fully understanding it—was the siren's song; the ability to mesmerize with her voice. He'd been ready to grant it to her, despite its destructive tendencies. But in the end he hadn't. Failure to meet his end of the bargain meant he didn't get to collect. No matter, he still believed the deck was stacked in his favor. Given the circumstances that were about to unfold, she would believe he had made good on his end of their bargain.

"Pull over up there," Haden directed, leaning forward towards the driver. He handed the gypsy cab driver an amount of cash, double the actual fare. "She's at Greenwich and Perry. Make sure she gets home," he said. He reached over and squeezing Persey's shoulder, whispered, "It's going to be alright." He ignored the way she seemed to shrink from his touch. "Go to him and remember what I said. He is not to blame."

She nodded without looking at him.

"I'll be in the studio late tonight. If you need anything—anything at all—call me or come to the studio."

She nodded again then looking at him for the first time said, "Haden, wait." Her voice had a little quiver to it. "What if he's not alone?"

He pushed her hair back from her face. "Don't worry, my beautiful Persephone. You have everything you need. I promise you, your husband will never look at anyone else. It will be you and you alone, until his dying day." He kissed her on the forehead then slid out of the Town Car. He closed the door behind him and watched while the car sped away to its final destination.

Haden climbed the stairs to Studio H and unlocked the yoga practice room. Inside, it was dark save for the light from surrounding buildings which gave the room an unearthly glow. The oversized windows were propped open and a lone figure stood balancing on the windowsill of the center window. She peered out over the city, oblivious to the cold December wind or her precarious perch. Her white skin gleamed in the semi-darkness, punctuated only by the dark tangle of hair that hung halfway down her back.

"You've returned," she said without turning away from the cityscape beneath her. "Is it done?"

Haden walked over to the window and traced a finger down the spine of her bare back. "Almost, my dear Leucosia, almost—but first I have one more service that I require."

She turned on the windowsill to face him. Opening her beguiling mouth, she began to sing.

Haden smiled. He waited a moment, indulging her whim before he said, "Eternally charming, but not what I had in mind."

The laugh that had enchanted thousands of men burbled up from deep in her throat. "Tell me then, what did you have in mind?" She slid off the windowsill and, in one sinuous motion, pressed her naked body against his.

He took her in his arms and quickly, before she could protest, tossed her out the open window. "Fly off little bird and watch over my Persephone," Haden called after her departing form, which already dipped and soared in the wind. He stared in the direction Leucy had taken and settled into wait, until Persey sought him of her own accord.

Chapter Thirty-One

Aaron stopped calling Persey's cell phone after the woman with the Hispanic accent began to answer it. Who else should he call? They had no family in New York, and if Persey had any friends, he didn't know their names. Out of desperation, he finally called her office.

The after-hours secretary picked up the line. "She's not home yet?" asked the woman with concern. "She left hours ago."

"She had to run back to the office. She realized she forgot something." He hoped she couldn't tell he was lying. "Maybe you could just check with the receptionist to see if she's seen her."

The secretary put him on hold for several long minutes. "I checked with reception and the front desk. She hasn't been here." The woman sounded less friendly than she had before.

"All right," said Aaron. "If you happen to see her, let her know I'm at home."

He considered calling the police and filing a missing persons report, but somewhere in the back of his mind he thought he remembered a person had to be missing for more than twenty-four hours before the police would take it seriously. His anxiety was such that he almost called anyway. In the end, the only thing that stopped him was the prospect of explaining the circumstances leading up to her disappearance.

He had to do something. He couldn't just stay in the apartment waiting for the phone to ring. He wandered the neighborhood hoping to catch a glimpse of her somewhere. He peered in the windows of their favorite restaurants, coffee shops and even stopped at the yoga studio where he'd given her a membership.

"Classes were canceled tonight," said the woman with braids who sat behind the desk.

When he ran out of places to search he went to their favorite breakfast place. The waiter had brought Aaron his bacon and eggs almost every weekend for the last two years. They'd shot the shit a million times. Aaron didn't know his name but he knew the guy was a Knicks fan and had a regular music gig in the East Village. Without Persey, the waiter didn't seem to remember him. Without Persey he was unrecognizable.

When his food arrived, he pushed it around on his plate until it was cold. He let a busboy take it without protest and—ignoring the check sitting on his table—drank cup after cup of black coffee. God, what had he done? Why had he done it? He still didn't know. The thought of those white feathers floating out the window made his flesh crawl. He shuddered with disgust.

"Hey man," said the waiter as he came up to the table. "We're trying to close up."

"Sure, sure, I understand," said Aaron.

He opened his wallet and tucked a twenty under the bill. Maybe she'll be home, he thought as he stood up from the table. That gave him a ridiculous pang of hope. Pathetic! Why was he so pathetic? She wouldn't be home and he knew it. He didn't deserve to find her at home.

He was halfway down the block, on the opposite side of Seventh Avenue, when he saw her. Like a thirsty desert traveler coming upon a waterhole, at first, he couldn't believe his eyes. She was getting out of a black gypsy cab. When she straightened up, the breeze caught her hair and rearranged it around her face. It was her. She wore the same clothes, work clothes she'd worn earlier that day, a lifetime ago. Even though her face was pale with fatigue, she was still the most beautiful girl, the most perfect person he'd ever known.

He'd been an idiot. He'd been given a chance to protect her and he'd messed up. He'd hurt her. If she would give him another chance, he'd spend the rest of his life making it up to her. He'd never let anything hurt her again. He'd be the perfect husband. "Persey," he called out and somehow—despite the cars, taxi cabs, buses, noisy restaurants and pedestrians that habitually crowded Seventh Avenue late into the night—somehow she heard him.

"Aaron." Her lips formed the word and she smiled.

"Persey," he called again.

He could feel his face hot and wet with his own tears. She'd come back. His own Persey had come back. In a moment he would take her in his arms again. He would never let her go. He would do whatever it took to erase the memory of the pain he'd caused her. She was his and he had always been hers. She was the only girl he'd ever loved. He stepped out into the street, drawn back into her orbit as surely and swiftly as a wayward planet returning to circle its sun.

Her saw her face shift and her eyes grow round with terror. "Aaron!" she screamed as though the word was being torn from her body.

She was frightened. She was in pain but he would make it better. Nothing would ever hurt her again. "I'm coming." The words almost made it out of his lips.

The force of the impact only hurt for a moment. The searing pain and crunch of bone took his words away. Sirens wailed in the distance and traffic drew to a halt but he heard none of it. All he knew was she was next to him.

"Aaron, Aaron," he heard her cry.

Why was she so sad?

"Oh, Aaron."

He wanted to wipe her tears away, tell her not to cry. He wanted to tell her he loved her, would always love her. But already the sounds of the street were beginning to fade.

"Aaron, I love you."

He heard her voice as though it was coming from very far away. It was being drowned out by something more powerful than life, and for the second time that day, Aaron Strait was powerless to resist.

Chapter Thirty-Two

Haden never minded waiting—especially not tonight. The night he had foreseen so long ago was here. Aaron Strait had already fulfilled his destiny by walking haphazardly in front of a New York City bus. Haden felt Aaron's soul as it left his body behind. He concentrated on one soul—as he had been doing ever since he bid farewell to Persey—he could feel the small shudder it sent through the world of the living as it shucked off its human shell. He relished the sensation of death, this one in particular. It sent a delicious thrill through his borrowed human skin. Soon, very soon, Haden would reap the fruits of his patience.

Almost an hour passed before Leucy lit on the windowsill. Her feathers hardened and transformed back into opalescent skin before Haden's eyes.

"Where is she?" he asked, eyeing her gleaming form with detachment. Her head was still in its bird form. The small bird eyes darted away from his gaze. It was a tell. Haden picked up on it immediately. "Where is she?" he repeated in a low growl, walking towards the spot where Leucy stood.

"I did as you asked," said Leucy. The words issuing out of her bird's beak were high-pitched, too high-pitched.

"Tell me what happened," he said.

"I was there to watch his blood spill. After the police finished with their questions, I expected her to come to you but instead she walked uptown. She went to an office building. It was near the place where we found her before—the place where you first introduced her to me. She went inside…"

"Did you use your charms to follow her?" interrupted Haden, even though he already suspected the answer to his question.

She was silent.

Haden understood the answer in that silence. "You disobeyed my directions?"

"I followed her as you asked me to do," Leucy replied. "The building was dark. She's alone. I thought it prudent to let her come to you on her own terms."

"Did you?"

"Yes," she replied, moving her silver white body across the dimly lit room until she was in front of him. She was growing more confident in her explanation. "If you like, I will go retrieve her," she said. She ran one hand suggestively over her breast until it came to rest against the inside of her thigh. "Or you could just satisfy yourself with me instead." She tipped back her bird's head and released a wild inhuman song from her beak.

Haden reached out to stroke the place on her neck where her feathers hardened into skin. "You think your song calls to me as it does to mortal men?"

"No, my master, it is only for your enjoyment that I sing. You know I exist only to please you."

"Do you think I am pleased?" he asked, tightening his fingers around her neck ever so slightly.

"I think I could make you pleased, if you would allow me."

He looked at her without speaking. She took his silence for invitation and began to sing again. As her voice filled the air, he tightened his grip until the music choked and died in her throat. Her hard bird eyes glittered up at him. She knew better than to struggle. She allowed him to strangle her until her body went limp underneath his hand. He released her, letting her fall to the floor, a bundle of gleaming skin and feathers.

Haden knelt down beside her and felt for a pulse. Once satisfied, he stroked the feathers on her head with one finger. "The boy might have been blinded by your charms, but he was—after all—only human. As you well know, I am not. See that you are careful not to repeat the mistake of thinking you offer me anything in the way of satisfaction." He stood up and nudged her with his foot.

When she opened her eyes, he said, "Never underestimate my feelings for Persephone. You are not an acceptable substitute for her, nor will you ever be. If you manage to retain anything within your tiny bird brain make sure it is that." She blinked up at him in understanding. "Now I must go succeed where you have failed." Without sparing her another glance, he strode out of the yoga studio leaving the unfortunate siren bruised and prone on the floor.

Haden had told Persey he could always find her. It was true. He could find any of them, if he so desired. Of course he had to know they existed before he could find them. There was something to the peasant idea of escaping notice—hiding your child behind ugly names. However, once he'd caught the unique scent of their soul, he could always find its human form in much the same way an animal knows the scent of its prey.

Outside, his unfailing senses led him across town. Leucy might have left Persey at her office building but she was no longer there. He knew that much already. Leucy had failed him. She should have brought Persey to him. It was how he'd envisioned this night. He'd long anticipated putting together her broken pieces and collecting his long awaited prize. Instead, he—the lord of the Underworld—was forced to hunt her down. He swallowed another surge of displeasure at Leucy's bad judgment. After all, he reminded himself, it didn't matter. Soon, very soon, Persey would be his.

Chapter Thirty-Three

It wasn't unusual for Daniel to work late into the night. He liked the uninterrupted flow provided by the solitude of the office. Issue spotting was a hell of a lot easier when no one was around to interrupt his train of thought. He also had to admit, he got a certain macho sense of pride from sending out emails at two-thirty in the morning. It was a form of intimidation. It let other people know that while they'd been off resting their pretty little heads on their comfy down pillows—he, Daniel Hartnett, had been hard at work. Working into the wee hours allowed him to set the tone of other people's days.

Tomorrow, lawyers in New York, Chicago and L.A. would turn on their computers and spend the rest of their day scrambling to respond to issues framed by his emails. His early morning missives also sent a second unspoken message. They said, "Don't fuck with me because I will go longer and harder than anyone else." He always cc'd his clients on these emails. Clients, in particular, liked it when their hired guns burned the midnight oil on their behalf.

He'd already outlasted the night cleaning crew and was just getting into a groove when he heard something. It must be his imagination he thought, as he peered out into the blackened hallway. Except there it was again and he was suddenly aware his heart was pounding loudly in his chest. I'm being ridiculous, he thought. Even so he moved stealthily down the hallway to investigate. His brain was busy cataloging the horror stories. There was the disgruntled client who'd broken in and gone postal in a law office downtown or—he told himself sternly—it was someone from the cleaning crew who'd forgotten something. Whatever he'd been expecting, he wasn't prepared for the sight that greeted him when he rounded the corner.

Persey Campbell-Strait was standing in the dark hallway leaning up against her office door. Her eyes were squeezed shut. Even from where he stood, Daniel could hear the sound of her breath coming in jagged gulps. His first thought was the giant smears on her bare arms and down the front of her shirt and pants were dirt. Even her golden hair was matted with it.

"Persey," he whispered, instinctively lowering his voice. She looked up at him and her deep blue eyes were so empty that—for a moment—he thought she didn't recognize him.

"It's locked," she said, rattling the doorknob again and Daniel identified it as the noise he'd heard.

"Are you alright?" he asked, edging closer to her.

For the first time her eyes seemed to focus on him. She said in a barely audible whisper, "Go away Daniel. You shouldn't be around me."

Ignoring her warning, he edged closer still. As he did so, he caught a tangy iron scent that he recognized. "Oh my God," he said looking back at what he'd thought was dirt. "What happened? Are you all right?"

Without looking at him she slid to the floor. She hugged her knees to her chest and rocked back and forth ever-so-slightly.

"Persey," he whispered, squatting down on his haunches in front of her. Even in the darkness of the deserted hallway he could see she was covered in blood. It was matted in her blonde curls and clotted on her shirt. The pants she'd worn to work earlier that day—the same ones he'd noticed when she walked out of his office because of the way they hugged her ass—were soaked with the dark red substance. There were deep red streaks on her face, as though she'd been crying and wiped away her tears only to leave behind more smears. Her hands were spattered with a fine coating of the same substance. She was literally covered in blood.

He reached out to her slowly not wanting to frighten her, the way you might approach a wounded animal. When his hand made contact with her knee she flinched but didn't protest.

"Are you hurt?" he asked.

She shook her head. Even though the office was warm she was beginning to shiver.

"Come on," he said, prying one of her hands away from her knees. "You're cold. You're probably in shock." He half-led half-carried her down the hallway back to his office. Once inside, he locked the door behind them and wrapped her in a suit jacket that he left on the back of his door for emergencies. This hadn't been the type of emergency he expected when he hung it there, but all the same, he was glad to have it.

A quick search through his office cabinets turned up a bottle of water and a half-empty bottle of vodka. He filled a glass half full of water and spiked it liberally with vodka before handing it to her. When she made no motion to take the glass from him, he held it to her lips and tipped it up the way he'd observed young mothers do with their small children. She drank obediently then started coughing as the vodka hit the back of her throat. He patted her on the back until her coughing fit subsided. She took another sip, on her own this time and he thought he saw the muscles in her jaw relax a fraction.

"He's dead," she whispered.

Her voice was so quiet that Daniel wasn't sure if she was aware she was speaking out loud. Then she turned and looked at him with her dark lifeless eyes. "Dead," she repeated.

He swallowed his strange need to ask her questions. With anyone else he would already know what the words meant. With anyone else he would have heard who was dead and what had happened this evening. He wouldn't feel so frustrated and helpless. It struck him that most people spent their entire lives in this state. Never hearing more than the dusty tip of what words revealed to him.

"He's dead?" he repeated, hoping this technique would be more effective than subjecting her to an interrogation.

"It's my fault," she said. She took another drink and then paused for a moment to let the taste subside. "I wanted to be like her, to make him feel like nothing else in the world mattered." She looked up at him with anguish. He felt a twinge of his own anguish at making her relive whatever had happened. "All he could see is me. I tried to warn him but it was too late. I watched it happen but he never saw it coming. All he could see was me," she repeated. "It's what I wanted. I wanted him to see me and nothing else. I couldn't stop it because it's what I wanted," she repeated and then broke into sharp jagged sobs.

It was becoming clear. This must be how everyone else did it. They took the bits and pieces and drew conclusions. Someone had died. That much he knew for sure. He glanced over at his laptop. His fingers itched to Google Aaron Strait's name. Was that what you did when someone died? He wasn't sure how long it took before that type of information became available online. Persey emitted a small whimpering noise which quickly wiped the thought of research from his mind. She was in shock. She was a mess. He had to get her out of here before anyone saw her.

"Stay here," he said. "I'll be right back." He sprinted up the two flights of stairs to the litigation department and down the hall to Ellen Abram's office. He tried the door and finding it unlocked muttered a small thankful prayer. He rifled through his fellow partner's desk until he hit 'pay dirt'—a white bottle labeled Lunesta. He shook it experimentally before tucking it into his pocket. Every time he talked to Ellen she told him—in not so many words—that uppers got her through the day and downers through the night. Daniel hoped Ellen had another bottle at home because she wouldn't be getting this one back.

When he returned, Persey was sitting exactly where he'd left her. He poured her a fresh glass of water and placed two pills in her hand.

"Take these," he said. "They'll make you feel better."

"What are they?" she asked.

The question caught him off guard. "Sleeping pills, I stole them from Ellen Abram's office. She won't miss them." The truth slipped out before he could stop it but she didn't seem to mind or even notice. Instead, she placed them on her tongue and washed them down with the glass of water he handed her.

The moment she swallowed them he realized his error. He should have gotten her out of the office first. Now the clock was ticking. He wasn't sure how long he had. If she passed out, he was going to have to carry her out of the office and maneuver her into a cab. At the very least—a scene like that would make an amusing tale for the night doorman to relate to the morning doorman when it came time to switch shifts. That was the last thing Daniel needed.

"Come on," he said, pulling her up out of her chair. The way she was already beginning to sway on her feet told him he didn't have much time. "Let's get you cleaned up a little."

He steered her down the hallway to the women's bathroom. The harsh fluorescent lights revealed even more blood. Most of it would be covered if he buttoned up his jacket that she still wore. No one would look twice at a woman wearing a man's suit jacket late at night.

Her hair was another matter. Her long blonde curls were matted and dark in places. He considered washing her hair in the sink, but when he removed his jacket from her shoulders she began shaking so violently, he quickly buttoned it around her again. In the end, he settled for tucking the more matted pieces under the jacket and wiping her face and hands with a wet paper towel.

"Come on Persey," he said to her as her head nodded. "All you have to do is walk out of here. Just hold it together for a few more minutes. Come on. I know you can do it." He continued to babble encouraging words to her as they waited for the elevator and then descended down to the lobby.

"You need a cab, sir?" asked the night doorman glancing up from his newspaper.

"I got it," said Daniel as he swept Persey outside, past the doorman's prying eyes. Daniel raised his arm and a taxi screeched to a stop at the curb. He opened the door and poured Persey into the backseat. "Gramercy Place, just off of Twenty-Second," he said to the sleepy cab driver whose registration tag identified him as Jean-Pierre.

Jean-Pierre glanced back at them when they stopped at a red light. "She have too much to drink?" he asked.

Daniel was relieved to hear nothing behind the question except fatigue, and a belief that conversation insured more generous tips. "Yep, one too many. She's just going to have to sleep it off," he replied. Persey's head came to rest heavily on his shoulder.

Chapter Thirty-Four

The dating scene wasn't the only thing about Manhattan Daniel eschewed. He also refused to buy into the whole stick-up-your-ass Upper East Side thing. His colleagues could have their Eli's, Metropolitan Museum and Agata & Valentina. It wasn't worth the trade-off. Not that Gramercy Park was a dump. If anything, he'd paid more for two floors in an old brownstone then he would have paid for some pre-war, off Park. It was still a nice neighborhood. There was no denying it when apartment sales regularly topped the seven digit mark. What he liked about downtown—why he'd been happy to fork over the big bucks for his apartment—was the energy.

His neighborhood was grittier, hipper, more filled with youth and simultaneously more anonymous. He never had to make nice with some uniformed doorman watching his every move. There was no need to make polite elevator conversation with fur-wrapped women—their faces stretched into a grotesque parody of youth. Also missing was the phalanx of delivery boys that spread over the Upper East Side each night, like magical food fairies, the crowds of nannies slogging home to the lesser boroughs of the city, the dog walkers, the dry cleaner delivery people, the housekeepers, the limousine drivers idling along the side streets and avenues and the myriad of other parasitic satellites which rotated around the rich animal that was Manhattan's Upper East Side.

As the cab pulled up in front of his building, he had a surge of renewed thankfulness for his refusal to follow the pack uptown. There was no doorman to greet him tonight—no one to scrutinize the beautiful blood-soaked girl in his arms. Anonymity, he thought as he fitted his key into the front door of his apartment, was highly underrated.

He carried her into his bedroom and set her down on the bed. She didn't move. In fact, the only way you'd know she was alive was from the slight rise and fall of her chest. She still wore his jacket. It had fallen open to reveal her blood-stained shirt. He contemplated putting her in the bathtub but was overcome with irrational fear that he might accidentally drown her. Was it his imagination or had she stopped breathing? Panic shot through him and he grabbed her wrist trying to locate a pulse. It was strong. For a minute, he sat next to her on his bed and just savored the feel of her blood pumping through that delicate pressure point at her wrist. He tried to remember the last time a girl had spent the night in his apartment then quickly discarded the memory. It wasn't relevant—different time, different place.

He contemplated her blood-stained clothing again. She couldn't sleep in these clothes. He unbuttoned her blouse and eased her arms out of it. Then he turned his attention to the pants he had admired less than twenty-four hours ago. He unfastened them at the waist and tugged them down over her hips, doing his best not to disturb her. She groaned and turned on one side which allowed him to finish the job.

It must be habit, he thought as he adjusted his pants. How else could he explain his raging hard-on? He wanted her even when she was passed out and he was removing her blood-soaked clothes. Before his body had time to have any other reaction to the visual stimulus lying in his bed, he slipped one of his old t-shirts over her head and covered her with a blanket.

Back downstairs in the kitchen, he grabbed a beer out of the fridge. He picked up his laptop and headed for the couch. He pulled up the New York Times website and typed in the name Aaron Strait; no dice. He typed the name into Google but still didn't turn up much of anything besides a few mentions in connection with USB deals. On an impulse, he pulled up the local NY1 website and there it was—the lead story. He didn't even have to look for it.

Local Man Dies After Being Hit By Seventh Avenue Bus

The victim, Aaron Strait, a Manhattan resident, was pronounced dead this morning at St. Vincent Hospital, according to the Manhattan County medical examiner's office. An autopsy is scheduled for Wednesday.

    Police said Strait was struck by an M7 bus traveling South on Seventh Avenue. Onlookers said it appeared as though Strait walked directly into the path of the bus. Strait attempted to cross Seventh Avenue mid-block and was struck by the oncoming bus at approximately 11:12 p.m. on December 14th. Strait was briefly pinned underneath the bus, authorities said. The bus driver, Sheryl-Lynn Pruitt was interviewed by the police but no citations were issued.

    Authorities have not yet ruled out the possibility of suicide or intoxication. Strait was an employee at the investment banking firm of USB and leaves behind his wife, Persephone Campbell-Strait. Mrs. Campbell-Strait was unavailable for comment at the time of this article.

There it was in proverbial black and white. He pushed his laptop to one side and leaned forward to pick up the beer he'd set on the coffee table. Half a beer later and he was still trying to locate the appropriate emotions. Pity, sorrow, sadness, he knew those would all be appropriate. Instead, all he felt was delirious hope and unbearable guilt. He'd wished for this to happen. In his darkest moments, he'd wanted nothing more than some convenient accident to wipe Aaron Strait off the face of this earth. Now his wish had come true. The girl he'd imagined a future with was asleep in his bedroom. He pondered this a moment and suddenly something Persey had said earlier tugged at the back of his brain.

What was it? He knew he needed to dredge the memory up to the surface before it floated away on the tide of sleep headed his way. "It's my fault. I wanted him to see me and nothing else." Now he remembered it clearly. He remembered the way she whispered it just before she brought the glass of vodka and water to her lips. What had she meant?

Then it came to him. She'd said, "I wanted to be like her. I wanted it to happen." That was it. It all made sense to him. The bastard was cheating on her and she'd found out about it. She'd been understandably hurt and jealous of the other woman.

What an asshole Aaron Strait must have been to cheat on someone like Persey. He could imagine the conversation where she told her cheating husband she wished he was dead. Now it had happened and she hated herself for it. Well it wasn't her fault. Even though he'd occasionally wished for Aaron's Strait's death himself, it wasn't his fault either. It was like the old saying "If wishes were horses, beggars would ride."

Aaron Strait had screwed up. Now he was gone before he'd had a chance to make amends. His widow was asleep in Daniel's bedroom. Whatever had happened in the past was over. The future belonged to Daniel. It would be up to him to comfort and assure Persey that Aaron's death was not her fault.

He picked up the beer can and drained the last of it. Honestly, he thought shaking his head again, had Aaron Strait experienced some kind of temporary insanity? He must have, otherwise, how could he possibly manage to think about another woman when he had Persey? That's what Daniel would tell her when she woke up the next morning. From the warm recesses of his pants, his opportunistic penis stirred happily at the thought.

Chapter Thirty-Five

Haden followed Persey's trail uptown from Studio H and across Fifth Avenue. He paused in Union Square, momentarily thrown off guard by the lights and sounds of rushing technology. Then he caught it again. It led him up Park Avenue and onto a sleepy side street.

He stopped mid-block in front of an ivy-covered brownstone. There was nothing to distinguish it from the other brownstones lining the street; nothing except for the fact that Persey was inside. Haden could feel her there, one story up. She was safe and warm. Those were the only emotions he could glean through the brick walls.

A light came on in the main room and from his position in the street, Haden could see a man. The man walked back into the farther recesses of the apartment before returning to the front room carrying a sleek laptop computer. He sat down on the couch and began pecking away on the laptops keys. Who was this man? Why was Persey in his house? Whoever the man was he was excited. Haden could feel the unmistakable buzz of his emotions, his racing heart. He was also comfortable. This was his home. Haden was sure of it.

How had he been unaware of this person Persey sought out in her darkest moment, her hour of need? She should have come to him. He'd been waiting for her at his studio while she'd been finding comfort in the arms of another. A surge of jealous rage shot through Haden. He thought once again of that moment when her soul invaded him. How much had she seen? Was it possible she understood the dark secrets residing at the core of his being? Even more worrisome, did she know what he'd planned? Haden took a deep calming breath. He must act cautiously, be clear-headed. There was the chance—he must acknowledge it—she had seen enough to deny the claim he intended to make. Was she running from him or had a simple twist of fate brought her to the apartment of this inconvenient stranger? He needed to understand what motivated her before jumping to any more conclusions.

Haden quietly mounted the steps of the brownstone and leaned against the front door. He would not disturb her sleep. He didn't need to. There were things he could learn about the man on the other side of the door without ever breaching the privacy of the apartment. Haden stood there for a moment, probing the man's soul for information. It was clear the man she had turned to was no different than any other human. He had an end. Haden searched deeper, hunting for that crucial piece of information.

The last moments of the man's soul were ingrained within it. They had—in fact—been ingrained upon it since the moment of its creation. Haden could see this man just as clearly as any of the rest of them. The fact that he could see this human's end wasn't what made him turn away from the door. It was the vision of what he saw. His new knowledge pierced through him. It demanded a new strategy. Slowly, Haden backed down the steps and retreated away into the night.

Chapter Thirty-Six

Rudy Turner had known Persey Campbell for as long as he could remember. Persey Campbell—that's how he always thought of her—full name, no stop, no hyphenations or abbreviations. Her marriage to Aaron notwithstanding, she was still Persey Campbell to him.

Even when they were both kids he'd thought of her that way. She'd been the kind of kid who warranted thinking about. Pretty, that was a given, but there was something else. Where Persey was concerned there was always something else. It was the way you desperately wanted to know her, sit next to her, become her friend, despite all apparent evidence she wanted nothing to do with you. He'd had a lot of time to study her because his mother was always inviting Persey over. He could still hear his mother, patron saint of lost souls, on the phone with Demi Campbell.

"Now Demi," she'd say. "You don't need to worry at all. She'll be just fine over here. Drop her off as long as you need to."

It must have been hard on Demi, raising a kid all by herself like she'd done. His mother had understood that but Rudy hadn't. It was the kind of thing you didn't realize until you were no longer a kid yourself.

Persey would arrive and his mother would fuss around, offering her cookies and other snacks that were not standard fare at the Turner residence.

"Rudy, ask Persey what she wants to do. She's your guest. Make her feel welcome," she'd coach before Persey came over.

"Wanna play a game?" he'd ask.

Even as a kid, he'd known what Persey wanted to do. He'd also known it didn't involve him. Left to her own devices, she would curl up with anything in print between two hard covers. He also knew if he didn't make the offer, he would be in for a lecture after Persey went home.

"Be nice to her Rudy-rudes," his mother would always say to him. "She may act like she doesn't want to talk to you but you've got to understand she's not like us. The poor little thing never even got to meet her father."

In one respect, his mother hit the nail on the head. Persey wasn't like them. In response to Rudy's offer to play a game she would always shrug an 'okay'. They'd go to the game cupboard and sometimes he'd make her go through the charade of playing Monopoly or Life. A game meant talking to her, real interaction that held out the possibility—however infinitesimal—of taking one step closer to the warm promised land of her friendship.

Sometimes, as they stared into the contents of the game cupboard, he'd find the willpower to say, "If you want, you can just hang out in my room and read." That offer never failed to earn him a genuine smile of gratitude.

"Are you sure?" she'd ask in a voice that let him understand there was nothing she'd like better.

"Yeah," he'd say, trying to make it sound like the truth.

"Okay," she'd say with another smile. "But only if you're sure."

Clearly, he wasn't the only one who'd been briefed on manners. More often than not though, he would choose the board game. It was always with the vain hope that today would be the day she would enjoy it. They would become friends, real friends. The kind of friends that call each other on the phone, not the kind where your mother needs to call their mother before you get to spend time together. He wanted them to be the kind of friends who hang out after school, on the weekend or whenever they get the chance. He wanted it and he knew it was never going to happen. He also knew he shouldn't make her play board games. He knew better but it was almost like she was a drug and he couldn't help himself. Later on, he would remember that feeling and realize how prescient he'd been.

They'd set up the game in the basement and he would chatter away at her like some little kid. She always had that effect on him. She turned the tables and made it seem like she was the one who was a year older instead of the other way around. He would tell her things, the kind of things that made him shudder if he happened to think about them later. After she'd gone home, he would try to forget what he'd told her. It was just too damn embarrassing. Then, the next time she came over, the whole charade would start all over again. At some point, she must have reached an age where Demi felt like she could be safely left alone at home because the play dates, as his mother referred to them, just sort of petered out.

Then one morning, after those forced afternoon play dates had faded to a faint memory of middle childhood, Demi spotted him in front of Shari's.

"You have to come over and tell Persey about what you're doing," she insisted. "I know she'll want to help out. It's exactly the kind of thing she loves."

Demi Campbell had acted like he, Rudy Turner, was a find, some kind of prize. Didn't she know, couldn't she tell, that he was nothing more than a big high school loser? Hanging out with a group called the Sir Hacks-a-Lots—he still couldn't think about that name without a little inward shudder—trying to raise money for new computers. He might as well have worn a sign around his neck that proclaimed, "Beat me up, please!"

But Demi was insistent and his mother's training ran deep. He couldn't be rude. He'd agreed to go to her house and talk to Persey because he was a nice guy. More than that, he wanted to show Persey he wasn't some annoying kid anymore. He was all grown up now.

He'd been all of sixteen that day. Even so, when she entered the room, he knew with complete certainty he would never see another girl as beautiful as Persey Campbell. It wasn't just that she was beautiful. It was something more and simultaneously less. At first he'd thought it was because she just didn't give a damn. She was the polar opposite of the cutest girls at Clear Lake High. The ones he sneaked passing looks at from a comfortable distance in the hallway. Those girls knew they were objects of desire. They owned it, traded in on their good looks with alarming regularity as though it was a cash account with an unlimited balance.

Persey didn't need to draw on any kind of account. She just drew you in. He felt almost helpless sitting so close to her gravitational pull. When she asked him about the computer drive—God, he was such a nerd in high school—he had to fight the strangest impulse to tell her all about the computer games he and the other Sir Hacks-a-Lot guys played, the really dirty ones. He had a sudden flash of fear that once he opened his mouth to start talking he would never be able to stop. The only thing that restrained him, pulled him back from the brink, was the solid fact of Demi Campbell, beaming at him from across the kitchen table.

His close call, his brush with apoplectic confession, had been fresh on his mind as they drove into town that day. They'd been silent, Rudy, by necessity and Persey, by choice. Later, it all made sense, the way she kept everyone at a distance. Life must have felt like—must still feel like—a treacherous obstacle course. His first clue there was more to Persey Campbell than met the eye came that afternoon, although he didn't put the clue together with the rest of the pieces until much later.

It was the effect she had on those Neanderthals on the football team. She was an incoming freshman, not even in high school. Yet, as he watched them buy droopy strawberry plants from his plant sale, he saw a reflection of his own desire and need laid bare upon the other boys' faces. It made him feel better for nattering away at her over drawn-out sessions of *The Game of Life, the Simpsons version*, somehow more justified. Around Persey, they were all children. No one was immune to her pull. It didn't matter if you were a Rudy Turner or a Luke Leister. Persey rendered everyone the same.

Luke and his friends followed a certain code. The members of the Sir Hacks-a-Lots were intimately familiar with that code. If the code had ever been discussed—which it wasn't—it would have been something like the law of the jungle. The strongest and best shall prevail. Those football kings of the jungle were quick to remind anyone who stepped out of line or forgot the code of their rank. Verbal abuse was a favorite tool. When that failed, they resorted to physical reminders.

Girls—especially girls who hadn't even started high school yet—were at best accessories to the kings. At worst, they were a source of locker room stories. One thing Rudy knew for certain was that, until that day in the Shari's parking lot, Luke and his followers would never have dreamed of following the mandates of a lesser primate—a mere incoming freshman—in order to benefit the "Geek Squad."

It took him a while, but one week in late October the clues came together. It was all because of Aaron Strait. After all, Aaron asked him to keep an eye on her and so that's what he did. Every day at lunch, Rudy watched Persey eat her sandwich out of the corner of his eye. Even if golden boy Aaron Strait, captain of the football team, honors student and all around nice guy, hadn't asked him to watch out for her, he would have done it anyway. She was hard to ignore. Now he had an excuse, a mission.

The rest of the Sir Hacks-a-Lots followed his lead. They all watched her even if they never talked about it. They barely even mentioned her name. There was no point in discussing her finer points when she was so far out of their league. It went without saying that if she hadn't been dating Aaron Strait she would've been dating someone else. It also went without saying, that the someone else would not have been a member of the Sir Hacks-a-Lots.

Soon, lunch hour became Rudy's favorite part of the day. It wasn't just because he got to see Persey. It was because he got a secret thrill out of the way she refused to play by the code that governed the rest of them. Aaron could no more convince her to reign as queen bee of the high school social scene than Rudy could ever convince her to happily play board games. It was good to know that failure, where Persey was concerned, was egalitarian. Rudy started to think of the Sir Hacks-a-Lots as "Team Persey" on a protective detail. He was sixteen, after all. In retrospect he realized he was lucky to have kept that conceit to himself because even a group called the Sir Hacks-a-Lots, were not above ridiculing one of their own.

Every day in the lunchtime hideout for losers and misfits, he observed how people watched her. They would drift closer and closer into her orbit until the pull would become too strong to resist. They would sidle up to her, sometimes taking a seat at her table.

That was where Rudy came in. He would grab a book and sit at the table next to her. Often, his mere presence was enough to discourage the sidler. If it wasn't, Rudy would pretend they—he and Persey, as though that coupling of names existed on any sphere—had to work on a project and didn't need any interruptions, thank you very much. The only hard part about this role was it required him to quell his urges to divulge his most tawdry thoughts. She'd been graceful about his inadvertent admission on the way home from the computer drive but he didn't want to suffer through a repeat performance. He was pretty sure she didn't either.

Late summer became fall and it never occurred to Rudy to question his need to tell Persey things. It had always been like that with her. It turned out it was just another piece of the puzzle that hadn't quite fallen into place yet.

Then came the day when Luke paid a visit to the library during lunch hour. The unexpected presence of a predator in the land of zebras and gazelles put the entire room on high alert. People shifted in their seats and busied themselves with projects so as to avoid the predator's eye. They needn't have worried. The predator had already chosen his prey.

He was headed directly towards the one person in the room who seemed to be completely oblivious to his presence. Despite the fact that Luke targeted her like some kind of teenage version of a heat-seeking missile, Persey continued to read. She sat at her table twisting a piece of flaxen hair around her finger as was her habit when she was deeply engrossed. Rudy, one table away, ostensibly working on some new piece of coding, sat frozen to his chair in a kind of mute terror.

"Hey, you," he heard Luke say as he slid easily into the wooden chair opposite Persey.

Persey glanced at the obstruction in front of her then her eyes met Rudy's for a fraction of a second. Her look managed to convey she would be handling this particular interloper on her own.

"Hi Luke," she said. Her tone was resigned, as though she was expecting something.

"I was wondering where Aaron stashes you every day." Luke's voice was low, intimate but not quite a whisper. He still thought he was in control.

Rudy, watching from behind Luke, saw something shift deep in Persey's eyes. It was at that moment he understood two things. Luke was about to have an unpleasant experience and Persey Campbell was fully capable of taking care of herself.

Luke plucked the book she'd been reading out of her hand and glanced at it. "Any good?" he asked, flipping through its pages.

"You didn't really come here to ask me what I'm reading," Persey said, allowing her deep blue eyes to meet his.

From Rudy's vantage point two tables away, he could feel his own secrets and confessions bubbling inside of him in response to the invitation in her eyes and the radiance of her smile.

"I, umm," said Luke. His ready confidence seemed to wilt and flee under the brilliance of her full attention.

"We're here," said Persey. Her eyes never left Luke's. "It's just the two of us. If you want to tell me something, this would be the perfect time to do it."

Luke leaned his head towards hers like an obedient child. He whispered something into her ear. This time it was a real whisper. The kind meant for Persey's ears alone.

"It's okay," Rudy heard her say. She laid her hand on top of Luke's. "Don't worry," she said. "I'll keep it a secret."

Luke stood up and looked around the library with a stunned expression, as though he couldn't remember how he had managed to come to this particular spot. Then he walked quickly towards the door, a victim of his own aggression.

It was that moment that led to Rudy's "Persey epiphany". What Rudy could never understand afterwards was why it had taken him so long to pull it all together.

Rudy was smart. "Too smart for your own good," his mother said. "One to watch," was how *Wired Magazine* phrased it. But those accolades had nothing to do with his insight into people. He understood physics and gigabytes. It wasn't the kind of knowledge that translated to insights about beautiful girls. But then, Persey had always been more than just a beautiful girl.

As he watched Luke walk out of the library, a collection of tiny remembered moments came whizzing together to form a complete picture. Some of the moments were excruciating—who tells the most enchanting girl you've ever seen that you're going to be thinking about her while you whack off? Some were merely odd. In the end, they all led to the realization that Persey Campbell was more unique than he'd ever understood. He sat there in the library marveling at his discovery. When he glanced back at her again, she was reading her book again as though nothing out of the ordinary had taken place. But it had. Information was like that. Once it was disseminated there was no going back.

Chapter Thirty-Seven

Rudy saw the piece while he was drinking his morning coffee. He choked, literally choked, spraying coffee all over his screen and keyboard.

"What the fuck, man?" said Bradley.

He and Bradley were partners, only in the business sense. They'd met at MIT—graduated the same year with degrees in software engineering. Over the last ten years, their paths had crossed so often they'd developed a healthy mutual respect. During Rudy's last gig, he and Bradley had come up with their current brainchild over an all-night caffeine fueled work session.

Now they were holed up in this shabby office space in order to combine their collective genius. The brainchild was actually Rudy's, but the inspiration (unbeknownst to Bradley) was Persey Campbell. "It's the next step after Facebook," was how Rudy had phrased it to the angel investors in the funding meeting. The idea was simple, as most good ideas are.

The website they were building combined the connectivity of social networking with the adrenaline rush of confession. Bradley was working on code that would analyze each user's retinal patterns as their eyes viewed a webpage. What they'd discovered was the movements of each individual user's retina were as unique as a human fingerprint. Rudy was building the program that converted the retinal analysis into an instant feed of individual predilection. The website, when it was up and running, would be called Confess.com.

Users would view its content. While they read the website, it would read their retinal patterns and translate them into a newsfeed indicating the users most appropriate mate, most sought after merchandise and—most interestingly in Rudy's opinion—predilection for vice. At the user's option, their personal information could be published into a wider social network feed.

When Confess.com was completed, it would translate into big money from big business. Rudy already had execs pissing in their pants with excitement over the idea of a website that would bring in the very consumers who were most inclined—whether they realized it or not—to purchase whatever corporate America was shilling.

Rudy was convinced Confess.com would take the addictive nature of a website like Facebook and up the ante. What could be more compulsive and addictive than a newsfeed composed of people's secrets? Rudy had been an early adopter of Facebook and an even earlier adopter/observer of Persey. Given his experience with both of them, he firmly believed that Persey style confessions and realizations were far more interesting than anything Facebook had to offer.

"Who's going to want to publish their secrets?" his mother asked when she heard the business plan.

"Everyone under twenty," Rudy told her. "And then it'll age up. That's the way technology works."

"It's the death of life as we know it, that's what it is," his mother replied, shaking her head.

"Maybe," he said with a grin. "But once we're up and running, it might mean a vacation house, or two, for you and dad."

"Rudy," she said shaking her head at him. "Your father and I don't need a vacation house. You know what I dream of?"

He'd been foolish enough to take the bait. "What Mom, what do you dream of?"

"Grandchildren, that's what. Any progress on that front?"

Oddly enough, this was the conversation playing in his head as he scrolled through his list of contacts with shaking hands. It couldn't be true. People like Aaron Strait, kings of the jungle, didn't get mown down by buses. He hesitated for a moment before he punched in Persey's work number. She'd tell him it was some kind of joke, a misprint. Maybe she'd tease him about being gullible enough to fall for it.

"Ms. Campbell-Strait's office, how may I help you?" said a woman on the other end of the line."

"Yeah, is she in?" asked Rudy.

"I'm sorry she's out of the office today. May I take a message?"

"No, um, no message. Actually, can you just let her know Rudy Turner called?"

"Yes sir, I'll make sure she gets the message."

He dialed Persey's cell but it went directly to voice mail. A sick feeling crept over him. It couldn't be true. He'd seen Aaron last night. He was going home to Persey. It just couldn't be true.

"Hey man, take a look at this code," said Bradley. He pushed his chair back from his desk and rode it over to Rudy's side of the office. "Dude, what's up? Are you okay?" The article was still maximized on Rudy's computer screen. Bradley read it over his shoulder. "Holy shit, that's not your high school friend at USB, is it? You met him at Maru yesterday."

Rudy nodded. It felt like his head wasn't connected to his body. "I've got to go," he said quietly.

"Yeah, go, do what you need to do. The code can wait," said Bradley as though Rudy were waiting for his permission.

Rudy was already disconnecting his cell phone from the charger and grabbing his keys. He threw on his coat and headed down the stairs without looking back. She was out there somewhere, all alone, but this time she needed him. For the first time in his life, he might be able to give her something she didn't already have.

Chapter Thirty-Eight

On the icy cold morning of December 15th, Daniel Hartnett did something he'd never done before. He called in sick—make that two things he'd never done before because he also called in sick for Persey. He'd fallen asleep on the couch and woken up, as was his habit, around 7:30. The harsh December sunlight was glaring in his eyes but doing nothing to warm the room.

He tiptoed back upstairs and found Persey just as he'd left her. She'd turned over on her side. Her face was hidden underneath her hair. He stood there for a moment listening to the soft cadence of her breathing. His bedroom chair was piled with documents. He put them down on the floor and sat down to watch her sleep. He wanted to be there when she woke up. He wanted to be in bed next to her. He wanted to be there for the rest of her life. He shook his head in an effort to expel the images those thoughts conjured. What the hell was wrong with him? He was there to comfort a woman—insanely desirable as she may be—who had watched her husband be hit and killed by a bus.

He tiptoed back out of the room and down the hall to take a piss. When he came back, she was sitting up, knees hugged to her chest, staring out the window. She heard him come in and turned toward him. She looked at him, letting her eyes rest on his. Daniel realized that all the eye contact he'd experienced up to this moment was the equivalent to a quickie in a bathroom stall. This, what he felt right now, was the joining of two souls.

"Tell me it didn't happen," she whispered hoarsely. "Tell me it was just a bad dream." Her eyes reached inside of him. It was as though they were one person.

Desperate as he was to tell her something comforting, soften the blow so to speak, the words poured from him as though they weren't his to control. "It's true," he said frozen in the entrance of the room. "He's dead."

She buried her head against her knees, hugging them even more tightly. As soon as their eye contact was broken, he felt some semblance of his much practiced self-control return. His words became his own again. He walked over to the bed and sat down next to her.

"I'm so sorry," he said.

He wondered for a moment whether it was appropriate to pat her on the back or not. Instead, he settled for lamely repeating, "I'm sorry. I don't know why I said it like that—"

"It's not your fault," she said into her knees. "It's my fault. Everything is my fault and now he's dead."

"No, it's not your fault," said Daniel. "It was an accident. I know you love him but you can't believe what happened is your fault."

"He was crossing the street to see me," said Persey. "I wanted to be like her, irresistible. He couldn't help himself. I might as well have pushed him in front of that…" Her voice broke off choked with sobs.

"Look," said Daniel. "I will be the first one to admit you are ridiculously beautiful but you didn't push him into the street. It was an accident."

"No, it wasn't," she insisted. "It was his gift to me. He said no one can resist her. Aaron couldn't. I wanted to be like her. I wanted Aaron to want me as much as he wanted her."

Despite all the questions that came to mind, the first one that he was able to formulate was, "Whose gift to you?"

"Haden's," she said.

The name meant nothing to him. He listened carefully, hoping something else might reveal itself but like always where

Persey was concerned, Daniel could only hear her spoken words. He would have to go on instinct.

"Listen to me," he said. "I don't know who this Haden guy is but that's not the kind of gift anyone can give. "But," Daniel added, holding up his hand to staunch her protest. "Just for the sake of argument, let's say he did give it to you. Here I am, a grown man who has admitted he finds you beautiful. I'm sitting in bed next to you and I'm pretty sure I'm in control of all my faculties. Let me see," he said, standing up and walking out of the room then quickly re-entering. "Yep, still in control. And let me add that I managed to take off your clothes and put you in a t-shirt last night. It was difficult," he said, hoping his deprecating tone would belie the truth of the statement. "But I managed."

"It's not the same," said Persey shaking her head.

"It is the same," said Daniel. He placed his hand under her chin, lifting her head so he could look in her eyes. It was a mistake. Everything inside him surged to the forefront, desperate to be told. He quickly shut his eyes. He took a deep breath and then reopened them, focusing on the safer regions of her forehead.

"I'm guessing he made a bad choice," he said. "And now he never gets the chance to make it up to you. That sucks. It really, really sucks but in no way does it make it your fault. It was his time to go. You know, as well as I do, that if somehow he could be sitting here with you right now he'd say the same thing. He'd say he loves you and it's not your fault."

"You're right," said Persey with the shadow of a smile. "That's exactly the kind of thing he would say."

"It was his time, Persey," said Daniel. "No one gets to live forever. As fucked up and unfair as it is, yesterday was his time. But, that doesn't make it your fault."

Tears welled up in her eyes. Had he ever seen anything so mesmerizing in his life?

"I want him back," she said.

Her voice wiped away all his selfish thoughts. She was in pain. He needed to make her better. This time he didn't have to think about it. His arms wrapped around her. He held her close as she buried her face against his shoulder.

"I know you do," he whispered, rocking her in his arms. They stayed that way for a long time; Persey's muffled sobs soaking the fabric of Daniel's shirt. He patted her back and smoothed her hair. He noticed Aaron's blood in her hair had dried and matted while she slept. He waited until her sobs became more intermittent before he said gently. "Come on Persey, you'll feel better if you take a shower." She nodded mutely, allowed him to guide her to her feet and lead her down the hall to the bathroom.

Daniel's bathroom was only slightly newer than the apartment which, if the date stamped into the cement on the front steps was to be believed, was built in 1855. The harsh bathroom lights quickly revealed the full extent of blood covering Persey's body. Daniel was instantly grateful for the general lack of reflective services offered in his antique bathroom. It might make his morning shave a daily challenge, but right now Persey didn't need to see herself. His shower was fitted to the bathtub by means of a long metal pipe which ferried the water up to the shower head. He turned it on to let the water warm up and went back out into the hall to locate a fresh towel.

When he returned Persey was standing where he'd left her. In his too big t-shirt that hung almost to her knees, she looked like a little girl.

"I thought you left," she said with a strange little gasp.

"No, I'm right here. I was just grabbing you a towel," he said, holding it up as evidence.

"Daniel," she said grabbing his arm. Her hand was shaking. "I can't do it." She gestured helplessly at the blood, now dried in brown patches on her legs and crusted underneath her fingernails.

"Can you help me?" She closed her eyes and tears squeezed out from beneath her eyelids and rolled down her cheeks.

"You want me to, um, help you in the shower?" asked Daniel.

She nodded without opening her eyes. "It's him. It's everywhere." She made another noise, somewhere between a gasp and a gulp. "I'm covered with it. I don't think I can do it."

"So you...um," stammered Daniel.

She opened her eyes and looked around as though searching for an escape. "I'm sorry. I know it's too much to ask. You've already done so much. I should go."

"No," said Daniel a little too forcefully. "No, no, it's okay. Just give me a minute. I, umm, I'll put on my swim trunks." He ran back down the hall to the bedroom and brought himself to orgasm, more quickly than he had at any time since he was fourteen. Then he slipped on his swimming trunks and ran back down the hall to where Persey stood, rooted to the same spot.

The water was still running and clouds of steam were billowing out over the top of the shower curtains. "All right," he said, pulling back the shower curtain as though he was holding a door open for her.

Without looking at him, she stripped off the t-shirt he'd dressed her in the night before. Then she took off everything else and stepped past him into the shower. He stepped in behind her, trying to give her as much space as the narrow confines of the bathtub would allow. He was immediately thankful that her back was to him because despite whacking off less than two minutes ago, his penis was already becoming stiff underneath his baggy swim trunks.

"Let's start with your hair," he said, reaching for the shampoo.

She stood silently in front of him as he worked her curls into a deep, red foam.

"Close your eyes," he instructed as he rinsed and sudsed again and then a third time until the foam was no longer tinged with blood. He picked up a washcloth and—covering it with soap—went to work on her arms and legs. "Let's have your hands," he said. His voice had taken on a strange peppy quality that he didn't quite recognize. He cleaned both of her hands, scrubbing under each fingernail, until every trace of blood that had stained her body was gone.

The entire time she remained inert. She was passive, allowing him to handle her like a doll. Despite that—or maybe because of it—Daniel had never experienced such exquisite torture. The feel of her skin sliding beneath his hands—even with the washcloth as a protective barrier—was like an invitation. The back of her neck with her wet hair hanging down on either side, those fragile tiny bumps making up the individual knobs of her spine, the roundness of her ass, the hardness of her nipples under the water's spray; it all begged to be touched. He wanted nothing more than to cup his hands around her breasts, turn her to him and feel her lips against his as he plunged himself inside of her.

He was almost certain she would allow it, expected it even. Almost as though it was the price she was willing to pay for something she hadn't been able to do for herself. He'd never wanted anything or anyone as much as he wanted her in that moment. Still, he held back. He was a model of forbearance. It was the right thing to do. It was the kind of thing someone does for someone they love. As he washed her beautiful body, Daniel understood (as some part of him had always understood) he had never loved anyone the way he loved Persey.

Chapter Thirty-Nine

Daniel was determined to give Persey a Hartnett style sick day. Some mothers believe if you are too sick to go to school, then you are too sick to watch television, play video games or do anything that involves leaving your bed. Daniel's mother was not among this camp. She believed the most direct route to recovery necessitated sitting in front of the television wrapped in a blanket. Chicken soup on a tray with Saltine crackers, a glass of ginger ale with a bendy straw, ice cream (if your throat was sore), new comic books and unlimited video game time were all a given. "A happy kid is a healthy kid," she liked to say. The only times he could ever remember her threatening to spoil his sick day with a trip to the doctor's office were the rare occasions when he was too sick to eat, watch T.V. or play video games.

Daniel knew Persey wasn't sick. He also knew what he had to give was of limited value. After all, none of it was going to make her better. There was no quick fix for what she was feeling. Still, a sick day meant you were loved. Under the circumstances, it was the best thing he could think of.

He'd left her behind in the bathroom to dry off in private while he found another t-shirt and unearthed an old pair of sweats that had shrunk in the dryer. He dressed quickly and then walked back down the hall.

"I put some clean clothes on the bed for you," he said to the bathroom door. He was beginning to wonder if she would respond when he heard her say, "Thanks."

"I'll be downstairs if you need me," he added. This time he didn't wait for a reply.

In the kitchen, he surveyed his supplies. Food was the easiest. He put a quick call into the local Food Emporium and was told he could expect his delivery in under an hour. After he hung up, he remembered the magazines. Two blocks down was a newspaper kiosk but he didn't want to leave her. He called Food Emporium again and asked them to add an issue of People and Entertainment Weekly. He turned on the television and scrolled through the pay-per-view menu. Romantic comedies were out, as was anything violent or bloody. He hesitated for a moment before settling on *Strictly Ballroom*. It seemed unlikely to remind her of any of the trauma she had suffered in the last twenty-four hours.

His computer was still on the coffee table where he had left it the night before. Everything was still quiet upstairs so he logged on to check his email—old habits die hard. He scanned through his inbox but before he could click on anything, he heard her feet on the stairs.

She came into the room and wiped all thoughts of email from Daniel's mind. Her hair was just beginning to dry. The small strands that were no longer wet curled away from the rest of her hair giving the effect of a fuzzy golden halo. She wore his old Goldman Parke t-shirt over the blue sweat pants—which despite having shrunk—still hung loosely on her slim frame. She looked perfect.

He wished he could see her wearing that outfit every morning for the rest of his life. It occurred to him, he would give a lot to repeat the events of this morning, except under different circumstances. If the circumstances were different then maybe the whole shower thing would have had a different result. That would be nice. Still, even given the present circumstances he couldn't remember a more perfect morning.

"Hey," she said.

Daniel listened intently—another old habit—as if somehow, now that she had shown so much of herself to him, he might have access to everything else. But all he heard was her words, nothing else.

"Hey," he responded, jumping up from the couch and heading back toward the kitchen. He pulled out a frying pan and called, "I make a mean omelet if you're hungry."

"I am," she said. She followed him into the kitchen and leaned on the shiny granite bar. The kitchen, unlike the bathroom, had been a selling point of the apartment.

"Orange juice?" he asked.

She nodded and then said, "Actually, I'm starving."

He poured two glasses of orange juice and handed her one. She stood there watching him crack eggs and grate cheese. When it was finished, he flipped it onto her plate, adding a piece of parsley as a garnish.

"It's pretty," she said.

"You sound surprised."

She shrugged one shoulder. "I didn't know you could cook."

He was tempted to expand on the many things she didn't know about him. Instead, he exercised his self-control and brought his own plate over to her side of the bar and sat down next to her on a barstool.

They ate without conversation. When she was finished, she turned toward him. She looked at him without quite looking at him. It was what she always did. Daniel had never fully realized it but now that he had felt the impact of her direct, unfiltered gaze the difference was clear.

"Thank you seems somehow insufficient," she said.

He shook his head. "Don't speak too soon. Wait until you see what I've got lined up on pay-per-view."

"Daniel," she protested. "I should go..." She stopped, unable to get any more words out. Tears welled up in her eyes.

"You don't have to go anywhere," he said.

She looked down at her lap and her hair fell around her face, protecting her from scrutiny. "You've already done too much," she said. "I don't expect you to babysit me all day."

"As your employer, I am telling you to go sit on the couch," he said.

She glanced up at him for a moment before standing up and walking over to the sofa.

"If you're cold I can get you a blanket," he said, following her into the living room. "I left the remote, let's see….where did I leave the remote?"

"Daniel," she said.

Something in the tone of her voice made him abandon his search for the remote control.

"At some point I'm going to have to go home. I'm going to have to make funeral arrangements. Then I'm going to have to go back to work and most of what I do at Goldman Parke is work for you. I need my job, now more than ever. I can't just stay here and pretend like nothing happened. You've done so much. I don't have the words to tell you how much I appreciate it. You've gone above and beyond the call of a good friend. I'm just afraid…." Her voice trailed off.

"What are you afraid of, Persey?" he asked.

"My husband died last night," she said. Her eyes met his, the way they had earlier that morning. He was silent but inside he could feel his secrets and desires stampeding, answering the call of their true master. Mercifully, she turned away and looked out at the frigid cityscape framed by his front window. "I'm afraid I can't give you what you want."

"I don't want anything from you," he said. The lie slipped out before he could stop it.

She turned back towards him training her dark blue eyes directly on his. The rest of his life, everything he'd ever known became a distant memory, edged out by the completeness of this moment. He was the core of her attention. He belonged to her.

"Nothing?"

It was one word, a simple word, but he felt the force of it. It pulled him closer to her. It demanded the truth.

"Not right now." The faint voice was almost unrecognizable. Was it his? "All I want right now is to make you feel better."

"And what about tomorrow?" she prompted still holding him in her dark gaze.

The voice, his voice continued as though it didn't belong to him. It confessed his feelings for her—everything he'd bottled up for so long.

"And tomorrow, I will love you just as much as I've loved you every day since the first time we met."

Something in her face softened but she still didn't look away. "I'm not ready for that Daniel," she said.

"Then I'll wait."

The words surprised him but even as he said them he knew they were true. Truth was his only option.

She looked away from him, back out the window. After a moment she said softly, "I think I actually would like that blanket."

"Sure," he said.

He jumped up, happy to have the excuse to do something, and returned with a large quilt.

"We can share," she said as he laid it over her legs.

"Are you sure?" he asked.

In response, she held up one edge in invitation. He scooted underneath and hit play on Strictly Ballroom. Halfway through the movie, her cold hand came to rest near the crook of his elbow and her head, scented with his own shampoo leaned up against his shoulder.

Carefully, so as not to disturb her, he looked down. She was asleep. He sat immobile on the couch as the rest of the movie played out in a series of flickering light and noise before his eyes. He hadn't been so happy to just be near someone since, well, never.

Chapter Forty

Haden had spent too much time at East 23rd Street. He hated East 23rd Street. He hated its charming coziness. He hated the view through the window that allowed him to see Persey dressed in Daniel's clothing, crying in Daniel's arms and snoozing on Daniel's shoulder. But most of all, with an intense searing passion he hated Daniel.

Haden had been patient. No one could argue that he hadn't been. He'd bided his time while a human defiled his chosen bride, the future queen of the Underworld. He rationalized it, reminding himself again and again of his plan to use the circumstances of Aaron's death. He had personally put each individual wheel into motion, pulling the strings like a grand puppet master. And how was he rewarded for his patience? With a front row seat to the Daniel and Persey show, that's how. Haden was beginning to think he'd overestimated Aaron's usefulness. Things hadn't panned out as he'd anticipated, not at all as he'd anticipated.

Why had Persey never mentioned Daniel? Of course, Haden knew who Daniel was now. Now that it was too late. He could see his whole plan had been wrong from the start. He should have instilled himself so that he could work alongside her, as Daniel had been doing for the last year. It would have guaranteed the kind of intimacy necessary for the proper fruition of his plan.

Now Daniel Hartnett was picking up the pieces, wrapping them in a blanket and snuggling with them. It made Haden seethe. He wanted to break into their cozy love nest and rip Daniel's head off of his shoulders. Unfortunately, he couldn't. He'd seen Daniel's end indelibly etched on his soul. The natural law had a plan for Daniel. Even if he chose to incur his father's wrath and the wrath of that law that governed all immortals, Haden still couldn't act as he wanted. Not when he'd seen how Daniel's fate was linked to Persey's.

When Haden could no longer bear witness to the quiet companionship developing in the brownstone on East 23rd street he called for Leucy.

"Stay here and watch them," he directed. "Let me know as soon as she is alone. Be careful not to fail me again. Your continued existence will depend on it."

Leucy nodded. She had learned her lesson well.

Haden took leave of East 23rd Street secure in the knowledge that Leucy would do exactly as he instructed. He stopped at the bodega on the corner and purchased a pack of cigarettes. He proceeded to chain-smoke the entire pack as he walked back to the yoga studio.

The rightful owner of this body had been stupid enough to barter away two years of life in exchange for success. Success! The sheer shortsightedness of the desire was enough to make Haden snort. At least the man had been intelligent enough to define his terms of success. He hadn't, however, thought to bargain for the return of his body in pristine condition.

Haden smiled as he maliciously ground out the glowing end of another cigarette on the tender flesh along the inside of the arm. The smooth skin there was already lined with round burn marks. He studied them with a sense of satisfaction. He was pretty sure those marks would leave scars. Scarred or not, the idiot who would soon re-inhabit this body had a devoted following and a yoga studio with cache. He also had a nice long life to enjoy it all. Haden had made good on his end of the bargain. It wasn't his fault if the man had a simplistic definition of success.

That night he vacated the body of the yoga teacher and returned to his kingdom. Leucy would come to him as instructed. Until then, he needed to think. He didn't do his best thinking in a human body. In his most recent incarnation, he'd made miscalculation upon miscalculation. The ache of those errors followed him down into the emptiness of his Underworld. Haden had anticipated controlling Persey through her own desires, but he'd been unable to grant her simple wish—strike one. He thought she would turn to him in her hour of need because he provided her freedom from human need, the one thing she'd always wanted. He had misread her—strike two. He'd anticipated she would come to him, agree to be his wife while he searched for a means to ensure her immortality but she hadn't—strike three and he was out. He wasn't even close to where he thought he would be.

In his dark kingdom, Haden turned the pieces over. He was finished with games and waiting. He was determined Persephone would be part of his eternity. He had hoped to have her securely hidden in the Underworld—where Kronos's sight could not reach—before he made this trip. Now he realized that he was tired of waiting. Aaron was gone. He was not content to wait until Daniel was gone too. There was no way around it—he needed assistance from his father, sooner rather than later.

Father, it was a word that made humans tender and sympathetic. Haden held no such tender sympathies for Kronos. Emotion would have been a foolish weakness. When dealing with the fierce cannibalistic God of Time, there was no room for either foolishness or weakness. Haden knew no favors would be granted on the grounds of familial privilege. Kronos amused himself by wreaking havoc and destruction at any given opportunity. The only thing his father respected was strength. In his dark Underworld, Haden formulated a plan designed to whet his father's peculiar appetites. Hopefully, Kronos would take the bait.

Chapter Forty-One

Kronos—ruler of both the world and immortals—lived on Mount Titanus. From his mountain-top palace, he pulled the strings of time which governed all human life. His palace was carpeted with the ever-changing map of time. He walked over it as he observed and guided the timing of all events in accordance with the dictates of natural law.

The mandates of natural law were clear on the subject of human death. But they were less so about the passage of time. Instead they served as a guideline with ample room for manipulation. When Kronos was well-occupied, time passed quickly in the human realm, allowing the mortals below to be almost unaware of their mortal suffering. It was Kronos's restless days that were troublesome for humankind. He had the power to slow the passage of time at his whim. He was notorious for stretching the length of days coinciding with natural catastrophes, in order to more fully savor the suffering below.

When Haden entered his father's palace, the old man was unsurprised to see him.

"You've come," Kronos said without looking away from the shifting map of time beneath his feet.

"As you expected I suppose," said Haden.

"You dare disturb me with your petty longings even as you neglect your own realm," growled Kronos.

Kronos harbored no affection for any immortal, but of all the immortals, his distaste was strongest for his own children. And of all his children, he despised Haden the most. He viewed his son's ability, to—ever-so-slightly—subvert the mandates of natural law by granting human requests in return for the promise of souls, as a direct challenge to his own authority.

"You've been following my activities, then?" asked Haden.

"It is my duty to follow the activities of everything, everywhere. I do not shirk it."

"Then you know why I've come," said Haden.

"You are as foolish as ever," Kronos snapped. "You forget that where immortals are concerned, I see only their past, not their future? I can assure you, however, that your mission, whatever it is, is pointless." He returned his attention to the glittering, evolving carpet of time beneath his feet.

"What if I could offer you something you greatly desire?" Haden asked.

Kronos's laughter was silent and mirthless. "You think your petty little bargains interest me? I assure you—there is nothing you can grant me that I desire."

"Are you sure about that?" asked Haden. "What if I could promise you both bodies and souls? Once I've fulfilled their desires and they have met their end they belong to me. I am freed from the constraints of natural law. What if I gave them to you? They would be yours and you could use them in any way you like."

"Free from the natural law," whispered the old man.

"Yes," said Haden. "Free from the natural law."

"What is your price?"

"You've seen my past. You must know what I seek," said Haden.

"Immortality for the girl," Kronos said. Kronos eyed Haden with appraising, crafty eyes. "What makes you think I can bestow this gift upon her? She is as bound by natural law as the rest of them."

"I will use her to search out the weakness among humankind," said Haden. "She is already an object of their need and desire. She will use her special talents to seal the fate of others, the ones I will deliver to you. In the end, she will gladly bargain with me in order to stop the suffering of her fellow man. When she gives me her soul, you will give her immortality."

"In return," said Kronos, "you will deliver unto me a million humans, body and soul. Their bodies will be mine to use as I see fit. Their souls will be sacrificed upon my altar. I expect I shall derive great comfort and succor from the eternal anguish that will be visited upon them."

"A million bodies and souls?" asked Haden hesitating. The sheer magnitude of the request would not be easy to manage. The idea of it gave him a brief twinge. Was it not a perversion of his duties to sacrifice the souls he was bound to protect?

"Yes, my son," said Kronos interrupting his thoughts with an ironic twist to his lips. "Is the price too high? Do you fear you cannot pay it? Or maybe you prefer to guard the fruits of your labor for yourself instead of sacrificing them for this creature you desire?" He erupted once more in silent laughter. "Alas, I fear my price is too high. Leave, bother me no more with your childish demands."

"No," said Haden quickly. "I'll do it. I will give you what you desire if you grant her immortality."

"Very well, my son," said Kronos. "After you have delivered the bodies and souls I require, you will find your Persephone graced with immortality, not unlike your own. However, be warned. If you fail, I will give her a choice of my own."

"What kind of choice?" Haden asked with alarm.

"And here I thought you were so certain of your success," Kronos sneered. "If you fail, I will exact my own terms from the fair Persephone. Does that frighten you? Are you afraid to barter for that which you most desire? Is my son a God among men or a coward among Gods?"

Ignoring the spiteful words of the ancient ruler, Haden pictured Persey standing next to him, a beacon of beauty, lighting the darkness of his Underworld. He would have her body and soul forever and together they would rule for eternity. It was his only chance.

"I'll bring them to you," he said. "But I must warn you, subversion of the natural law on this scale may have unforeseen consequences."

"So often," said Kronos, returning his attention to the glittering map of time beneath his feet, "we fail to understand the true nature of the thing we most desire. But, do not fear for me, my son. I do not suffer from this flaw."

Chapter Forty-Two

The first time Persey opened her eyes in Daniel's bedroom all she wanted to do was die. The pills Daniel had given her the night before had made her sleep but they'd done little to prevent the dreams. All night long, she dreamed dreams within dreams. The kind where she woke up only to realize she was still in the dream. In her dreams, she followed the irreversible path towards Aaron's death. She knew where she was headed but she was powerless to stop what was coming.

When she woke up for real, in the chill of a December morning, she realized being awake was only a continuation of her nightmares. Sleep was not an escape. Neither was consciousness. There was only one escape and it beckoned to her from the nightstand. It was the small bottle filled with pills. If she took enough of them she would be free. She could not stop reliving the events of yesterday. Somehow, death seemed infinitely preferable to a world without Aaron—a world where she was the reason Aaron was no more.

She'd been contemplating how many pills she would need to swallow when she heard Daniel enter into the room. He set something down and then stood over her for a moment before tiptoeing back out of the room. Daniel, she thought with a pang of conscience. He'd be the one to find her. He'd taken care of her last night, brought her to his home and given her his bed.

Now she intended to repay him for kindness by swallowing half a bottle of the pills he'd pilfered for her benefit. He'd be questioned by the police. He might be asked to leave the firm. Her death would bring him nothing but trouble and disgrace. She sat up in bed and hugged her knees to her chest. With a small sigh, she relinquished the idea of chemical escape.

All through that horrible morning Daniel listened to her. She talked to him and he listened. He couldn't bring Aaron back, no one could do that. But just having someone to listen seemed to ease her pain, take the edge off. She couldn't remember the last time she'd been able to talk—just talk while someone listened. She was used to being the one who listened.

"It's not your fault, Persey."

He said it over and over, like an incantation. His words seemed to wash her guilt away. He was the calm source of logic in the face of her crazy grief. She wasn't to blame. No matter what Haden claimed, it wasn't real. He hadn't imbued her with magical powers of irresistibility. Daniel was the proof. He was able to spend time with her, lots of time, without being overcome by the need to ravish her. His constant, calm presence reassured her that she'd been possessed by some sort of temporary insanity—the kind that occurs when you walk in on your husband having sex with another woman.

Over the next three days, her guilt over Aaron's death started to subside and in its place grew grief. It wasn't the kind of grief she had felt at first—the grief of a woman for her dead husband. This was an angry grief.

She acknowledged the possibility that she had not summoned Aaron into the path of an oncoming bus. The problem with that acknowledgment was it forced her to think about what had led them to that point. He'd been with another woman. No matter how she tried to spin it, she had to accept Aaron wasn't the person she thought he was. The grief that grew inside her was for the relationship she thought she'd had. At one time, she'd believed she knew her husband better than anyone else in the world. But he had deceived her. She'd witnessed his betrayal with her own eyes. The evidence was incontrovertible. If she'd been so wrong about Aaron, what else had she gotten wrong?

The first day at Daniel's—the first day after Aaron's death—she tried to leave. She didn't want to saddle Daniel the responsibility of caring for her. She might have made a stronger argument if she had someplace else to go. The truth was she couldn't bear to think about the apartment she'd once shared with Aaron—let alone go back to it. The question came to her again.

What else had she gotten wrong? The next day she heard Daniel tell her secretary she wouldn't be coming in for a few weeks. "I have to go back to work," she protested. "Besides, she's going to think it's strange that you called in for me."

"Everyone's going to understand that you need a little time," he had said.

"Having me here like this...I'm afraid it's going to be awkward when we go back to work."

"Don't worry," he said, shrugging off her concerns as though they were meaningless. "We'll figure it out."

Not I'll figure it out, or things will work out but we'll figure it out. The together part was implied. He loved her. She forced him to tell her the truth and he admitted his feelings. Yet he resisted. He was patient. She found herself replaying his words in her head.

"I will love you just as much as I've loved you every day since the first time we met."

He loved her, had always loved her. He loved her but he didn't need or demand anything from her. It was a completely new experience. To be perfectly fair, she'd always understood Daniel's interest in her was more than professional. "A work crush," that was how she'd heard other people refer to it.

She hadn't given it much thought because she'd assumed if it had amounted to anything Daniel would have told her. That was the way it worked. People always told her things—especially people who spent as much time with her as Daniel did. But now, she realized Daniel was in love with her. Had been in love with her for some time but managed to keep it a secret until she asked him directly. Once again she asked herself the question that replayed in a constant loop in her head. What else had she gotten wrong?

It was impossible not to compare Aaron to Daniel. Daniel kept things to himself while Aaron held nothing back. It was as though Aaron's brain had been merely a membrane through which information passed directly to Persey. So much of who Aaron had been was lighter and less penetrating than Daniel. His sandy blonde hair and fair skin that burned so easily without sunscreen were the physical foreshadowing of his inability to tell Persey anything but the whole truth and nothing but the truth so help him God.

She'd accepted his secrets as inevitable, but now as she compared him to Daniel, she wondered if that was just one on the laundry list of things she had gotten wrong. She'd assumed she was at the root of Aaron's compulsion to tell her every slightly scandalous thought that passed through his brain. Maybe her special brand of truth serum could be resisted with practice. It seemed like Daniel was able to manage some restraint.

Daniel's restraint was quite possibly the source of her quickening pulse. She reacted to him when his knee accidentally bumped hers, or the stab of desire—strong and sudden—to feel the touch of his lips when he smoothed her hair back from her face.

These were not appropriate feelings for a woman who had just watched her husband die. She knew this. She knew it and she filed it away with the guilt she felt about her failure to properly grieve her husband. It was in good company with the other guilt she felt about her inappropriate and selfish focus on all the things she'd gotten wrong.

Even on that first morning, as Daniel scrubbed the blood from her naked body, some basic animalistic part of her longed for him. Had he felt the same way? She didn't know. If he'd been Aaron she wouldn't have had to wonder. He would have told her. But he wasn't Aaron. He was Daniel and she was beginning to be confident he wouldn't tell her anything unless she insisted.

Friday afternoon, she awoke and for a single blissful moment all she knew was she was safe and warm in Daniel's bed. Then it all came crashing back, one basic realization after another. Aaron was dead. She'd watched him die. It had been her fault. Despite

Daniel's assurances otherwise, every morning those were her first three thoughts.

There was a light knock on the door and Daniel pushed it open just a crack.

"Hey," he whispered. "You awake?" His dark brown hair stuck out from his head and his face was shadowed with stubble.

"I am," she said, tucking her legs underneath her and sitting up. "I was thinking…"

He was in front of her before she could finish the sentence. He placed two fingers over her lips to seal in the words she'd been about to say.

"It's not your fault," he said. "I promise you. It's not your fault."

She laughed. He had that effect on her, making her laugh unexpectedly. "How did you know what I was going to say?"

"It's what you say every morning, every day," he said.

His hand had moved from her lips. It hovered there in the air between them as if waiting for an invitation to touch her again. He looked at her, making eye contact for a moment. Persey felt an unexpected sensation of longing in the pit of her stomach.

"So," he said glancing away. "There's this unwritten rule that no major holiday can occur without at least one of the deals you're working on threatening to blow up. And since it's almost Christmas…"

"You have to go in to the office," she said, finishing the sentence for him.

"I have to go in," he repeated. "It'll only be a couple of hours. You think you'll be okay?"

"I've been alone before," she said, tugging another one of his borrowed t-shirts down over her knees.

"No," he said reaching over and smoothing her tangled curls away from her face. "No, you haven't, not like this."

He looked at her for a long moment and then slowly closed the distance between them. She closed her eyes as she felt the gentle pressure of his lips against hers.

"I won't be long," he said, placing his finger on the space his lips had just occupied. "Not long at all." Then he backed quickly out of the room as though he was afraid he might change his mind.

Chapter Forty-Three

Three days after her vigil began Leucy came flinging into the Underworld. The scent of the human world still clung to her wings.

"She's alone," the siren told Haden breathlessly as her feathers hardened and became inviting white flesh before his eyes. "The man has gone to his office building. I followed him there."

"Good work, my Leucosia," he said, running one finger along the knife edge of her collar bone.

She responded automatically to his affection, however scant, by pressing her body against his hand.

"Return to him. Watch over him. You must warn me if he leaves." He squeezed her arm gently and Leucy sighed, luxuriating in his touch. "Go," said Haden, tightening his grip, making it painful.

Leucy shook herself once causing her flesh to ripple and transform back into gleaming white feathers. With a single cry, she raised her wings and flew back to the human realm to carry out the commands of her master.

The first thing he required was a new body. The thought of it gave him a temporary pang. He forced himself to extinguish it. What was one, when he needed a million? This was, as humans put it, simply a cost of doing business. The one he chose was an undeniably handsome specimen—tall and well-built. His hair was dark and close-cropped with a face that could be described as handsome, or arrogant. The mental aspect of this body wasn't anything like its physical potential. The man had sold himself—body and soul—for money. Typical New Yorker, thought Haden, to be so relentlessly focused upon monetary reward.

Money was what the man had bargained for and that was what he had. He should have asked for good taste, thought Haden, glancing around the man's penthouse apartment with its floor to ceiling walls of glass overlooking the East River. The furniture, like the walls, all seemed shiny and stiff.

On impulse, Haden glanced into the man's refrigerator. It was empty save for several white Styrofoam take-out boxes. Haden opened one with the tip of his finger. The open box revealed the remains of a well-marbled steak. It had been cooked rare and was sitting in a puddle of congealed blood. That explained the heart attack the man would suffer in three years time. Haden shut the refrigerator door and headed out of the kitchen. Daniel wouldn't be gone forever. The clock was ticking and he had other more important places to be.

Despite the constraints of the human body Haden occupied, it didn't take him long to reach his destination. He could see her from the street sitting in almost the exact same spot she had been when he left her. Only now there was an important difference. This time she was alone. There was no one there to interfere with Haden's plan. He studied her. She was framed in the window, almost like a piece of art. Bad art, he decided as he assessed the litter of magazines and newspapers covering the couch and coffee table, not to mention the ill-fitting sports attire she wore. The clothes belonged to Daniel, he supposed. It was the only rational conclusion since Leucy would have informed him if Persey had set foot outside of the apartment. He wondered how far the relationship had progressed over the last three days. Not that it mattered. She would belong to him now. She owed him. Or at least she thought she did.

The door was fitted with an old-fashioned brass knocker. He lifted it up and let if fall heavily against the door three times. From within, there was silence, then the unmistakable sound of locks clicking and turning. The door opened a crack. Haden saw the heavy chain that held it shut, protecting the people inside from those on the outside. Except now she was alone and Haden was confident the chain across the door wouldn't protect her for long.

"Can I help you?" she asked.

He looked at her with appraising eyes. "Don't you recognize me Persephone?"

She looked at him, meeting his eyes for only a moment before a gasp of recognition stained her face a deep red. At first she tried denied it. "I...I've never met you before," she stammered.

"You have met me," he said, placing his foot in the crack of the door before she could close it. "In fact, if you stop to think about it I'm sure you'll realize you've known me most of your life."

"No," she said, shaking her head even as he saw the truth of his words slide together and rearrange in a tumble of recognition on her face. "It's not possible," she said, looking around desperately for some means of escape.

"You might not recognize the body but you recognize what lies beneath it. It proves the depth of our connection. You feel me just as I feel you."

"You're not Haden," she whispered, shaking her head in disbelief. "You're completely different."

"And still you recognize me. Open the door Persephone," he said, removing his foot from the crack allowed by the chain.

She closed the door. There was a moment of silence, inner hesitation. Then he heard the chain slide off and the door swung open. He was inside.

She stared at him. He could feel her fear emanating from her in waves. Her instincts recognized and feared him, regardless of his form. He remembered her childhood distaste for him. At the time, she could have only suspected the darkness hidden within his protective human shell. Now she knew it was there. Whether or not she understood what she'd seen, Haden knew she recognized its presence. It was her old instinct, reawakened. He'd fought hard to overcome it but now it had found its mark. The only problem was now her instincts were useless. They had awakened too late because she'd already let him in.

"How did you find me here?" she said. Her eyes were wide, the pupils dilated with fright.

"Don't you remember Persephone?" he said, sliding through the door and shutting the winter chill firmly behind him. "You've asked me that question before and I told you I can always find you."

She looked away, shaking her head as if to deny the truth of his statement.

He stepped closer to her, cradling her head between his hands. "The last time we were together, you asked for something and I gave it to you. Do you remember what you promised me?"

"Yes." Her voice came out in a hoarse, frightened whisper.

"Then tell me, tell me what you promised me."

"Anything," she said. She looked down unable to meet his eyes. "I promised you anything you need."

"That's right," he said while stroking her neck with his thumb.

"Who are you?" she asked, stiffening underneath his touch.

"You know who I am, Persephone. After all, you've seen my secrets."

"I don't believe it," she said shaking her head. Her eyes darted around the room looking around for some means of escape, but Haden was confident her only escape route would be with him.

"Every culture, every time, every religion has its own name for me—Satan, Lucifer, the Devil, the Dark Lord, the Grim

Reaper. Those are the names favored by modern Christianity—although, I must say the negative connotations might be insulting—if I cared enough to be capable of insult."

"I made a deal with the Devil," she said staring at him. "And now you've come to collect?"

"No, my darling," he said gently. "You made a deal with the ruler of the Underworld. All souls, both good and bad, enter my domain, including the soul for which you mourn."

"Aaron," she said his name as though it was a defeat.

"Yes, Aaron—your beauty is such that, even in death, he pines for you." Haden walked to the window through which he'd observed her less than ten minutes ago. "I believe I am a just ruler," he said. He was careful to keep his back to her as he spoke. It was crucial that his eyes not reveal any more of his secrets. "The souls in my keep are given the respect—or lack thereof—that they earn during their brief lives. But in Aaron's case, justice will depend on your actions." It was a bluff. He waited to see if she would call it. One quick glance in her direction told him he needn't have worried.

The invocation of Aaron's name filled her eyes with tears. She collapsed back on the couch, defeated. Her hands covered her face. When she finally spoke her voice was muffled with tears.

"It was my fault."

Haden was at her side in a moment. He crouched down and placed his hands on her knees. "I know you are in pain but it is my hope that time will lessen that emotion. One such as you was never meant for a mortal. I know you, Persephone," he said, pulling her hands away to expose her tear-streaked face. "I know you as you know me. Finally, you understand how long I've known you and how patient I've been. Do you remember what I told you once?" he asked, moving to sit next to her on the couch.

"No," she said, shaking her head. Her whole body trembled with fear at his proximity.

"When you were a child, I told you need doesn't prove love and true love doesn't need. Do you remember that?"

She nodded hesitantly.

"You see," he said, taking her hands between his and pulling her closer to him. "All this time I've loved you. But have I ever burdened you with my need? No, I waited patiently for that moment when you would give yourself to me freely. And you did. Someday, my dear Persephone, you will come to understand the full extent of my love for you. On that day, you will become my wife, queen of the Underworld destined to rule with me for eternity. But before that can happen, you must give me what you promised. You must give me your love because it is what I desire."

He pulled her closer to him even as she shook her head frantically. "No," she gasped. "I can't."

"But it's what I desire. What I've waited for," he insisted. "You forget how well I know you, Persephone. My depth of understanding into your nature gives me great hope. I've already exhibited my capacity for patience. After all, I deal in death and death is nothing, if not patient. I have great confidence that in time you will come to return my love. Until that time, we have much work to do to ensure our future together."

He allowed his hands to slide down the length of her body, pulling her to him, touching his lips to hers. He felt the heat and fragrance of her skin entwining around the solid defenses he'd erected, searching for a way inside. But this time Haden was prepared. As long as he didn't delve into her hidden realm he was confident his own secrets would remain safe. His borrowed human body kissed her hungrily and she acquiesced. Haden felt joy surge through his human skin. Everything was falling into place. Persephone would be his. Soon her mysterious end—whatever it was—would no longer matter. She would be with him for eternity and every moment of eternity would be as rapturous as this one.

Chapter Forty-Four

She could wish it was a dream—hope it was a dream but—in the end, she knew it was reality. One moment she was on solid ground in a safe place. Then a moment later, she was inexplicably somewhere dangerous and out of control. How did she get from one place to the other in the space of a few minutes? It must be the same type of feeling—she realized—as crossing the street to reclaim your spouse and being mowed down by a bus. Opening the door and meeting Haden's eyes wasn't exactly death, it just felt like it. The man standing before her was a stranger. She'd never seen him before but still she recognized him. Or more aptly, she recognized what was inside of him. She knew those eyes and they held all her darkest fears. They'd come to claim her.

The realization dawned that she'd always recognized him but until now she'd chosen to ignore it. She'd told herself the familiarities and similarities amounted to nothing more than odd coincidence. She'd ignored her inner urge to get to safety—sold her instincts down the river for the price of hot cocoa and yoga. Haden had warned her about need and love. Despite what he thought, she hadn't needed the reminder.

The words from her trusted favorite librarian had found their mark. They'd become part of her, ingrained so deeply that it seemed as though the distinction was something she'd always known. For someone who had spent their life running from other people's need, it was the ultimate irony. But it was too late to do anything about it because this time she had been the one to need something. Her own need had led her into his debt and now he was here to collect.

Chapter Forty-Five

Haden whisked Persey past the doorman—who gave him a knowing smile—and up to the waiting penthouse.

"You know I can't love you. It's not something I can give on command. You'll have to figure out something else," she said as he led her through the expansive living room and toward the bedroom.

He smiled at her indulgently. "Don't worry my love. I've already figured out what that something else—as you so charmingly phrase it—will be."

It was the first thing he'd said to her since they had left Daniel's apartment. She'd gone with him, leaving everything behind. There was no point in arguing. She understood the implication in Haden's words. Daniel had been wrong all along. It was her fault. Now Haden was ready to torture Aaron's soul for all eternity if she didn't live up to her part of the bargain.

It changed everything. Her grief, misplaced as it had been, flooded over her anew. She had been wrong to doubt Aaron's love for her and the bond between them. Her worst fears were real. Aaron was no more than a badly used pawn. She herself was a pawn with no choice other than to go with this man, this creature that some hidden instinct had warned her against ever since she could remember.

Over the last three days, she had spent her time doubting and wondering what she had gotten wrong. Now she realized that the most important thing she'd gotten wrong were those last three days. She'd believed in them. She realized that they were the dream—the warm cozy dream. Now she needed to let go of the dream because this was going to be the rest of her life, her eternity.

Haden led her into a bedroom dominated by a bed draped in black velvet and situated prominently in front of floor-to-ceiling windows. The sight of it filled her with revulsion.

"What do you want from me?" she asked, hating the way her voice shook.

Haden didn't look at her. Instead he held her at arm's length, assessing her. Before she could protest, he pulled the ill-fitting t-shirt up over her head as though he was undressing a child. Then he slid his hand under the waistband of her borrowed sweatpants and removed them, efficiently, unceremoniously.

She stood before him—shivering and naked—save for her underwear. Her breath became ragged as he placed one hand on her smooth bare stomach. He ran the other hand appreciatively down the back of her leg until he was kneeling before her.

"You know what I want," he said as he removed the last piece of fabric protecting her from complete exposure. He pressed his face against her hot uncovered center, cupping her buttocks with his hands. She gasped with involuntary pleasure as his tongue found its mark. Her legs felt unstable, as though they were no longer capable of bearing her weight.

As though he sensed her weakness, he stood up and pulled her to him supporting her weight momentarily with one arm. "Your body wants me," he said, running one hand lightly over her erect nipples. She felt his other hand move down between her legs and she moaned in response to its rhythmic movement. "Someday the rest of you will want me too."

His hands lifted her, pulling her roughly against his hardness. "I've waited so long," he whispered as he buried his mouth against the smooth skin of her neck. "I've been patient, so patient."

She could feel him pressing against her, seeking that hot dark place that unaccountably longed for his touch. His hands cruelly squeezed and touched her body in ways that made her long for more. She reached out to him, but as though her desire held some hidden signal, he pulled away leaving her panting and burning with shame at her own need.

He moved over to the window and contemplated the city below them. "Patience doesn't always come easily to me, Persephone," he said without turning toward her. "But the pleasure will be so much greater when we are joined together for eternity. Besides, I believe the physical pleasure would only serve as a distraction when we have so much work to do."

He turned away from the windows and surveyed her naked body appreciatively. "An immense overwhelming distraction," he said, moving back to her side. He tucked her hair behind one ear and leaning close whispered, "One that I will gladly engage in for the rest of eternity, but eternity is not yet ours. We will take the time necessary for your heart to follow where your body goes without question." He moved around her, taking in her every curve and nuance, as though she were a nude on display in a museum. "You will learn to be my lover, in every sense the word implies."

Chapter Forty-Six

It was ten days before Rudy made any real progress. He went to Persey and Aaron's apartment in the west village. He'd only been there once but he still remembered the address. Where Persey was concerned he remembered everything. He talked to the doorman who confirmed that neither of them had been seen in several days. He spoke with Persey's secretary every day.

"I'm sorry Mr. Turner," she told him. "She won't be in all week."

"She told you that?" he asked. He sounded like a desperate man even to his own ears.

"Yes, she did." He could tell the secretary wasn't going to tell him anything so he let it go.

Why wasn't she at her apartment? This was the question he wanted to ask but he knew that even if the secretary knew where Persey was, she wasn't about to share that information with him.

He called his mother to see if Persey was in town for the funeral.

"It's all anyone's talking about," she reported. "The funeral's tomorrow and no one's heard a word from her. You know how the Campbell's are. Well, they're just mortified. Her Aunt Jen, that's her father's sister, told my bridge club she never believed that girl was really a Campbell. And she was serious. She said the timelines didn't match up and Mike couldn't have been her father. Well, it's just silliness if you ask me, everyone knows how crazy in love Mike and Demi were before the accident but it sure tells you a lot about the Campbells, doesn't it, willing to throw one of their own under the bus—oh, sorry hon, poor choice of words—rather than admit that she's just a little odd. Personally, I'm worried about her. Poor girl, have you tried her office?"

He flew home for the funeral, of course. Going back to Clear Lake was always strange. Everything still looked like childhood. It was a little like being a child all over again.

After the service, Luke Leister grabbed Rudy by the shoulder. "Good to see you, man," Luke said, clapping him hard on the back. For a moment, Rudy was thirteen again, tense and ready to take a beating. Then meaning attached to Luke's words.

"Couple of us are gonna raise a toast to Aaron down at the Fire Pit. You should come," Luke said.

Rudy turned to look at Luke and realized not everything in Clear Lake had remained the same. Not ten years out of high school and Luke's six-pack abs had disappeared with the help of another type of six-pack. "Nah, man, I can't," said Rudy. "I've got a flight back tonight. But if you're ever in the city look me up."

"Sure thing," said Luke, who lost interest when it became clear Rudy wouldn't be part of his evening drinking plans. "Sure thing," Luke repeated but they both understood it would never happen.

Rudy's mother drove him back to the airport. "Are you sure you can't stay for Christmas?" she asked for the hundredth time.

"I'd like to Mom. I really would but...."

"But work calls," she said finishing his sentence.

"Yeah," he said lamely.

"I thought for sure Persey would show up for the funeral," she said as they approached the departures terminal. "Remember how we used to have her over? Poor girl, she's never had an easy time of things. Will you let me know if you hear from her?"

"Yeah, I will," he said as she pulled over to the curb and put on the parking brake.

"Just remember, Rudy, there's a difference between work and life. If you put off life for too long, it'll pass you by." She paused for a moment and pressed her lips together turning them into a thin white line of worry. "I just can't seem to quit thinking about Aaron Strait. Remember sweetie, you never know when your number's going to be up. You've got to make the best of life while it lasts."

"I do my best, mom," he said leaning over and giving her an awkward hug. "Don't worry so much. My life's not all work. I've got a few irons in the fire."

"I'm sure you do, honey," she said, squeezing his chin in her hands. "I just don't want you to get burned."

He wasn't lying. He really did need to get back for a meeting. But the meeting had nothing to do with business. At home in his parents 1970's split level, confined to the four walls of his childhood room, Rudy realized he was no longer content to wait for Persey to return his phone call. A series of Google searches turned up a virtual history of Persey's career at Goldman Parke. When deals were big enough, they were published in publications like *Deal Makers Quarterly*.

It seemed Persey had spent much of her career working on the kind of deals that filled the pages of *Deal Makers Quarterly*. It didn't take long for Rudy to discover the pattern. In every article, her name was paired with that of another Goldman Parke lawyer—Daniel Hartnett.

From the Goldman Parke website, Rudy was able to glean that Daniel Hartnett had a lot of clients. He was a power player. It wasn't much but it was a place to start. Maybe Daniel Hartnett would have a clue as to where Persey was hiding. He left a message with Hartnett's secretary and had been surprised to receive an email within the hour from the man himself. He was available to meet on Christmas Eve. Rudy tried not to get his hopes up. In all likelihood, Daniel Hartnett was a power player precisely because he was the kind of person who Googled other people and agreed to meetings on Christmas Eve. Still, Rudy couldn't help but hope it was the mention of Persey's name, instead of the mention of his own name in *Wired Magazine*, that played the primary role in getting the meeting.

The offices of Goldman Parke had the festive, absent feeling of any office on the day before a major holiday. The receptionist was talking on the phone when Rudy walked in.

"Just a minute," he heard her whisper into the receiver. She looked up at him without bothering to take the phone away from her ear. "Yes?"

"Rudy Turner. I have an appointment with Daniel Hartnett."

"Have a seat," she said, motioning to the stiffly modern waiting area. "He'll be down in a minute." True to her word, a man who seemed to be a pale imitation of his picture on the Goldman Parke website appeared several minutes later.

"Daniel Hartnett," he said, sticking out his hand.

"Rudy Turner," said Rudy. They shook hands.

"You eaten lunch yet, Rudy?" asked Daniel with a smile.

Rudy shook his head.

"Come on then," said Daniel, propelling him out the door toward the elevator. "I'm buying."

Daniel steered Rudy across the street to a crowded noodle shop packed with Japanese business men. The host acknowledged Daniel with a curt nod. He led them through the maze of tightly packed tables until he set down two menus at a small table against the wall.

"Pork soup dumplings and a beer," Daniel said to the waiter who appeared before they'd had a chance to take off their coats.

The waiter glared down at Rudy who was trying to quickly peruse the menu. "I come back later?" he asked.

"I'll have the same," said Rudy. The waiter scribbled furiously on his notepad and then disappeared through the crowd and into the kitchen.

"The shrimp dumplings are good too," said Daniel.

"Next time," said Rudy.

Daniel looked at him sharply but before he could say anything their beers arrived. "Here's to next time," said Daniel, picking up his glass and clinking it against Rudy's.

"I'm a friend of Persey's. I know you work with her," said Rudy without preface. "I just came from Aaron's funeral. She wasn't there and I'm worried about her."

Daniel took a long drink from his beer glass and then shook his head. "So you don't know where she is either."

Daniel's words extinguished any small hope Rudy had allowed himself to feel. "Were you..." Rudy began but Daniel interrupted him.

"No, I wasn't banging her. I try to avoid being a cliché whenever possible. You got any other pressing questions you want to get off your chest?"

Rudy started to protest. That wasn't what he'd been asking. Except—he realized—maybe it was. They settled into an awkward silence, broken only by the arrival of two bowls of steaming soup dumplings.

"So what happened to her?" Rudy asked after the waiter had gone.

Daniel cut a large dumpling in half and stuck it in his mouth before answering. "That's the million dollar question, isn't it," he said shaking his head. "I don't fucking know."

"No one knows where she is," said Rudy. "I thought for sure she'd be at the funeral. I've known her since I was a kid."

Daniel downed the rest of his beer and motioned for the waiter to bring him another one. He studied Rudy, sizing him up before he said, "Let me guess. You were the nerd. She was the beautiful girl who never wanted you. She married her high school boyfriend while you carried a torch. You never thought Aaron was the right guy for her. He didn't understand her, not the way you did. You think you know what makes Persey Campbell-Strait tick. Now you've got your big shot with her and she's nowhere to be found. Does that pretty much sum up the situation?" Daniel recited these facts coldly, as though the formative events of Rudy's life were no more fascinating than multiplication tables.

Rudy stared across the table at Daniel and weighed his options. "Yeah," he said after a long moment. "So what makes you so different from me?"

Daniel looked surprised for a moment, but then an almost unwilling smile appeared on his face. "I wasn't a high school nerd."

"I guess there had to be one thing we didn't have in common," said Rudy.

"Yeah," said Daniel. "I guess you're right."

Chapter Forty-Seven

Daniel had never experienced loss. He realized this, now that Persey was gone. Both his parents were healthy and relatively happy. His father still drove over to Trinitas Hospital in New Providence every day to make his rounds. His mother, having raised Daniel and his sister, now sat on the board of three—or was it four—charitable organizations. He was lucky, he knew that. In his lifetime, the words pestilence, famine, and war were more like biblical terms than actual threats to his well-being.

His closest brush with loss—other than the obligatory passing of childhood pets—occurred in high school when three kids the year ahead of him had died in a car crash. He attended their memorial service with the rest of the school. A montage of snapshots taken during their short lives played on a huge screen. He had shed some tears along with everyone else in the school while the high school band played *Forever Young*. He'd felt sad. But this was different.

This was a sick gaping hole inside of him. He'd only been gone three and a half hours. He came home and the front door of his brownstone was standing oddly, unaccountably open. The sight of it filled him with a sense of dread. The outline of light from inside the apartment spilled out through the open rectangle. It would seem homey and inviting in a small town. But here in lower Manhattan it was all wrong.

He rushed up the steps, calling out her name. At first he ignored the deep silence that told him she was gone—irretrievably gone. He's conducted a desperate search for her, exhausting every possible lead.

He went to her apartment and talked to the doorman. The doorman's words told Daniel he hadn't seen Persey. The meaning behind the words said Daniel wasn't the only person who'd come looking for her. He reported her disappearance to the police. "A little food for thought," said the officer as he wrote down Daniel's report, "it sounds like the lady's been through a lot. You ever think she just don't want to be found?"

Daniel considered the officer's words. Had he made a mistake by kissing her? Was it somehow his fault? He couldn't bring himself to believe that. It didn't matter anyway because—no matter what he believed—she was gone and he couldn't find her. Deep inside, he'd known it from the moment he saw his door standing open to the cold December air. All his life he'd heard the hidden meaning behind people's words. This time the hidden meaning came without words but it was no less definitive. Persey was gone. He wouldn't be able to find her.

When his secretary gave him Rudy Turner's message, Daniel had been hopeful—so ridiculously hopeful—that this person might know something. He was certain Rudy was the other person who'd been making inquiries of Persey's doorman. Who else would have bothered to track him down? Hope alone floated Daniel through the two days leading up to Christmas Eve.

Those hopes were punctured before they even got their food. He didn't even need to hear the uncertainty and history behind Rudy's words to understand he didn't know anything. In fact, he knew less than Daniel. He hadn't held Persey as she cried. He hadn't washed dried blood from her hair—although it was evident Rudy would have welcomed the opportunity. Persey was still lost. The thought of life without her made Daniel cruel. His cruelty was fueled by his realization he wasn't alone in knowing her secret. Rudy knew it too. Daniel could hear Rudy's knowledge behind his fumbling words. Rudy had known Persey first and longer. Suddenly he inspired a fierce and blinding hatred in Daniel.

At the very least, Daniel expected his attack to guarantee him an afternoon of semi-solitude. He'd anticipated spending Christmas Eve alone. He would numb his pain in lonely misery buffered by the unintelligible din provided by the restaurant's Chinese clientele. But it hadn't happened that way. Rudy didn't take the bait. Instead, he sidestepped the shit Daniel was slinging and called him on it. He wasn't alone. That's what Rudy's words told him. Although Daniel was new at loss, he realized it was preferable to suffer with someone else than to suffer alone. They would numb their pain together.

They didn't talk about her anymore. What was there to say? Daniel didn't want to hear about Rudy's memories of Persey and he was certain Rudy had no desire to hear his own reminiscences. So they sat at their table, drinking beer until the waiter brought them the check.

"We close now," said the waiter tapping his watch, "Christmas Eve."

They found a cab and—at Rudy's suggestion—they headed downtown to Maru. More bars followed Maru but by then the sequence of events became hazy.

The next morning, Daniel woke up in his own bed with a pounding headache. He was halfway out of bed—headed to the bathroom—before he realized someone was lying next to him. She was a pretty blonde. And she was young—very young—Daniel realized as she stretched and opened her eyes.

"Merry Christmas," she said with a giggle as she propped herself up on her elbows. "You were a bad, bad boy last night but Santa told me to give you something anyway."

"He did?" he said. He stood up and caused the blonde to giggle again.

"I see you're all ready for your gift," she said, eyeing his boxer shorts.

"I'll be right back." He let himself out the door and headed down the hall to the bathroom. He gulped some ibuprofen and relieved himself. Through the door, he could hear sounds coming from his spare bedroom. Clearly, he wasn't the only one on the receiving end of an early morning Christmas present. What the hell—he thought, as he let himself out of the bathroom. He opened his bedroom door and assessed the pale imitation of Persey occupying his bed. "Hey there," he said, grabbing a condom from the top drawer of his dresser and sliding back under the covers.

"Hi," she said, giggling and moving closer to him.

"Wanna sit on Santa's lap?" Then he kissed her before she could unleash another torrent of high-pitched giggles. He was hopeful that the ibuprofen would kick in before he had to hear that sound again.

He and Rudy took the girls out to breakfast. The blonde's name was Brittany. Her friend was Chelsea. Behind their chatter, it was clear that both girls would forego their Christmas plans if he or Rudy were to ask. The whole thing was reminiscent of college—where lifelong friendships were formed over the course of a single night. It wasn't until Brittany showed him her driver's license that he realized there was nothing weird or reminiscent about it for either of the girls. What the fuck? Was she really only twenty? After breakfast, they made the ritual exchange of cell phone numbers before putting the girls in a cab. It turned out they were roommates. Of course they were roommates—he thought as he slid his phone back into his pocket. They were still in college.

Daniel glanced at Rudy. "Where you headed?"

"Back to my place," said Rudy. "I'm gonna get a shower and then catch up on some work."

"What the hell?" he chided. "It's Christmas. You CAN take the day off."

"I can't," said Rudy shaking his head. "I've got a lot to catch up on."

He didn't have family in town. He didn't want to think about Persey. Work was the best way to drown out everything else. Daniel could hear it all behind his words. "Doesn't matter," said Daniel. "Whatever you've got, it'll wait. You're coming with me. I'll pick you up around four but I'm warning you man," he said with a wink, "my little sister's in town and I've seen what you're like with college girls."

Rudy glanced in the direction of the disappearing cab. "Yeah," he said with a shake of his head. "I think I've had my fill of college girls for the day."

"So you're in?"

"Yeah," said Rudy again. "I'm in."

Chapter Forty-Eight

Persey understood what she had to do. The fright that threatened to paralyze her that first day in New York was gone. Haden wouldn't hurt her. She understood that—even though sometimes, perversely—she wished he would. Her own pain, however unbearable, was preferable to condemning Aaron's soul to an eternity of damnation. That was how she thought of it, even though she understood those words weren't quite right.

The truth was she still didn't understand what type of power Haden held over Aaron's soul. Whenever she asked Haden, he always said the same thing. "There will come a time when all will be explained." Try as she might, she had nothing—no religious instruction or moral belief—that equipped her to come to terms with what Haden alternately referred to as his Kingdom of Darkness or the Underworld.

Persey had grown up with nominal religion. She was baptized Lutheran at her grandparent's insistence. But she and her mother were infrequent churchgoers, at best. She knew the basic tenets of Christianity—Heaven, Hell, Adam and Eve, Noah's ark, King Solomon. When she was little, she'd gone through a phase of reading the *Big Book of Children's Bible Stories*. It had never occurred to her they might be based on truth. They seemed like obvious parables, stories, no different than the *Blue Fairy Book* or the mythology of any other civilization.

She'd written a paper about religious mythology in college. In it, she'd argued that such stories formed a necessary part of any functioning society because they provided a basis for morality. The class was Philosophy of Religion and she'd gotten an A on the paper. How could an A paper be so wrong? How could she explain Haden? There was no place for him in her world view and yet he was real. She knew—with the cold certainty that accompanied all statements of truth—that Haden was what he claimed to be.

"Are you Satan?" she asked him during that first night.

"I told you before," he said. "Some people call me that. I've been called a thousand names, in a thousand languages, but the names don't matter. What matters," he said moving closer to her—allowing his eyes to rest upon hers. "What should matter most to you, Persephone, is that I exist. I am the ruler of the Underworld and someday you will join me there. Not as a soul but as my eternal bride."

"Not everyone goes to the Underworld, do they? Where do people go if they've been good?" she asked, still searching for a parallel to her limited religious knowledge gleaned from Lutheran Sunday School.

"All souls come to the Underworld," Haden replied. Then, answering her unspoken question he confirmed once again, "Even Aaron's."

Haden wasn't always so forthcoming. Information and confessions didn't spill from him the way they did from most people in her life—probably because he wasn't a person. It was something she needed to keep reminding herself. He met her eyes and kept his composure—although, she observed he turned away from her when she asked him questions he chose not to answer.

The subject of what became of the souls in his keep was one of those questions. How were they tortured? Was there a place of peacefulness? How was it decided where each soul went? Was everyone who had existed since the beginning of time in his keep? These were the questions she wanted answered. But time and again, he refused to satisfy her curiosity. "In due time," he would say each time she asked. "You will have the answers to all your questions."

Her last attempt, to look into his eyes and ask a question in that vein, was met with a sharper response. "I warn you, Persephone," he had said sternly. "I am aware of your unique skills and I have little patience for your repeated attempts to compel my answers. I am not human. It would serve you well to remember that fact." The threat was implicit and so she checked her curiosity. She had murdered her husband with her vanity. She wouldn't allow her curiosity to bring Haden's wrath down upon his soul.

Chapter Forty-Nine

Persey was a world away from everything familiar. Haden had taken her from New York under cover of darkness. They'd flown through an endless night until their plane landed on the other side of the world.

"Welcome to the Asian capital of vice," Haden said as they disembarked. The lush, wet heat enveloped her the moment they disembarked from the plane. A bead of sweat slid down her back as Haden guided her through the crowded airport and into a waiting taxi cab. The car's feeble air conditioning did little more than stir the warm air that surrounded them.

They hurtled through the night toward brightly lit buildings in the distance. The driver spoke into a cell phone in a strange language. Every few moments, he would stop to glance over his shoulder at Persey. She became fascinated with his ability to keep the car on the freeway. This is life and we all plunge blindly through it, she thought, as the car—without any warning—veered onto an off-ramp and deposited them into congested narrow streets. The driver closed his cell phone and carried on a conversation with Haden while he steered the car deeper and deeper into the foreign landscape, choked—even in the wee morning hours—with traffic and people.

Haden interrupted Persey's jetlagged reverie by leaning over and whispering into her ear, "His name is Sampan. He wants you to know he would like to murder his brother. His brother is sleeping with his wife. Sampan's known about the affair for several months but he hesitates because he doesn't know how to dispose of the body." Haden leaned forward and said something to Sampan in his native tongue.

Sampan made a sharp left turn into a gated driveway. At a signal from Haden, two men uniformed in white hoisted the gate aloft. The car passed through and came to rest before a glowing monolithic building. The door of the cab was opened by another man in a similar uniform. Before exiting, Haden leaned forward and said something else to Sampan. Then, he too, slid out of the taxi cab.

Haden put one arm around Persey and said, "I think we're going to be very happy together in Bangkok. It's already proving to be the perfect place for your particular skill set."

Chapter Fifty

Haden ushered her inside and Persey recognized—with a sense of relief—a hotel lobby. It was dark, cool and cavernous—full of hard surfaces and clean lines. The walls and floor were covered in polished black marble. Thin, attractive people pressed their hands together at their chests and bowed their heads as Haden guided her towards the elevator.

"Namaste," she half-whispered, pressing her hands together and returning their gesture. The elevator shot them up towards the top of the building. It opened into a small hallway with one door.

"Our room," said Haden, passing a key card over the electronic eye. He opened the door allowing her to enter first. The room was vast and opulent. Haden shut the door behind them and then walked over to the window. He opened the blinds so she could look out at the glittering city below. "Do you like it?" he asked.

Instead of answering, she just pressed her face against the cool glass like a child.

"Come," Haden whispered, taking her by the hand and leading her away from the window. "You must sleep." He led her through another door.

She realized, in the foggy way of someone suffering from serious sleep deprivation, that the last time she'd slept was at Daniel's.

"You'll find fresh clothing in the closet," he told her.

But even as he spoke, she was already sinking down into the welcoming softness of the enormous bed. The sound of drawers opening and closing and the feeling of clothing being removed and replaced came to her as though it were all a dream. Then awareness was gone and she was lost to the delicious welcoming death of sleep.

Hours—maybe days—passed before her eyes opened again. There was a moment of confusion. She had no idea where she was. Then it all came back to her. It was all real—the room, the bed, the unfamiliar silk negligee that had twisted and tangled itself around her body while she slept. It wasn't a dream.

The door to her room opened and Haden came in carrying a bamboo tray, laden with food and adorned with a single white flower. It was fragrant with small waxy petals. He set the tray down on the bedside table before sitting down next to her on the bed. "Drink," he said, picking up a tall frosted glass from the tray and placing a straw to her lips. "You'll feel better."

She swallowed the unfamiliar liquid and found he was right. She did feel better. She allowed him to feed her like a child, gobbling exotic fruits from his fingers without protest. Strength returned to her body as she swallowed the last forkful of familiar scrambled eggs.

He bent down and kissed her on the forehead. "My beautiful Persephone," he said, looking at her with a trace of a smile. "You are irresistible."

"Because it's what I wanted. It's what I bargained for," she said, her eyes filling with unexpected tears. She felt him hesitate for a moment—as though caught off guard.

"No," he said, smoothing her hair back from her face. "I see you as you've always been. To me, you've always been irresistible." Then, as though remembering something important, he sprung up from the bed and walked toward the door. "I've run you a bath," he said. Then he left the room, closing the door to her bedroom behind him.

The oversized white marble tub was situated in front of tinted windows. She eased herself into the hot water and scrubbed the scent of fear, international travel and sleep from her skin. Below her was the hazy city, bisected by a winding river choked with boats. Modern buildings crowded next to golden temples. From her vantage point, she could see the maze of streets below. Despite everything, they called to her. She wanted to explore them—lose herself to the push and heat of the exotic city framed beneath her bathroom window. She pulled herself out of the water and wrapped a heavy towel around her body.

She returned to her room to find the bed already made up and the closet door propped open suggestively. A drawer had been pulled out an inch or two in order to hint at the contents contained within. She pulled open both doors of the closet and found it well-stocked with simple, elegant clothing. She quickly selected a white linen shirt dress and a pair of sandals with a small wedged heel.

Haden returned while she was brushing her hair. "I have one more improvement to make upon perfection," he said as he stood watching her from the doorway. "Lift up your hair." She did as he commanded. He moved behind her and fastened a heavy braid of gold around her neck. "A gift," he said, kissing the delicate exposed skin at the base of her neck, "and the first of many." He studied the tableau they made in the mirror before adding, "Come to the living room when you've finished."

Persey entered the main room of the suite and took in the details, the previous night's sleep-deprivation, had prevented her from noticing. Haden was seated on a white leather couch with one leg crossed over his knee while he read the newspaper. The couch he sat on was positioned across from another identical couch. Where a coffee table would usually sit a small pool of water was sunk into the floor. As Persey moved closer, she could see water lilies floating at the top of the pool while the bottom was covered in pebbles the same shade as the couches. Haden looked up and smiled at her.

"Come, sit down," he said, motioning to the spot beside him. "Do you remember Sampan?"

She shook her head trying to remember—why did that name sound familiar?

"The driver that brought us from the airport," he prompted. "In your presence, he was unable to prevent himself from sharing his secret. While you slept I found him. I offered him his darkest desire, the thing he couldn't bring himself to do. The price was high but he was eager to pay it. He traded his soul for the life of his brother. The deed was done as he wished and now his soul is mine. You see, Persephone," Haden continued, uncrossing his legs and setting aside the newspaper, "now more than ever, I require human souls. Until now, I've never had a way to ascertain human desire and longing unless they chanced to share what was hidden in their hearts. Now I have you and that obstacle has been removed. With you, there are no secrets. They tell you everything. When I know their weakness it is a simple thing to make their soul mine. We make a unique team, don't you think?"

"You killed Sampan's brother?" Persey asked.

Haden shook his head and a strange, modest expression passed over his face. "No, I merely had the good fortune to know what Sampan most desired. As luck would have it, Sampan's wife did the killing. The unfortunate brother had the temerity to suggest he would end the relationship if the good woman continued to refuse him certain pleasures she deemed unsavory. She flew into a rage and stabbed him to death. The police took her into custody last night. I was just reading about it in the paper. You're welcome to read the story yourself," he said, reaching for the newspaper he'd set aside.

"No," said Persey. She stood up and walked over to the window. Far below them, the river wound its way through the city. "What happens to Sampan's soul?" she asked without looking at him.

"It's mine," said Haden. "To do with as I choose."

She turned away from the window and walked back over to him. "And what do you choose?" she pressed, looking into his eyes.

"I shall sacrifice it for your immortality," he said. He smiled at her and although his words should have frightened her she took comfort in them. She finally understood the worst. Choice was a luxury she'd relinquished that night in Central Park. This was to be the rest of her life. It was worse than she could have ever imagined but at least she understood what was expected of her.

Chapter Fifty-One

Persey was gone. She was nowhere. That's what the private detective Rudy hired told him. "It's mostly what was already in the police report," the detective said, handing Rudy the forlorn, thin manila envelope. "Usually, I can dig up something those guys miss but this time I got nada."

"Do you have any hunches?" asked Rudy, using language gleaned from Hardy Boy mysteries read so long ago.

The detective shook his head and tapped the report. "It's all in here. I wrote up my own independent analysis, but to paraphrase it—people who disappear the way she did, don't usually reappear—if you get my drift." Something in Rudy's face caused the detective's face to soften. He reached over and squeezed Rudy's shoulder. "I'm sorry, so sorry for your loss," he said.

Rudy loved her. His current project was nothing, if not a dedication of his life's work to Persey Campbell. Now that she was gone, he was able to admit what he'd never acknowledged. He knew Daniel loved her too. Rudy wondered if Daniel had hired a similar detective and been rewarded with a similar slim report and funereal wishes.

He didn't know because Persey was something he and Daniel never talked about after that first night. It was their unspoken rule. In any other circumstance, the relationship between him and Daniel would have been adversarial. Rudy was no longer willing to step aside because she was "out-of-his-league", as they used to say. If anything, he'd convinced himself he was what she needed most. Who else had known her since she was a child? Who else had understood her secret for almost the same length of time?

In high school, Rudy had understood why Persey chose Aaron. Girls always chose guys like Aaron. It made sense. It wasn't like he had much to offer her back then. Now everything was different. As long as Aaron Strait was alive, the point was moot. He'd never thought about it because Persey's future was a done deal. The only role Rudy played in it was that of a friend. But from the moment he'd read the notice of Aaron's death something had reawakened in Rudy. Despicable as it might be—he'd begun to dream about the possibility of a future together with Persey Campbell. Once he'd opened that door there was no going back. In her absence—the unlikely substitute became Daniel. They both shared a hidden passion. They were both trying to kill the pain.

At first, his friendship with Daniel was based on mutual loss. Misery loves company, Rudy would think as he headed uptown to meet Daniel for a beer. It was their shared experience that brought them together but they never talked about it. That didn't mean they didn't talk. In fact, in the eleven months that had passed since Persey first went missing, they discovered how much they had in common. They were both night owls, their brains revving up to do their best work somewhere in the wee hours, when most of their colleagues had long since tumbled into bed.

By the end of January they'd developed a routine. They met for lunch a couple times a week, often returning to the soup dumpling shop where they'd spent a good portion of Christmas Eve. They met after work at least twice a week to hit the bars. Meanwhile, the detective's report sat on Rudy's desk unopened. In February—after she'd been gone for two months—he stuffed the pathetic little file in his desk without bothering to read it. What was the point? The detective had already told him his conclusion. Even though Rudy felt certain Persey was very much alive, he was realistic enough about his own abilities to realize there was little chance of him succeeding where the private detective had failed.

On a Wednesday night in late March, Rudy broke their unspoken rule. He and Daniel had met at a new bar in the meatpacking district. It was an unseasonably warm evening and the place had opened the large garage doors running along the sidewalk so that the party could spill out onto the street. They'd just ordered their second round of drinks and Daniel was eyeing two young women three tables away when Rudy said, "Do people ask about her at work?"

Daniel's eyes flickered down to his glass. "She's on a leave of absence," he said without looking up.

It was all the confirmation Rudy needed. He wasn't the only one who still believed Persey was alive.

During the next eight months, work became the drug of Rudy's choice. He shut himself into his office with Bradley, leaving only to forage for food or when Daniel insisted that he needed to get the fuck out of his office. He could lose himself in his work. Work was a way of being with Persey without having to think about all the questions that didn't have answers. The project was called Confess.com but he never thought of it that way. To Rudy, it was always the Persey Project.

Chapter Fifty-Two

The Persey Project was in the testing phase and the initial numbers were shocking. It was almost as though—through the script and code written into the virtual pages of Confess.com—Rudy had managed to bring some essential piece of Persey to life. Rudy had encrypted consumer products into the Facebook-like news feed. The retinal scanning technology did its work and fed into Rudy's code. What came back to Rudy and Bradley was a feed of which products most appealed to the test consumers. The website then suggested friends and groups based on other consumer's similar interests.

It still wasn't exactly Persey-style truth serum but the longer Rudy worked on the code, the closer it got. All it took was a slight tweak to the encryption database and the feed could focus on preferred pornography and—in a test run on college freshman—preference for sexual experience. A surprising number of the female freshman, who volunteered for Rudy's test sample, displayed a distinct desire to be handcuffed during sex. It was the kind of information Rudy would have loved to have had access to when he was still in college.

The reason Rudy never talked about the Persey Project with Daniel was because it came too close to breaking their unspoken rule. One night in November, almost a year after Persey disappeared, Daniel and Rudy were trudging downtown through an early winter snowfall in search of cab. As the anniversary of her disappearance grew closer, they had resumed their twice-a-week bar routine.

"Did you give her your number?" asked Daniel as they walked.

"Who?" asked Rudy, distracted by his feet which—clad in sneakers—were going numb.

"That girl in the bar, she was into you."

"The hot redhead?" asked Rudy. "She told me she had a boyfriend."

Daniel laughed and shook his head. "No," he said, holding up one finger in a drunken correction. "What she really said is my boyfriend is a jerk and I'm looking for an excuse to dump him. She thought you were the perfect excuse."

"When did she say that?" asked Rudy. "When I went to the bathroom?"

"Man, you were sitting right there," said Daniel. "You've got to listen to what people are trying to tell you."

A taxi took pity on them and pulled over to the curb. Before Daniel could give the driver his address, Rudy leaned forward and said, "We're making two stops. I need to head back uptown to a place called Kennedy's. It's on Fifty-Seventh between Eight and Ninth." The cab pulled up to the bar they had just left and Rudy hopped out saying, "I'll be right back."

He dashed inside threading his way through the drunken crowd until he found the red head. "Call me sometime," he said, thrusting a scrap of paper at her with his phone number scribbled on it.

"Maybe I will," she said looking at him with a startled expression as though he'd somehow read her thoughts. She called the next day. "It's Lisa, from the bar. I was just wondering, do you want to meet me for coffee?"

At first, Rudy attributed Daniel's way with people as easy charm—the kind that people like Daniel had and people like Rudy lacked. In all likelihood, if Lisa hadn't called him, Rudy would never have given it another thought. But she did call him. It led to a hunch—there was that Hardy Boys word again. If someone like Persey existed then it wasn't too much of a stretch to believe other people might exist with similar abilities.

Daniel had said Rudy wasn't listening to what people were telling him so Rudy decided to tune in. He paid attention to Daniel with the same kind of focus that led to his discovery about Persey. Back then it had been easy. At sixteen years of age, it was easy to devote a startling and singular amount of attention to one beautiful, compelling girl. He was no longer sixteen and—even if he had been—Daniel would not have attracted Rudy's attention with the same kind of intensity. All the same, he forced himself to follow Daniel's advice. He paid attention, close attention.

Chapter Fifty-Three

Rudy had plenty of time to observe. Daniel seemed as focused on sleeping his way through the bar scene, as Rudy had been focused on work for the last eight months. It didn't take Rudy long to conclude that Daniel's gift was not the same as Persey's. People weren't drawn to him the way they were to Persey. Although, that wasn't quite right, people were drawn to Daniel but the quality of their attraction was different. For one thing, it was usually just girls and gay men who fawned over Daniel. The Persey effect was more democratic.

As Rudy observed, he became convinced that Daniel's confidence with women was born from something other than good looks and success. It was as though, somehow, Daniel had direct access to the exact information he needed to navigate any woman he wanted back to his Gramercy Park bedroom.

It didn't click until December. They were at a Christmas party standing by the bar. Daniel was eyeing a group of women across the room. "Be back in a minute," he said, grabbing his drink and weaving through the crowd. Rudy followed at a distance. He watched as Daniel leaned up against the back of one girl's chair. He bent down and whispered something in her ear. She glanced at him with something like disdain and made a face for the benefit of her friends.

"Sorry, not interested," she said.

An expression of satisfaction passed across Daniel's face. It was fleeting, lasting only a moment but Rudy caught it. Daniel leaned back down and whispered something else to her. Whatever he said made her put down her drink and look at him.

"I don't," she said, trying for vehemence and failing.

"I think you do," he replied with his charming smile.

Rudy had seen the rest before. He knew the sequence of events, even as he watched them unfold. The girl followed Daniel to a quieter corner. They would talk and by the end of the night, Daniel would take her home. The sequence of events wasn't important because he realized the crucial part had already happened. Somehow, by denying her interest, the girl had given Daniel the exact information he needed to secure it. Rudy remembered Daniel telling him about Lisa. "What she was trying to tell you." Rudy was certain Lisa hadn't said anything. Then how had Daniel known? Was he some kind of mind-reader? Rudy was beginning to think he was.

What had begun as Rudy's initial reluctance to talk about Persey took on a broader scope. Rudy had never said much about his work and now he said even less. It wasn't that he didn't trust Daniel. It was just that he didn't trust anyone with this particular piece of his life. The Persey Project was going to be big. He was sure of it. He didn't want to do anything that would jeopardize it. The problem was he wasn't sure whether Daniel had already mined his most private thoughts. It was possible Daniel knew as much as Rudy did on the subject but was just keeping quiet out of respect for their unspoken rule.

Despite all this, or maybe because he wanted to test his theory, Daniel was still the first person Rudy called when he finished the Confess.com beta site. It didn't hurt that it was almost one o'clock in the morning and Rudy knew Daniel would be awake. It occurred to Rudy as he hit speed dial that he needed to celebrate and he wanted to do it with someone who knew the source of his inspiration.

Daniel picked up on the second ring.

"Hey man, can you meet me for a beer?" Rudy said.

"What are we celebrating?" Daniel asked.

"The project I've been working on," said Rudy. "The beta site's finished."

They met at Kennedy's. Daniel listened while Rudy talked.

"Holy shit," said Daniel when Rudy paused for air. "This is huge, you know that right? Fucking huge!"

"Yeah," said Rudy with a laugh. "Response on our initial pitches to advertisers has been through the roof. I'm gonna take it live next week so we can get some initial numbers."

"No, no, no," said Daniel, shaking his head. "People are going to jump all over this thing. You go live and all your work is out there begging to be imitated by all the other big guys who've got better capitalization. You can get the numbers you need with a limited test audience. Keep the Persey Project under wraps and use your test numbers to fully capitalize it. When you go live and streaming, this thing is going to fucking blow up. You know that, right?"

"I do," he said, nodding his head. "I do, indeed." Rudy took a sip of his beer. This was the moment. He wondered how much else Daniel knew about the Persey Project. It was time to find out. "How'd you know that's what I call it?" he asked.

Daniel looked at him sharply. "That's what you said—the Persey Project."

"No," said Rudy shaking his head. "I didn't. As a matter of fact, I made a point not to call it that. So how'd you know?"

For a split second, Daniel's face wore the surprised look of a little boy caught in the act of doing something he shouldn't be. His face grew red and his eyes narrowed. Then he looked away. "How long have you known?" he asked. Waiting, he continued to study the table between them.

Rudy was silent.

Daniel looked up from the table. "What the fuck? You're giving me the silent treatment?"

"I'm 'thinking' the answer," said Rudy. The words sounded ridiculous when said out loud.

Daniel laughed. "It doesn't work like that," he said.

"Then how does it work?" asked Rudy.

It made more sense after Daniel explained it—as much sense as something like that could make. Now he understood why Daniel had never brought up the Persey Project. It wasn't out of some particular sensitivity or reticence on Daniel's part. It was because Daniel hadn't known any details.

"It's just like listening carefully to what people say," said Daniel.

"Like with the red head?" asked Rudy.

"Yeah, exactly," said Daniel as he drained the rest of his beer. "I don't know how you figured it out but I gotta hand it to you. I'm thirty-eight years old and this is the first time anyone's ever called me on the crap-o-meter. Two more beers," he said to the waitress as she picked up their empty glasses.

The waitress set two more glasses of beer on the table. "To the crap-o-meter," said Daniel as he picked his glass up and drained half of it.

Rudy smiled and followed suit.

"So, can we talk about something else now? Let's get back to the Persey Project," said Daniel.

Rudy shrugged. "What's to talk about? Haven't you already heard everything there is to know about it?"

Daniel shook his head. "Listen, I can't read your mind. All I got from your words is that you were too nervous to talk about it. That and you think it's going to be huge." Daniel leaned across the table. "Why don't you let me help you out by doing what I do best," he said. "I can make this happen in a major way. I can get the funding you need. You know I can do it. Persey may be gone but we can still build a million fucking dollar memorial for her."

Daniel's drunken reference to Persey jarred Rudy's tongue loose. "Do you think she's still out there somewhere?" The question seemed to slip out before he could stop himself

Daniel paused for a second. "Just as much as you do," he said. "Why else do you think I've been hanging out with you for the last year?"

Chapter Fifty-Four

It wasn't so terrible. Worse things happened to better people. Persey had gotten into the habit of giving herself pep talks whenever self-pity threatened to overtake her. The only problem with the pep talks was sometimes she had trouble buying into her own logic. Worse things might happen to better people but if anyone deserved to be miserable—it was her. She was a menace to society. She sacrificed people's souls on a daily basis in order to protect the souls she cared about most. Although technically— the lawyer part of her brain argued—she wasn't sacrificing their souls. She was just smoothing the path that led them to sacrifice their own souls.

Each person had a choice. She understood that. Once upon a time she'd had a choice. And she'd made her decision. In a moment of weakness, she had bound herself to Haden. He gave her a gift and she accepted it. Now she belonged to him. There was no going back. The best thing to do was to not think about it. There was no point in thinking about it because—no matter how long she pondered the ins and outs of her situation—nothing was going to change.

"I'm no different than those girls," she whispered to Haden one night. They were seated in the lurid light of a Patpong bar watching young girls gyrate on-stage.

Patpong—Bangkok's infamous red-light neighborhood—was not far from their hotel. It supplied Haden with a steady stream of people ready and willing to enter into a business arrangement—on his terms.

"How can you make such a comparison? You're nothing like them," said Haden. He looked at her in a possessive, appraising way that made her feel like an object he was preparing to add to his collection. The corners of his mouth curled up in a smile. "You—my beautiful Persephone—are destined for eternal life.

You shall belong to me... and me alone. Those girls," he nodded contemptuously toward the stage, "are for public consumption."

For a moment, Persey was tempted to elucidate the similarities between herself and the girls on stage to Haden but it was already too late. He leaned over and kissed her cheek.

"I'll be watching," he said, standing up.

He was leaving now—leaving her alone and undefended in the midst of people with terrible secrets. She looked at the other patrons in the bar and wondered who would be her first customer of the evening. Those who frequented Patpong were foreign tourists. The bars in the sex district drew men from all over the world—Australia, Germany, Canada, Israel, and beyond. The lure of Thailand's sex tours, with their promises of naughty girlie bars and exotic Thai women, seemed to be universally irresistible. Tonight, the men in the audience were mostly white and ranged in age from early-twenties to late sixties. It was a given most of them spoke English. Almost everyone she met spoke English well enough to confess their secrets.

It didn't take long. It never did. Half of them were already drunk. Glances lingered upon her. She could feel them circling—working up their nerve. She was like bait in the middle of a school of fish. It wouldn't be long before the first one would strike. It was just a bar on the other side of the world. They thought whatever happened here wasn't real, wouldn't affect the rest of their lives. That's where they were wrong since she and Haden had arrived.

The owner of this particular bar had observed Persey on previous evenings and tonight he was ready to make his move. He sat down in the chair Haden had just occupied, studying her appreciatively.

"Drink?" he said, clapping his hands and motioning to a scantily-clothed cocktail waitress.

"Water," said Persey.

The bar owner scooted his chair closer to her. She could smell his unwashed skin and noticed the dirt compacted in the round crescents underneath his fingernails.

The waitress set a bottle of water down on the table. Persey opened it and took a long drink. Then—taking a deep breath—she forced herself to look into the eyes of the man sitting next to her. Her eyes met his and that was all it took.

"You like girls?" he asked, motioning to the stage. "They are all beautiful girls. You are beautiful girl too. You want—I put you on my stage?" He giggled.

"Is that all?" Her voice was dead and unfamiliar. "Was that all you wanted to tell me?"

"I like the girls too," he continued in his heavily-accented English. "You, me, we the same, we both like the girls. These girls, they come from North. You like?"

"Yes," she nodded. "They seem nice."

His eyes were still fixed on hers and he moaned a little under his breath as he leaned closer to her. "They come to me as virgins. It is best, you know. They so tight, so clean."

He gave another little moan and Persey felt a wave of disgust. She fought the impulse to jump up and run—run out of this bar and away from its terrible secrets. He was still talking.

"All men, they like virgins. They pay extra—so my girls—I teach them how to make blood on sheet. You cut in mouth. It bleed but no show. Girl spit blood on sheet and the men think they have virgin," he said.

He seemed almost proud of his cunning deceptions. Persey took another sip from her bottle of water and looked away. This was not an auspicious start to the evening.

And so it went—confession after confession. She knew that somewhere, Haden was watching—weighing the possibilities and assessing each of the confessions, as they were bargaining chips for the human soul.

That night—like every other night since she'd been in Thailand—people told Persey their vile, often criminal, secrets and she listened. The men sought her out first. They never lingered after they'd finished unburdening themselves. Instead, they moved on as though they'd been the victim of some sort of temporary insanity. For some of them, Persey experienced no crisis of conscience over the fate of their souls. She couldn't help thinking that whatever use Haden made of those men—it was no less than they deserved.

But the girls were different. Until she came to Bangkok, Persey had never given much thought to the confidences she inspired. Her life had been an exercise in avoiding people's secrets. The actual content of the secrets was always secondary. Now, for the first time in her life, she was stripped of all the protective mechanisms she'd relied upon. All she could do was listen and let other people's secrets flood over her.

At first it felt like death—like she was drowning in other people's horror. But little by little, her perspective changed. She started to listen—to really hear what was being whispered to her each night. She realized the things people told her fell into two categories. Night after night, Persey listened to confessions and gradually the secrets made their pattern clear; harmer and harmed, criminal and victim, powerful and powerless.

The other thing she realized is that the girls in those bars, approaching her shyly, hesitant but still unable to resist, almost always fell into the second category. Which category did she fall into? She often wondered as Haden made his silent inventory of the information she collected.

In the wee hours of the morning, Haden returned to her side. As they prepared to leave, a girl touched Persey on the arm. She was wearing hot pants emblazoned with the American flag and a half t-shirt with the words "Me So Horny" printed on it. She couldn't have been more than fifteen. Persey had heard secrets from these kinds of girls before and so she pretended not to feel the girl's touch—avoided her with her eyes.

Still the girl tugged on Persey's sleeve. Her voice was insistent as she whispered, "Madame."

Haden, standing to one side, quickly intervened. "I'll give you two a moment alone," he said.

Persey put her hand on top of the girl's, and—blinking back her own tears—met the waiting eyes.

"I don't send everything to family," the girl whispered.

"How long have you been here?" Persey asked. In response, the girl just shrugged.

"My father, he bring me here two, maybe three years ago. I work hard so my family can eat. But sometime I keep a little for myself, for Anchali. It's not so bad?" she asked, looking into Persey's eyes as though they offered benediction.

"No," said Persey gently. "It's not so bad."

Chapter Fifty-Five

If Persey was in a form of mourning, than Bangkok proved to be strangely consoling. She took comfort in the crowds of people, the push of vendors and food carts on every corner. The contrast between the primitive living conditions on display in back alleys and the ultra-modern high rise hotels and shopping malls intrigued her. It felt like a synonym for all the contrasts in Persey's own life. The city of Bangkok and the person Persey was becoming were constant juxtapositions of opposing forces.

One particular consolation of Thailand was the kindness of its people. Persey had a newfound appreciation for kindness. The secrets relentlessly thrust upon her during the last year had changed her—or more precisely changed her understanding of what it meant to be human. For the first time, she understood the gift of kindness. It was something people gave despite the foulness or pain of their inner lives. It was gratuitous. There was no requirement to be kind. That's why it meant so much.

"Do they all bargain away their souls?" she asked Haden one languid afternoon. They were sitting next to the private rooftop pool of their hotel looking out over the cityscape. "Because some of them deserve better," she added before he could answer.

He picked up her hand and caressed the back of it as he spoke. "They have a choice," he said. "The choice they make is a testament to their weakness."

"How can you say that when you already know their weakness, you know the thing they most desire?" She wanted to ask if he'd offered Anchali money but she didn't. She couldn't bear to hear the answer.

"What does it matter?" said Haden. "In the end, I only offer possibilities. I don't make the final decision regarding their fate."

She gripped his hand tightly in her own. "And what about me, Haden—did I ever have a choice?" she asked as his eyes met hers.

Maybe it was the tightness of her hand on his or the passion in her voice but for some reason she caught him off guard. His body tensed as though he was in pain.

"Yes," he whispered through clenched teeth.

Persey dropped his hand and turned her head away so he wouldn't see her tears. She understood her choice. It was the same choice given to the young Thai prostitutes she met in bars. Escape was possible but the cost was too high. The prostitutes knew their families would starve without the money they sent home.

Persey knew her loved ones would…well, she still didn't fully understand what would happen to them, if she failed to comply with Haden's wishes. All she knew is Haden was powerful. He might torture their souls and hers. The possibility terrified her. In the end, her options were no different than Anchali's.

"Persephone," Haden said, interrupting her thoughts. She turned back to him, letting him see her cheeks slicked with tears. "My beautiful Persephone," he said. "It pains me to see you grieve over these humans who bargain away their souls. You must understand their suffering is a small thing relative to what is to be gained."

He leaned towards her, touching his lips to her. For once she returned the pressure—sought the warmth of his lips in return instead of just succumbing to its seduction. She let go of her fear and sadness and surrendered to the darkness of his kiss. There was so much freedom in letting go. She felt the darkness of a thousand secrets surround her, calling her towards the center of their swirling vortex. The sensation made her giddy, as though just beyond the boundaries of her conscience, something was waiting to spin her away. It made her dizzy as it struggled to submerge her deeper into the kiss that connected her to Haden.

She felt him push her away with more force than necessary. He made a strange little gasp as he leapt up from his lounge chair. For a moment, he stood in front of her breathing hard. Then he wrapped himself in the heavy white cotton bathrobe supplied by the hotel and turned away.

"I'm going to take a shower," he said, walking back towards their suite without glancing back.

She watched Haden as he walked away. Her own breath still came in ragged gasps. There was a lot she didn't understand about what had just happened. But one thing she knew for sure, Haden was keeping a secret from her. She was certain of it. The image of a teenage Aaron, driving her home through the dusty Iowan cornfields, flashed into her head unbidden. His darkest, most shameful secret had been his desire to keep her safe. She'd always understood her attraction to Aaron was based on the things he didn't have. There was nothing hidden and dark inside of Aaron. He did more than protect her; he offset the darkness inside of her. Now Aaron was gone but inside of her—darkness remained—unchecked and unbalanced. She could feel it in her soul. It was still hidden but every day it grew stronger.

All her life, she'd known it was there—calling to the worst parts of other people. She had controlled it. She had refused to acknowledge it. Now, she realized she'd spent a lifetime pretending the horror contained within her didn't exist. In truth—since that was the only currency she was dealing in these days—her marriage to Aaron had been nothing more than a security blanket. She'd wanted safety and he'd wanted her, except Aaron hadn't known about the thing lurking in her soul. Neither of them had anticipated that it—whatever it was—would find Aaron's presence exhausting and stifling.

It was happy to be freed of Aaron. She could feel the hidden darkness surge up within her, forcing her to admit her own truths. Aaron hadn't had any secrets worth discovering, but Haden did. Whatever this thing inside of her was—its radar was never wrong about sensing hidden darkness. Secrets, she thought, picturing

Haden's sudden exit again. The image gave her a small unexpected thrill.

Chapter Fifty-Six

Haden loved Bangkok. He'd met with some of his greatest successes in this city. He'd prowled the banks of the Chao Praya River when Thailand was Siam, and the ancient city itself was referred to as Bang Makok bang. Its present day incarnation of crowds, chaos and humidity was just as appealing. He'd brought Persey to Bangkok because it was on the other side of the world, and he wanted to be able to work without interference. However, Bangkok's appeal went beyond its geographical location. Humans were at their weakest—most suggestible when they were in the throes of indulgence. A city which held the dubious title of sex-tour capital of the world seemed an obvious hunting ground. So far, his prediction had proved correct. Together, he and Persey made a most effective team.

The warm, enveloping nights were the perfect breeding ground for vice and corruption. Similar to the way bacteria multiply more quickly in the moist environs of the human body, people were more receptive to his offers in Bangkok's humid early morning hours. Persey's presence compelled their confessions, and Haden cataloged their desperate desires and secret sins. The confessions provided him with a window into their souls. With Persey's assistance—he could pinpoint the thing they most desired. He knew their bottom line from the beginning of the negotiation. Again and again, he was able to make an offer that convinced them to alter their fate. Everyone had a price. It was just a matter of discovering it. Despite having all the cards stacked in his favor, he was beginning to realize soul collection was a time consuming business.

His goal was deceptively simple. A million souls must be delivered to Kronos before Persey could choose to alter her unknowable fate. Haden was starting to realize a million souls was a high price. He understood right from the beginning that it was a large number, about the same amount of souls as there were people in the city of Dallas, Texas. What he hadn't fully understood was the actual physical time it would take to collect them all. How could he have known? He'd never been required to think in terms of human time before. It was probable—he thought grimly—that Haden's lack of comprehension about the passage of human time was exactly what Kronos relied upon when he'd made the deal.

And if he couldn't deliver the souls…the recollection of the other girl came to him. Is that what Kronos had planned for his Persephone? Haden had no plan to subvert natural law. If he couldn't gain her immortality, then he was prepared to let her die according to the dictates of natural law. Her mysterious fate would protect her from Kronos's wrath.

Then what—he asked himself with increasing frequency—what choice could Kronos offer her? What was the old man's plan? Kronos had knowledge of all human time—both past and present. Haden could only surmise that the choice would be based on some piece of Persephone's future revealed to Kronos, and unknown, as yet, to Haden. Whatever the information was, Haden knew that Kronos would not share it with him. The only path was forward towards his goal. Until he delivered the souls, Persey's human clock would continue towards certain death, a death that Haden was powerless to predict or prevent.

His blindness to Persey's end compelled him to work while she slept. Each night, he escorted her back to their grand suite and waited until her body succumbed to exhaustion. Then he returned to the teeming streets below to make eternal bargains with the information she'd gathered. He didn't regret the lack of sleep. Sleep wasn't something he required. It was the thought of leaving her behind in the lonely room—which despite its sumptuous luxury—was still simply a room in a hotel.

"Someday," he would whisper to her each night after her breath became slow and steady. "Someday we will never be apart." Then he would press his lips to hers and allow himself to indulge in their softness. They were a promise of what was to come—an indulgence he found safer to partake of while she slept.

On that dark night in Central Park, she had effortlessly penetrated the core of his being. Since then he'd exercised caution. After all, it was his initial lack of caution that almost ruined his plan. Failure to grant her desire that night could have been disastrous if Persey had managed to call his bluff. She hadn't, not yet anyway. She still believed Haden had given her the gift which caused Aaron's death. Going forward, he needed to step carefully. For the bluff to continue to be successful, he needed to keep his defenses up. It should have been easy but it wasn't. There were times—like earlier when they'd kissed by the pool—when he was almost helpless to resist her. If she'd asked the right question in those moments, he would be unable to deny her the truth.

Persey trusted him. She relied upon him. If she learned the truth, her trust would be destroyed. Everything would be destroyed. Her reliance and trust grew stronger every day. Haden was certain it would soon blossom into love. When the choice was presented to her—she would choose to spend eternity with him. He was certain of it. This knowledge only fueled Haden's resolve. He reminded himself that—in this crucial stage—desire of Persephone was fraught with peril. Time spent in Persephone's embrace put their future at risk. He must exercise self-control. It was vital. Still, there were moments when he found himself powerless to resist her.

Haden didn't realize he'd been pacing back and forth until Persey emerged from her bedroom. She was dressed in the floor length black gown he'd purchased for her. Her hair was pulled up in a simple chignon.

"Turn around," he said, more severely than he intended.

She obeyed—swiveling on her high heels so he could take in the long expanse of her bare back. He smiled and drew closer despite his best intentions.

"Perfect," he said, running his hand lightly down the ridge of her spine.

She glanced at him over one shoulder. "I'm glad you like it."

He caught her under the chin, holding her in profile for another moment. Then he forced himself to relinquish her. A trace of disappointment flashed across her face and it filled him with intense desire. Forgetting his resolve—he pulled her back to him—kissing her deeply. The silky smoothness of her skin slipped beneath his fingers and he reveled in momentary abandon.

The placement of the mirror across the room was fortunate. The sight of the rough human hands searching for the delicate prize hidden beneath the black silk brought Haden to his senses. He released her and turned away. Humans weren't the only ones vulnerable during indulgence, he reminded himself yet again.

"We should go," he said, keeping his back to her.

From behind him, he could hear her rapid breath and feel the heat her body generated in response to his touch.

She was silent for a moment before she asked, "Where are we going?"

"The Oriental," he said, walking towards the door. "The hotel is hosting a dinner for a group of Asian businessmen. I believe many of the guests will be anxious to sample the pleasures offered by the City of Angels. I thought it only fitting to have them make the acquaintance of my own personal angel first. That way, I shall be better equipped to propose business arrangements personally suited to meet each one's needs."

Chapter Fifty-Seven

Daniel was discovering he had a significant amount of untapped talent at raising capital. The talent didn't surprise him. What surprised him was that—until now—he'd never thought of raising capital as a viable career option. Law school had been the respectable route—kind of like becoming a doctor without all the science. But this—this was a hell of a lot more fun than spending his nights parsing sentence meanings and his days negotiating provisions. This was fast-paced and sexy.

Which was a good thing; it couldn't happen fast enough for Rudy, since he was anxious to take the website live. In fact, it took all of Daniel's persuasive powers to convince Rudy to keep it under wraps. Rudy's actual words had been way too modest when he described the Persey Project. Daniel could already see it—in all its permutations and enormous marketing potential. He could see it just the way Rudy could.

The glitch—the hard nut that needed to be cracked—was Daniel had no intention of raising capital from any of the usual suspects. He'd been a lawyer for high flying, financial industry guys for too long. He was confident he could pitch the project to any of the typical New York players, and they would cough up the cash needed to capitalize the Persey Project. But he didn't want to go that route. He'd been down that route many times before, albeit in the role of attorney. He knew the terms required for free and ready capital. In fact, he'd written many of the documents which elegantly extracted control and future revenues from cash hungry entrepreneurs. "A document fucking"—that's how he thought of it every time he watched someone sign their rights away. No way were he and Rudy going to be on the receiving end of that type of transaction.

Since Daniel wasn't willing to pay the price extracted by the usual channels, it meant he needed to be creative.

"What do you mean by creative?" Rudy asked over lunch the next day.

Daniel laughed. "What you really mean is, what do I mean by 'we'," he said.

Rudy looked at him and shrugged his shoulders. "Well, yeah, that too."

"Let me answer the first question first," said Daniel. "The major players aren't going to mess around. You don't need any kind of special gift to realize this thing is going to change internet usage. We'd be lucky—and I mean really fucking lucky—to walk out of the closing room with anything close to fifty percent control over Confess.com. That's why I'm looking outside the typical New York, Hong Kong, Tokyo markets for a funding source that came late to the tech table, and is hungry to get in on something new."

"But…" Rudy said.

Daniel shook his head in semi-disgust. "Give me a little credit. I'm not a novice at this. It's not going to be a name you recognize but I'll do the due diligence. And by 'we'," Daniel continued, "I mean you and me. Like it or not, we're in this thing together. I'm the best person to position Confess.com—capital-wise—and you know it. Your MIT buddy, Bradley, may be able to write code but he doesn't have the skill-set to pull the rest of this deal together for you."

"Yeah, I guess you're right."

"What the fuck, man?" said Daniel, shaking his head in disbelief. "I have no intention of screwing Bradley out of the deal. You understand that's not what I was talking about, right?"

Rudy's face colored a little and he laughed. "I'm over-communicating," he said.

"Don't call it over-communication," said Daniel, grinning as he ran his hands through his dark hair. "Call it our new model of efficient conversation."

It didn't take long for Daniel to zero in on China. The entire country was searching for a foothold in the tech industry. The problem was finding someone with the right track record. They needed somebody who had experience with small capital deals and was hungry to push into the next tier. He found what he was looking for buried on the eighth page of *The Economic Times*. It was a throwaway reference to something called the Allied Asia Fund Group buried in an article about another more prominent funding group. A night of online research gave Daniel hope that the Allied Asia Fund Group might be exactly the kind of investor he had been hoping to find.

The Allied Asia Fund Group was based in Beijing. They had completed a series of small capital investments, imitating the style and deal structure of larger more successful investment groups—hence the reference in *The Economic Times*. The English version of their website was rife with typos and misspellings. It was clear the group had yet to enjoy the level of success which secured them access to the kind of well-honed scrutiny offered by Goldman Parke caliber lawyers and advisors.

They were small-market all the way and Daniel's instincts—after his first night of research—told him the Allied Asia Fund Group was ripe for a pitch on the magnitude of Confess.com. This instinct was confirmed, over the course of the next ten days, through a series of email exchanges and calls with their director, Hu Chen (or Mr. Chen as he seemed to prefer). Eleven days after discovering the existence of the Allied Asia Fund Group, Daniel boarded a flight to China. He'd been summoned to Beijing to meet Mr. Chen in person.

Beijing Capital International Airport was a cacophony of chaos. Daniel wound his way through the crowded hallways—following the symbol for taxis—only to be confronted by a mass of drivers holding up hand-written signs covered in Chinese characters interspersed with inconsistent English. He stared at the signs in confusion for a moment. As Daniel hesitated, a small man wearing a wrinkled suit, rolled up at the sleeves, appeared at his side. In one hand, the man clutched a leather briefcase and in the other, he held a lit cigarette.

"Hello Mr. Daniel. I'm Mr. Chen. I recognize you from website," said Hu Chen, transferring his cigarette to his briefcase hand so he could pump Daniel's hand up and down in greeting. "You look like American movie star."

"And you look like a Chinese businessman," said Daniel. The words came out awkwardly, despite Daniel's clear understanding this was the response Mr. Chen wanted.

"Yes, yes," Mr. Chen said beaming at Daniel. "We think the same. I think already we do good business together."

Daniel followed Mr. Chen as he made his way through the people thronging the airport walkways. Outside, cars sped through the terminal—as though they were unaware of the masses of pedestrians. They made their way through the onslaught of people and oncoming traffic until they reached a driver, slouched against an Audi with tinted windows. The driver jumped to attention at their approach.

"Is expensive car. I buy in cash," said Mr. Chen as the driver opened the back door. The driver jumped in the front seat and they screeched away from the curb, only to come to an abrupt stop fifty feet later at the tollbooth. "You smoke?" asked Mr. Chen, offering a crushed pack of cigarettes to Daniel.

"Thanks," said Daniel taking one. He hadn't had a cigarette since college but it seemed a small price to pay in the name of diplomacy.

"In China, we say air already dirty so why not smoke?" said Mr. Chen, leaning back against the leather seats of the Audi and smiling at his own witticism.

The Audi deposited them, not at the headquarters of the Allied Asia Fund Group as Daniel had expected, but, a bar.

"Is good, American-style bar," insisted Mr. Chen. One American-style bar led to another and the alcohol-fueled afternoon slipped into the evening. Later, much later, Daniel collapsed into his bed at the Beijing Grand Hyatt.

He was awakened by the shrill ring of the hotel phone. He glanced at the clock and saw it was close to three-thirty in the afternoon. "Hello," he rasped into the receiver.

"Mr. Daniel." Mr. Chen's voice came through the receiver at a volume that made Daniel hold the headset away from his ear. "We wait for you in hotel lobby."

"Alright, give me a couple of minutes," Daniel said. He quickly took a shower and changed his clothes before heading downstairs for what he already knew was to be a repeat of the previous evening.

It wasn't until Daniel's third day in Beijing that Mr. Chen brought him to the headquarters of the Allied Asia Fund Group. The headquarters were, reassuringly, located in a modern skyscraper in downtown Beijing. By the time Daniel walked into Mr. Chen's office, he'd already spent two nights drinking and pitching key members of the group. As he was ushered into the conference room with its long, shiny mahogany table, he understood—in the way that had always given him the upper hand in business dealings—he'd done what needed to be done. The money was there, now he had to close the deal.

Daniel looked at the term sheet and was pleasantly surprised to find the Allied Asia Fund Group's slim grasp on English did not extend to their understanding of the basics of capitalization. The term sheet was everything he'd been hoping for, basic terms, nothing too onerous but still enough teeth to stand up in court.

"Looks good," said Daniel, accepting the lit cigarette offered by Mr. Chen's attractive young assistant.

"Yes, it look good," said Mr. Chen nodding. Then, as if the matter was settled, he asked, "How long you stay in Beijing, Mr. Daniel?"

Although Daniel had a return ticket booked for the next morning, he understood what Mr. Chen was asking. "What do you have in mind?" he asked, leaning back in his chair.

"Ahh," said Mr. Chen, narrowing his eyes and allowing a small smile to creep onto his face. "We go to Bangkok—for pleasure, you know—for relax. Is very short flight."

"Everyone in the office?" asked Daniel, feigning surprise.

"No, no," said Mr. Chen. He raised his eyebrows to indicate the significance of the trip. "Is special, only for hard-workers."

"Like an incentive trip?"

"Yes, is right. It is incentive. You come too. Is paid for and, 'like this', we celebrate and make better partner for next time," said Mr. Chen, clasping his nicotine-stained fingers together to illustrate the point.

"Great," said Daniel, thinking of Mr. Chen's analogy three days earlier. The air was already dirty so why not smoke. He'd done enough deals to understand that every transaction had its price. In lieu of future control and distribution rights, Daniel was bargaining with carcinogens and booze tours. When you put it that way, it wasn't such a steep price to pay.

Chapter Fifty-Eight

The charter flight to Bangkok was crowded with Chinese businessmen. The men talked in loud voices and ignored the flight attendants exhortations for them to fasten their seat belts. Before the plane had lifted off the runway, the air inside the cabin was thick with cigarette smoke.

"Have you been to Thailand before?" Daniel asked Mr. Chen after the flight attendant had served him a mixed drink. "Complimentary," she said, handing it to him with a smile.

"Yes, yes," said Mr. Chen. "It is—how you say—special pleasure."

Daniel nodded and Mr. Chen seemed to take this as confirmation of his own sentiments. "Very special," he repeated. He leaned over towards the man seated on his other side and repeated the exchange. Only this time, the conversation was punctuated by pointed grunts and lewd gestures that made everyone in the immediate vicinity of their seats laugh.

Mr. Chen looked back at Daniel and said, "Xiu—he say he think Thailand girls will find Mr. American Movie Star very special pleasure." Xiu looked hopefully across the aisle at Daniel and seemed gratified when Daniel joined in the general amusement.

It was late afternoon when they arrived at the airport and located the cars waiting to take them to their hotel. They were staying at the Mandarin Oriental. The elegant old hotel had sat on its perch, above the Chao Praya River, ruling over Bangkok like a dowager queen for more than one hundred and fifty years. In the lobby, Mr. Chen told Daniel, "We meet at seven for to eat and see beautiful, Thai dancer girls." Then he departed for his room.

Daniel watched his fellow travelers disperse to their rooms with a sense of relief. He was exhausted and he reeked of cigarette smoke. But still, he wasn't quite ready to succumb to a hot shower, followed by the fresh coolness of a pillow.

Daniel wandered out of the ornate lobby and down a hallway which led to one of the original wings of the hotel. The first room he came upon was furnished in white rattan. A small plaque beside the door told him he was in the Author's Lounge. The delicate colors of the room, combined with the golden afternoon light streaming in through the windows, only served to highlight his rumpled condition. Self-consciously, he rubbed one hand against his cheek and noted he was in need of a shave. A girl in a traditional Thai gown stood in one corner of the room.

"Sawadee Ka," she said, pressing her hands together and bowing her head.

Daniel repeated the words, pressing his own hands together in imitation of her gesture.

She giggled and said kindly, "In our country it is different for men. The man say Sawadee Kup." He repeated her words again and she nodded her head in approval. "Would you like a glass of iced tea?" she asked, picking up a tray from a table behind her.

Daniel accepted the tea, then he turned to look at the black and white photos hanging upon the walls. Joseph Conrad, Somerset Maugham and Noel Coward had rested their heads at this elegant hotel. The contrast between the framed photos and his present company occurred to him. Before he had time to find it amusing, a wave of dizzying jet-lag fueled fatigue washed over him. He desperately needed a shower and some sleep. He drained the rest of the tea from his glass in one gulp. Before he could move to set the glass down, the girl was again at his side.

"Sir, please," she said, reaching to take his glass.

"Thanks." He relinquished it to her.

"Khap Khun Ka," she said with a smile.

Despite his fatigue, Daniel realized he was about to receive another lesson in Thai. He started to repeat her words but before the first foreign syllable left his lips, something caught his attention. It was no more than a fleeting impression, black fabric, blonde hair, but something about it pierced the fog of his exhaustion and made his heart leap with an emotion he hadn't felt in over a year.

He felt hope.

"Excuse me," he said, stepping around the Thai girl. He raced out of the lounge and looked down the hallway in both directions. "Persey," he shouted. His voice sounded rough against the gentle murmurings of the hotel. "Persey," he called again, ignoring the stern looks directed at him by a pair of elderly German women. Aside from the ample frames of senior Germans, the hallway was deserted. She had been headed away from the lobby. He was certain of it.

Daniel raced down the hushed, plush hallway of the old hotel. It took him to a door that led outside to a manicured garden bisected by a pebbled path. He followed the path to a boat ramp on the river.

"Can I be of assistance?" asked another young Thai woman. She was dressed in a hotel uniform and spoke with a British accent.

"Did you see a girl?" asked Daniel. "She's blonde, very beautiful. You would have noticed her. I think she was wearing a black dress."

The woman shook her head, as though she was saddened by her inability to help him. "No sir, I'm sorry."

"Are you sure?" asked Daniel.

"I haven't seen anyone come by for some time," the woman assured him.

Daniel felt in his pockets until he located a grubby piece of paper. He scribbled his room number on it and handed it to the woman. "I'm staying at the hotel. If you see her, please let me know."

"Yes sir, of course," said the woman, taking the paper. As he turned to leave, she pressed her hands together and executed a graceful little bow of her head.

Chapter Fifty-Nine

It was all about efficiency and balance. Those two words were fast becoming Haden's new mantra. He needed to harvest souls as quickly as possible, and Persephone was essential to this plan. With the information he learned from her, he was able to convince almost everyone he approached to trade their eternity for some small token to be enjoyed during their short lifetime. It was balance that was the problem. He hadn't anticipated Persephone's use of her special talents would have an effect on her. He was aware the secrets were taking a toll. At the end of her long evenings spent listening to tales in bars, she radiated sadness and fatigue, fraught with something else. It was the unidentifiable something else that was most worrisome to Haden.

He could sense something stirring deep within her soul. It was something wild and uncontrollable. He understood he needed to treat her with more caution in order to avoid waking it. What Haden didn't understand was whether it was something that had always been inside of Persey—waiting for an opportunity to present itself—or whether it was something he had created by forcing her repeated exposure to the darkest parts of the human soul.

Although Haden wasn't given to soul searching, he was beginning to have misgivings about his methods. Persephone was a human. As such, it should be a simple thing to exert control over her. However, the thing awakening inside of her caused him to question his ultimate influence. He told himself the notion of a mere mortal—however beautiful and otherworldly—influencing an immortal, was ridiculous. It was impossible. He was sure of it. Still, the cold fingers of doubt paid him more frequent visits.

It was this concern, combined with Persey's general fatigue, which led Haden to switch tactics. Businessman, he decided, were just as ripe with confessions as sex trade workers and their clientele. Even more so, he thought as he contemplated the face of the body he currently occupied in the mirror.

This body belonged to a businessman who had possessed the typical business desire—he'd wanted money, nothing else. Greed was a powerful motivating force. It was possible Haden wouldn't even need Persey's special talents tonight. Greed was an acceptable twenty-first century vice that few bothered to keep secret. He only hoped this particular vice wouldn't provide any more fodder for the awakening emotions that lurked within his intended bride.

Tonight, two hundred businesspeople were expected to dine in the exclusive restaurant situated on a small island in the middle of the Chao Praya River. They were two hundred people, with the potential for vulnerability, who might soon join the ever-mounting ranks of souls to be sacrificed in pursuit of Persephone's immortality.

Their taxi made its way underneath the Oriental's protective awning. They stopped and Haden held his hand out to Persey to assist her out of the cab. A doorman held open the ornate hotel doors, which harkened back to colonial occupation, and Haden led Persey through the coolness of the lobby and down a hallway leading to the oldest part of the hotel. He opened a door at the end of the hallway, and once again, they passed outside into the heat.

"I thought we were having dinner at the hotel," said Persey, glancing back in the direction they'd come. Her cool fingers, pressed into the flesh of his borrowed body's elbow, pulled Haden from his thoughts.

"We are," said Haden, smiling at her. "Would you like to see the gardens first? Come and I'll show you." He led her down a pebbled path, veering off on a smaller—little used—path. They walked, past the Cassia Fistula trees covered in yellow flowers and underneath fragrant Golden Shower trees, until they came to a hedge maze. It was marked by enormous bushes meticulously clipped into the shapes of fantastical elephants, tigers and snakes.

"It's charming," said Persey, smiling at him.

"I thought you'd like it," he said. He pointed out across the river. "The restaurant is there, on that island."

They returned to the main path and followed it down to the water where a black lacquered boat decorated with carved dragon heads and lit with lanterns awaited them.

"It's beautiful here," said Persey as they boarded the boat. She looked up at him, her eyes guileless and yet searching.

Haden wondered what those eyes sought before desire overwhelmed him. For the second time that evening, he succumbed to need. He pressed his lips against hers, reveling in their soft fullness and allowing her presence in his arms to wipe away all his earlier worries. Their boat touched the bank of the island with a gentle bump and Haden moved reluctantly away from Persey. The boat attendant hopped over the side of the boat and moored it to a small dock. Then he climbed back aboard and opened the hinged black lacquer door. Haden took Persey's hand and led her onto the island.

The restaurant was decorated in traditional Thai style. The tables were low and made of polished teak. The walls were hung with silk tapestries depicting ancient Thai legends and stories. It was early but people were already beginning to filter inside as more and more boats delivered their human cargo onto the dock of the small private island.

"I'll get you a drink," Haden said.

He walked over to the bar, leaving Persey behind to watch the graceful movements of the Thai women, each wearing traditional Thai garb and dancing in stylized formation at the front of the room. The bar was already crowded with Chinese businessmen. Haden pushed his way through the men until he reached the front and placed his order. The bartender brought him their drinks. Haden was about to pick them up and return to Persey when he overheard a conversation that made him set the drinks back down on the bar.

A Chinese man in a shabby suit was speaking in rapid Mandarin to another man. "Tell me the name again," asked the second man.

Haden felt his shabby-suited neighbor surreptitiously assess him and then dismiss him as a non-speaker of Mandarin.

"Confess.com," replied shabby-suit in hushed Mandarin.

"How does it work?" asked the friend.

"The technology is proprietary," answered the man. "But they've created a website that accurately predicts the end user's preferences."

"For what?"

"For everything," was the gleeful response.

"It's not possible."

"Yes, yes, it is," said the first man, almost unable to restrain his excitement. "Our team has already finished their initial analysis of the test results. It's amazing. It predicts choice of girlfriend, what consumers want to buy. It reveals all, even what most would not want revealed. They've given us access to a limited-use test sight. I tried it myself. It knows me—like a mother. You will try it and see for yourself."

As Haden listened to the exchange his mind started to spin. Was it possible that something like this existed? Not only would it solve his problems, it could open up a whole new world of unforeseen possibilities and opportunities. A website with the ability to reveal that which most would not want revealed. The thought made the extremities of Haden's human body tingle. If such a thing existed then he must master it. It would bring about his success and so much more. An hour ago, he'd quivered with anticipation at the thought of two hundred souls. He realized how paltry that was in comparison to the vast reaches of a website.

A website could reach millions, even billions of people. If he could control the information extracted, he would have insights into humanity beyond the wildest dreams of any immortal. He would have Persey at his side and, heretofore, unimagined power. He would be even more powerful than Kronos! The thought of his father—the ruler of immortals, eternally hungry for destruction and pain—made him clench his fists in hatred. Haden took a deep breath, savoring the moment. The hour of his success was at hand.

"Excuse me," he said in formal Mandarin to the rumpled businessman at his side. The man turned towards him wearing a comical expression of surprise. He hadn't expected the western face to his right to be able to speak Mandarin. "I have to admit I've been eavesdropping. I'm not sure if you're looking for any additional investors in your project but if you're interested," here Haden handed the man one of his business cards. "I'm in the business of funding start-ups. Based on what I've already overheard, it sounds like your project would be a good fit with the rest of my company's investment profile."

The man looked at the business card. Haden saw him register a smile of recognition at the company name and the title of chief executive officer printed underneath Haden's name. "Of course," Haden continued, "typically, we focus on large capitalization projects but if yours is as interesting as it sounds, I might be willing to make an exception." As though the words "large capitalization" spurred him to movement, the other man fumbled in his pocket and managed to pull out a business card of his own.

"Hu Chen," he said, handing it to Haden with a broad grin. "I am Director of Allied Asia Fund Group."

Chapter Sixty

Persey stood alone in the middle of the room. She had hoped that tonight would be different. It sounded different when Haden told her about it. Yet—here she was again—alone amidst the circling sharks. She knew she wouldn't be alone for long but that knowledge did nothing to stem her tide of loneliness.

"Let me guess, you're American," said a male voice behind her.

And so it begins, thought Persey, turning around without bothering to disguise her reluctance. The speaker was Asian with a British accent. He looked to be about her age and was tall with handsome features. "What gave me away?" she asked without allowing her eyes to meet his.

"Nothing, until now," he said with a laugh. "I suppose it was cheating a bit to put it that way. I'm a good sport, though. If you like, I'm happy to guess which state you call home. That should be a bit more challenging."

"I'd let you," said Persey, her thoughts returned to the windswept plains of Iowa where she'd spent the first eighteen years of her life. "The only thing is, I don't really know anymore."

"I understand completely," he said, glancing back down at his drink.

Something in the gesture made her anxious to prolong the encounter. "Are you Thai?" she asked.

"No," he answered. Before she could say anything else, he gestured towards the bar and asked, "Is that your boyfriend, over there?"

"I don't really know that either," she said, allowing herself to glance up at his warm brown eyes.

"Ah-ha, now I understand. We're playing the game of questions, where we compete to see who can give the least informative responses. I've guessed it, haven't I?" he said.

"I'm not really familiar with that game."

"I knew it," he said and she couldn't help but laugh. "I'm very quick at this sort of thing, you know," he added.

The room was becoming crowded and Persey could feel the interested stares her laughter had provoked. "I'm Persephone," she said, holding her hand out to the man.

"Walter, Walter Yu," he said, shaking her hand. "Were your parents, by any chance, scholars of Greek mythology?"

Before she could respond, she felt a soft touch on her elbow.

"Excuse me, Madame," said a Thai woman outfitted in the hotel uniform. "I'm so sorry to interrupt," she added, twisting her hands together. "I did not tell him you were here but he seemed so very," the woman paused searching her English for the right word. "Concerned," she said at last. "My boss say he seemed very concerned to speak to you—very, very concerned," she stressed as she thrust a small piece of wrinkled paper into Persey's hands. Before Persey could respond, the woman pressed her hands together in the traditional Thai bow and then turned and melted back into the crowd until she was lost to sight.

"How very mysterious," Walter said with a wink. "Aren't you going to read it?"

Slowly, as if in a dream, Persey unfolded the grubby piece of paper and read the four hastily scrawled words.

Daniel Hartnett   Room 314

For a moment there was nothing else—nothing but the piece of paper she held in her shaking hands. Then the answer to

Walter's question came to her as though she'd known it all along. Home wasn't Clear Lake or Bangkok. It wasn't the place where you grew up or lived. Home was where you loved and were loved in return. She hadn't thought about Daniel since she'd left the safe haven of his home. It was pointless and painful, so she'd locked it all away. She'd convinced herself that life as she knew it had ended on that cold night in Central Park. But it hadn't. There were three days that passed between Aaron's death and the time Haden had come to collect on his bargain. She'd been pretending those three days hadn't happened. But they had. The note in her hand had opened the door to all the feelings she'd locked away. They came flooding back and threatened to overwhelm her with their intensity. Daniel! Daniel was here and she knew she had to see him.

"Persephone?" Instinctively, she crumpled the piece of paper in her palm. "Persephone, are you alright?"

It took her a moment to recognize the voice. She looked up and her eyes met Walter's. He was staring at her with concern. "Don't call me that," she said. Her voice sounded harsh and her breath came in jagged little gasps.

"Are you quite alright?" he asked again. He seemed on the verge of flagging down someone for assistance. She couldn't let him do that. It would catch Haden's attention.

"Are you staying at the hotel?" she asked, training her eyes upon him.

"Yes," he said without hesitation.

"I need to get off this island without anyone seeing. Can you help me?"

Walter nodded almost mechanically. He held out his hand to her. She took it, and keeping her head down, followed him as he negotiated the crowded room. They entered the kitchen and left the restaurant by a back door. A man was loitering outside the door smoking a cigarette and Walter spoke to him in rapid Thai.

"I've sent him for a boat," he said, turning back to her.

Despite her agitation, Persey looked at him in surprise. "You're not Thai," she said.

"No," he said with a smile. "But I speak a little."

The memory of Haden's facile ability with language came to her, making her instantly distrustful. "Who are you?" she asked. Once again she allowed her eyes to meet his, plumbing their depths.

"My father's a real estate developer," said Walter. "He owns chains of hotels—the rather nice ones. He's attempting a takeover of this one." He swallowed hard shaking his head. "You're not meant to know that. I don't know why I told you? It's all still very top secret."

From across the water, she could see the light of the boat heading toward them. It slid silently through the water until it bumped up against the dock with a soft wooden thump.

"Do you want me to come with you?" Walter asked.

Persey shook her head. "No, you should stay here," she said as she stepped onboard. "And Walter," she whispered into the darkness, "don't worry about what you told me. I'm good at keeping secrets."

Chapter Sixty-One

Daniel fell asleep for longer than he intended and awoke with a headache. His dreams had been a continual loop of his glimpse of the phantom Persey. In his sleep, he'd chased her down that long hallway only to lose sight of her time and again.

He showered for the third time that day and located some fresh clothes. As he dressed, he glanced at his watch and winced. Eight-thirty—he hoped Mr. Chen wasn't big on punctuality. Outside his room, a young Thai boy, no older than sixteen, sat dozing on a chair. At the sound of Daniel's door opening, he sprung up from his seat.

"Good evening sir, Sawadee kup," he said, making the greeting sound like a military salute. Unsure of the proper response, Daniel smiled and handed the boy a fifty baht note. "Khap khun kup," said the boy as he accepted the bill and bowed.

The concierge directed him past the Author's Lounge and down the same hall he'd visited earlier in the day. A boat was waiting for him at the dock and he boarded it. He couldn't help but wonder if Persey had disappeared earlier on this same boat. As he stepped onto the island, Daniel pushed all thought of Persey aside. He was jet-lagged and exhausted. His mind was playing tricks on him. The reason he had flown halfway around the world was to do business—get the deal done and that was exactly what he intended to do.

He headed toward the crowded restaurant lit with swaying lanterns. It didn't take him long to locate Mr. Chen. He was seated at a table with several other members of the Allied Asia Fund Group. Across from Mr. Chen sat a tall westerner who conversed with the rest of the group in easy Mandarin.

"Daniel," called Mr. Chen, waving as Daniel made his way toward the table. "Tonight we celebrate." He handed Daniel a shot glass brimming with amber liquid. "To continued success and funding." He clinked his glass to Daniel's and they downed the respective contents while the mysterious westerner watched. Mr. Chen wiped his mouth with the back of his hand and then turned his attention back to the table. "Daniel, I introduce to you Haden Black. He is very interested in our project." He refilled another shot glass and slid it across the table to Haden. Before Daniel could protest, Mr. Chen refilled the glass Daniel still held in his hand.

Haden nodded at Daniel and raised his shot glass. "To Confess.com," he said and downed it in one motion.

Daniel's hand froze halfway to his mouth. Then—before anyone noticed—he followed suit. "I take it you like what you've heard?" he asked, hoping his voice didn't betray any of what he'd just heard.

Haden nodded. "Very much so. I've told your partners I'd be willing to double their initial investment."

"Very generous," said Daniel. "What kind of terms are we looking at?"

Haden shook his head as though the terms didn't particularly interest him. "I'm happy to sign on to whatever Allied Asia has already negotiated." Haden glanced at Mr. Chen who smiled and nodded at him. "It's the website's potential that interests me. I'd want access to the end-users. I'm a market research guy at heart," he added with a congenial smile.

"Sounds like we could do business," said Daniel. His heart was pounding in his chest. It was miraculous everyone at the table couldn't hear it.

"Indeed," said Haden.

As they spoke, a cold trickle of sweat made its way down Daniel's back that had nothing to do with the sultry evening or crowded room. Daniel had never seen this man before. He was certain of it. Yet, the man knew him—instantly recognized him.

He heard it from the moment the man first opened his mouth. The meanings behind this man's words were excruciating and incomprehensible—like nothing Daniel had ever encountered. It was more than just meaning. The man's words produced pictures in his head.

He saw a vision of himself reading in his apartment, as though he was outside looking in. Then Daniel felt a suffocating wave of hatred and he understood, better than he'd ever understood anything before, that the man he was talking to knew and despised him. He could feel the meaning behind Haden's words as though they were reaching out to him, slithering around his throat, in hopes of ensnaring and choking him. The clarity and depth made him feel nauseous.

Then—just as he'd glimpsed her outside of the Author's Lounge—Haden's words brought forth Persey. This time it was much more than a glimpse. She radiated through Daniel's brain. She was dressed in a black silk dress. Her smile, her hair, her eyes, the image of her made his heart ache. Had he really expected to see her again? He'd said he was but he was unprepared for the painful surge of longing and loss that shot through him, as the images of her played through his mind. Persey was still alive and this man named Haden knew where she was. Daniel needed to keep him talking.

"So you're a market research guy." He forced the words out hoping they sounded casual.

Haden pulled out a card and handed in to Daniel. "Like I told your partner, I do mostly large cap stuff, but I'd be willing to make an exception for this project."

It was the project. That's what he was interested in. He needed it for Persey. There was something else there. Daniel needed Haden to keep talking. He needed to learn more but Haden was already standing up.

"We'll be in contact, then," he said with a smile that didn't penetrate his eyes.

She was somewhere close. Daniel could hear it. The image of her in the black dress blazed through his brain once more. Haden was leaving to go find her.

"Absolutely," said Daniel shaking the hand Haden held out to him. "Good to meet you," he added.

"You too," said Haden.

Daniel heard the final piece. Soon Persey would be Haden's forever but right now there was still a way out.

Haden turned and walked quickly through the crowd. Daniel watched him go for a moment before plunging into the crowded room after him. Haden would lead him to Persey. He'd heard it. Daniel followed him, not stopping to think or care about what he would do when he found her. He could see Haden up ahead moving through the drunken businessmen. Then—almost as if Daniel had blinked and missed it—Haden disappeared. His tall form seemed to meld into the crowd and in an instant he was gone.

Daniel pushed his way through the room in the direction Haden had taken in a vain effort to relocate his target. A man in a hotel uniform stood to one side of the restaurant's front door. "Did a man just pass by here?" he asked the hotel employee. "He was tall, white skin like me?" The man shook his head in apology. Daniel walked out the front door and looked out at the quiet river in defeat. Where had Haden gone? He'd disappeared like magic—like he wasn't human. A wave of comprehension swept over Daniel. That was it. That was why the meanings behind the words had been unlike anything he'd ever experienced. Haden wasn't human!

The realization triggered a memory of Persey. It was the first morning after Aaron's death. Daniel remembered the way she looked in his bed, her hair still matted with blood. Her eyes had connected to his and she'd been afraid. She blamed herself for Aaron's death. He'd told her it was an accident but there was something else—something she'd said. He remembered it now.

She'd said, "He gave me a gift." She thought she'd been given a gift and it caused Aaron's death. It was a ridiculous idea. It had been an accident—a horrible accident but still an accident. She couldn't blame herself. He wouldn't let her. Daniel had written off the strange conversation to shock.

But now, as if hearing the conversation for the first time he heard himself ask, "Who gave the gift to you?"

She'd hesitated—her dark blue eyes sweeping the room as though looking for an escape, but then she'd looked at him and answered his question. "Haden," she'd said.

All along, she'd been trying to tell him something. He just hadn't been listening to her.

Chapter Sixty-Two

Persey knew she didn't have much time. Haden would find her. He could always find her, much the same way death finds and lays claim to its victims. She raced down the halls of the old hotel. In the lobby, she pushed the elevator button then paced back and forth as the ornate elevator opened in slow motion. Had Haden noticed her absence yet? It was only a matter of time. He would come searching for her. She knew she didn't have long but maybe there would be enough time to say good-bye.

Her mother, the father she had never known and Aaron—everyone she'd ever loved. They were all dead and gone. Soon she would be the one who was gone. This was her last chance, her only chance to tell Daniel good-bye. She had to find him. She already understood she wasn't just saying good-bye to Daniel. This was a good-bye to everything that could have been. It was a farewell to the life they could have made together, and the person she might have been.

Haden had told her she would learn to love him. He loved her, inasmuch as he could love anything. Persey knew this. She understood now that love could take many forms. Haden's love for her felt like ownership. He loved her as a thing to be used and manipulated at his will. She also knew what she felt for Haden still wasn't love. It was more like acceptance. She'd grown to accept the inevitability of their future together, much as the terminal cancer patient comes to accept the inevitability of death. She'd lost the strength to keep Haden out of her soul. Or maybe she'd just realized it was impossible. His kisses still made her skin crawl with equal parts longing and revulsion.

It worried her that the longing had begun to grow stronger and the revulsion, well, it had turned into something she didn't quite understand. She knew the time was coming when she would be unable to resist him. She would give herself to him heart and soul, as he once predicted she would. Once she succumbed to him, she would never be able to come back. The darkness of other people's secrets and the dark thing inside her, longing to be appeased, would take over. This was her last chance to say good-bye.

She stopped in front of the door marked 314. Now that she was here, so close, she was nervous. She opened up the crumpled ball of paper in her hand reassuring herself once more of the correct room number before knocking on the door. She pressed her ear against the wooden barrier between them and listened. Inside all was quiet; no soft murmurings of the television, no footsteps on the other side.

"Daniel," she called, pounding on the door. Maybe he was sleeping. In the pit of her stomach, doubt took over. The hot tears that accompanied it slid down her cheeks. "Daniel," she called again, pounding upon the door, refusing to believe she could come so close and still fail. "Daniel," she called once more but knew the room was empty. She slid down until her body touched the floor. She pressed her forehead against the door as though it had some comfort to offer. "Daniel," she cried again, but this time the word had the sound of defeat.

A hand touched her shoulder, making her jump. "Persephone," said a voice quietly from behind her.

"No," she said, shaking her head. Her time was up. She'd lost. He'd come for her and now he would take her away again. "No, no, no, I won't go. I won't," she cried, refusing to look at him. She buried her face in her arms. He would have to carry her away—wrench her from the spot.

"Good God," said the voice. "She's absolutely terrified."

It took a moment for the words to register. Almost not daring to believe her ears, Persey raised her head and looked behind her. "Walter?" she said in a tone of disbelief.

He raised his eyebrows. "Here we are again. I can't remember when I've had such an unenthusiastic reception."

Persey looked at him. She was incredulous. "I was expecting someone else."

"Clearly," said Walter. A boy of about sixteen in a hotel uniform was standing behind him. Walter turned to the boy and gestured at the door. "Let her in, then."

"He's not here," said Persey.

"Yes, but he should be along any minute now," said Walter, glancing at his watch. Then, in answer to her unspoken question he added, "You seemed quite... how was it put? Oh, yes, concerned to speak with Daniel Hartnett. One good turn deserves another, and in light of my unfortunate revelation, I thought it might be wise to get my good turn in as soon as possible. Som was quite helpful," continued Walter as the boy held open the door for them. "I must say service at the Mandarin surpasses even its own reputation. It makes the prospect we discussed earlier all the more interesting."

Walter said more but Persey wasn't listening, coming down the hallway was a familiar face. One she had almost abandoned hope of ever seeing again. He looked tired and somehow older. But it was unmistakably him.

"Persey," he said. Halting in his tracks, he looked at her as though he didn't quite trust his eyes.

Walter turned around. "Right then, okay," he said, giving a brisk little wave before retreating down the hallway with Som following behind.

"Persey," Daniel repeated, and in one sudden movement she was in his arms. He pulled her into his room. The door closed behind them with a soft click and they were alone.

He held her there in his arms rocking her like a small child. "I thought I'd never see you again," he whispered, drying her tears with the cuff of his sleeve. There were so many things she wanted to say and yet all she could do was cling to him. She basked in the warmth of his arms as his lips touched hers. Their softness and warmth was like an antidote to the cold worm of grudging acceptance of her fate that had twisted itself into her soul.

"Daniel," she whispered, touching her hand to his face. She pulled away from his kiss so she could look into his eyes. "We don't have much time," she whispered. "He's coming for me. Before he comes I need you to know how much I love you..."

"I love you, too," he interrupted.

"I love you but I can't stay with you," she continued. Her voice sounded small and choked. "I made him a promise and he came to collect." She searched his eyes desperately looking for some indication he understood what she was saying.

"We can be together," he said.

"No, no," said shaking her head.

Before she could continue, he pressed a finger to her lips. "Listen to me, Persey," he said and his voice was urgent. "I know your secret. I know people tell you things. I also know about Haden. I understand what you were trying to tell me that morning after Aaron died."

"How do..." she started to ask, but Daniel cut her off.

"You were right. He's coming for you. We don't have much time. Go back to him, but before you go, there's something you need to understand. Haden has a secret too. There's still a way out. I know you can make him tell you. You have to make him tell you because..." his voice faltered and he looked away.

She finished the sentence for him. "Because once I become his, I can never come back."

Daniel shook his head as though to deny the truth of her words, then he repeated, "I know you can make him tell you."

For the first time since coming to Thailand, Persey was filled with hope. It flooded through her, making her impatient. She knew what she needed to do. "You're right. I can," she said.

Instead of releasing her, Daniel tightened his grip on her hands as though he had no intention of ever letting her leave. "I wish I could go for you," he said.

"We both know you can't," she said. "It's something only I can do." She pulled her hands out of his. "I have to go now," she said. "He'll come looking for me and he can't find me here. If he does, he won't trust me. If I'm going to find out what he's hiding, I need him to trust me." She stood up and walked toward the door. Daniel followed her.

"I'll be here waiting for you," he said.

She turned and kissed him one last time. "I love you, Daniel," she whispered. Then she ran down the hallway away from him before she lost her courage.

Chapter Sixty-Three

Outside the hotel, taxis were queued up and ready for passengers. Persey slipped into a waiting backseat and handed the cab driver the address of her hotel. As the car sped away, she sank back and prepared herself for what she was about to do.

She'd known Haden had a secret. What she hadn't fully understood was that his secret was the key to her freedom. Now, it was all so clear. The way he avoided her eyes, the way he passionately kissed her one moment, only to push her aside the next. He'd been hiding something from her. There was a way out but he hadn't wanted her to know. She still had a chance at freedom. Just the thought, the mere inkling of hope made her heart pound hard in her chest.

She had to be strong. He had told her right from the beginning that he would reveal everything to her when she was ready. She had to convince Haden now was the time—she was ready to become his. It was the only way she would be able to convince him to drop his defenses and reveal what he was hiding within. It was her only chance at learning his secret. Secrets were weakness. It was a lesson she'd learned from Haden. Now her future depended on passing the upcoming test.

The taxi stopped at a red light and the driver caught Persey's eye in the rear view mirror. She looked away quickly but it was too late.

"I have many unpaid parking tickets," he said as though he was commenting on the weather. "I gamble away my money. Tonight, I will probably lose everything I've earned and my wife will grow to hate me even more than she already does."

Persey looked back at him in the mirror. "Why do you gamble if it's ruining your life?" she asked.

"It is—how to say—I am not able to stop," he said.

"We all have things inside of us that are hard to control," she said as she met his gaze. "It's the choices we make in our moments of weakness that define who we are. In the end, each of us decides what kind of life we will live. Do you understand?"

He looked at her with surprise. "Yes," he said, ignoring the sound of the horns blaring behind them.

"Good," she said. Then she added, "The light's green. If you don't mind, I'm in a hurry."

She walked through the dark granite lobby of their hotel, where techno music played in an endless loop, and the attractive employees nodded and smiled at the guests. It all faded into the background. An essential change had occurred in the back of the taxi cab. She'd heard the driver's darkest secrets and for the first time in her life she'd done more than listen. She'd spent her entire life avoiding other people's secrets. In Bangkok, she had learned to listen.

All her life she'd been a passive listener—a vessel. But it didn't have to be that way. With her or without her, people she met would still have their secrets and their darkness. They gave her information and she had a choice. There was nothing she could do to change the past. Her role was to guide their future.

The elevator delivered her to the penthouse floor and she let herself into the luxurious suite. By now, it was familiar but it still wasn't home. She walked into her dressing room and deftly pulled out the pins that held up her chignon. She shook her head and ran her fingers through her hair, until it fell in loose curls on her shoulders. She still wore the black dress Haden had given her. She considered changing into a dressing gown or some of the more seductive lingerie that lay on her shelves—still unworn and wrapped in tissue paper—but then rejected the idea. It might give too much away. She wouldn't give Haden any reason to question what had precipitated her sudden change of heart. If anybody was going to keep secrets tonight, it would be her.

Persey walked back out into the living area of the suite. She pressed one cheek to the window and looked out at the glistening city spread below. Despite the aggressive hotel air conditioning system, through the window, she could still feel a whisper of warmth from the night. She closed her eyes. Out there—through the crowds and the hot, exotic heat—was Daniel. He was waiting for her and she was waiting for Haden.

Chapter Sixty-Four

It had been an interesting night, a very interesting night. Haden was ready to celebrate and the only thing he lacked was Persephone. He couldn't deny his initial vision of Daniel Hartnett's death had nagged at him over the last year. The man was fated to die in Persephone's arms. This was the disturbing vision that made him retreat into the darkness on the night of Aaron's death. The knowledge had ruined his night and the days that followed it. What should have been a night spent in celebration, as he consoled his beloved for her loss, stretched into several days of contemplation. What did Daniel's death mean for Persephone? She could alter her own fate. He knew they all had the power to alter their own fate but how would the change of her fate affect Daniel's? When fates were intertwined, what happened when one person chose to change their end?

This was the first time Haden had cared about a human enough to have cause to wrestle with this particular problem. After much agonizing thought, he realized the question was, at best, unanswerable. Once he achieved his goal, the question would be irrelevant. If Persey agreed to alter her fate, Daniel's end would lay the question to rest. He made the decision to press forward with his plan because once Persey made her choice, Daniel Hartnett wouldn't matter anymore.

And now, he'd had the good fortune to meet Daniel again. He was anxious to study Daniel's end again to see if any change had occurred. While the unsuspecting human engaged in business talk, Haden carefully studied his last moments. There they were. He saw it again as he had that first night on East 23rd street. Persephone held Daniel in her arms. She was young, beautiful and full of life. The man she held in her arms was an older version of the man who stood in front of him. Haden watched as she bent down and whispered something into Daniel's ear. She looked back up, waiting patiently for his final moments. Her face showed no sign of tears or remorse. It was the same face Haden had looked upon every day in Thailand. That was it! The import of the vision came to him all of a sudden. Persephone was unchanged.

The meaning of it started to sink in. The last time, he hadn't looked carefully enough. Time had moved on for Daniel but not for Persephone. Daniel's death was nothing less than the vision of Haden's own success. She was immortal. This vision could only have one meaning—she'd chosen to alter her fate and accompany him into the eternal land of the immortals. Now that Haden knew about the website it all made sense. Of course—Daniel and Persephone's fates were linked. It was the website.

They were joined by the website—the wonderful website which would soon give Haden access to all the souls he desired. Daniel's website would prove to be essential for the realization of their eternal union. As such, his death would be a sad day for Persephone. Someday, Haden would allow his wife to return to the land of the living to mourn this man. She would want to say good-bye. It explained why she wasn't wracked with grief. She was already beginning to display her immortal indifference to the small matters of human life and death.

Haden was almost unable to contain his excitement as he headed back towards the hotel. This was a moment for celebration. He had held back for so long but now he had the confirmation he needed. He was sure of her. At last, he could afford to lavish every generosity and indulgence upon his fair Persephone. He ignored the polite bows of the night concierge and the employees as he swept through the lobby.

All his energy was focused on one thing—Persephone. He could feel her. She was thirty-two floors above him in the suite he'd grown to think of as home. She was his. Why had she left without telling him where she was going? Had she been overcome with fatigue? It didn't matter now. Nothing mattered. He was freed from the duty of collecting souls. Tonight, he would luxuriate in the pleasure of watching her sleep. He stepped off the elevator and eased the door open so as not to disturb her slumber.

He needn't have worried because she was waiting for him.

"Haden," she said. She turned away from the windows as he entered. He let the door close behind him and walked towards her. Her eyes lingered on his and they contained a strange new hunger he'd never seen before. This time he made no effort to look away. He knew the future and she was his.

"You left," he said.

"Did I worry you?" she asked. Before he could answer, she added, "I knew you'd come find me."

"Like I always do."

"Yes," she said moving closer to him, "like you always do." She reached up and touched her hand to his face. "All this time and the only piece of you I've seen are your eyes." She pressed her body against his and despite his extended use of this particular human's body, it felt foreign and awkward. "Don't hide from me anymore," she whispered. "Take me—let me see inside of you. I'm tired of waiting."

He caught her in his arms with a swiftness that made her gasp. Her eyes were locked upon his. They didn't waver, as she pressed herself against him, urging him forward.

He'd been patient and now she would be his. "Persephone," he breathed. "Nothing will ever separate us. You have my promise. We will be together forever." His lips touched hers and this time he didn't hold back.

He had glimpsed the crucial moment in her future. Death would not claim her. He would achieve her immortality and they would be together forever. He opened himself to her without reservation and felt her delve into his darkness. He experienced one moment of caution as he remembered the night their lips first met in the cold darkness of a city on the other side of the world—but it was already too late.

Chapter Sixty-Five

The moment Persey heard the mechanical click and hum of the suite's front door; she knew her wait was over. The rest of her life would depend upon the next few moments. She turned to face Haden and was met with a terrifying spectacle. Light radiated, out of his every orifice, throwing his features into grotesque relief. The glow coming from within only served to emphasize the fragility and temporary nature of his borrowed body. It was as if the human shell that hosted him was no longer capable of containing the terrible power secreted within.

He moved towards her and Persey felt her heard pound in her chest. This was her chance—her only chance. She didn't know what had caused the sudden change in Haden. The only thing she knew for certain is Daniel was out there waiting for her. This wasn't a time for fear; it was a time for action. She forced herself to focus on Haden's words. She moved closer to him, pinning her eyes upon the horror contained within his. She would no longer be a passive vessel. The past was finished. There was only the future. His secrets were hers to find.

She reached her hand out to touch his face. Beneath her fingers, his skin burned radiating heat. "Haden," she said. Her eyes met his and words slipped from her lips as though, all along, she'd known what she would need to say. The heat of his body was no longer repulsive. It called to her—beckoning her towards the ultimate darkness contained in his eyes. She was barely aware of his touch as he pulled her into his arms. Everything she'd known prior to this moment disappeared.

A whole new future opened up before her as he proclaimed, "We will be one, my dear Persephone, entwined together for all eternity." His voice was choked with passion—making it sound deeper, less human. His lips fell upon hers, and once again she experienced the swirling vortex of darkness she'd first tasted on the night of Aaron's death.

Haden's kiss contained an eternity of secrets and suffering. It was no different than she remembered—just as dreadful and terrifying. Except this time, she was prepared for the horror it contained. She opened herself to Haden as though darkness was her fate without end or beginning. Wrapped in his kiss, she plunged deep into his abyss of death and dread. The darkness inside of her throbbed and swelled. It expanded, growing stronger, flexing itself like a muscle aching to be used. It was her hidden monster—cold and cruel. It responded without question to the call of darkness within Haden and he gave it free reign. He welcomed her dark monster into the deepest regions of his consciousness without fully understanding the consequences.

They were surrounded by a cold gray mist. The darkness was in control. It had brought them to this place.

"Where are we?" Persey demanded. Her voice was cold and brutal. The darkness has infected her throat and Persey understood she didn't have long before it consumed whatever was left of her humanity.

"You are in the kingdom of the dead," said a voice. She turned towards the voice and for the first time she saw his immortal form. It glowed brilliant as a sun in the middle of the blackest night.

"Haden?" she whispered overcome with awe. He stood before her in all his magnificent glory. The light she had seen pouring from his human body had consumed him. He was a beacon—radiating light and heat throughout the cold mist. Persey realized every other living creature she'd seen before was a sad imitation of what she looked upon at this moment. He moved to her side and took her hand.

"Do not be frightened, my Persephone. I welcome you to my kingdom. Together, we will pass eternity at each other's sides."

The small piece of Persey's remaining humanity fought its way to the surface before the dark queen residing within her could squelch it. "Is this Hell?" it asked.

"Not as you understand it," answered Haden. He led her through the mist that surrounded them. She could feel the dry touch of souls swirling in their wake as they moved. "All souls meet their judgment here. I walk among them and judge them before they are sent to their destiny." He paused and gestured out through the mist illuminating the darkness. "They welcome you," he said smiling at her. "They feel your call. Or maybe it is you who are called to them." He studied her, waiting for his meaning to become clear.

Every soul that had ever existed was here in this place. Already, Persey could feel the darkest souls creeping closer through the surrounding mist. They were approaching, encroaching, ready to envelope her. All of a sudden Haden's words made sense. It was her darkness. It was the monster inside her that had brought her to this place and called to these souls.

"It isn't all like this, is it?" she asked. Her voice was weak. In another moment, her human strength would be gone.

"No my love, it's not," said Haden. Even as he spoke, Persey ceased to care about any other place, any other moment than the one they were in. Her humanity was dying. In its stead grew a ravenous inhuman desire.

The evil and weakness of the soul's that surrounded her called to the thing inside of her. She was seized with insatiable desire to feed off of them—devour them.

"They desire me and I shall make them mine," said her monster. Persey felt her face stretch into a cold, hungry smile.

Haden shook his head. He held her by one hand and—although his touch was light—his strength was such that he effortlessly held her back. "No, my dear Persephone," he said. "You are correct that these souls are filled with evil. But they have already met their fate as ordained by the natural law. Even ones such as us must abide by the law that commands both mortals and immortals alike. It is only the souls who choose to alter their fate that we can use as we desire. Come, I will show you," said Haden, pulling her deeper into the darkness.

"We are almost to that place you call Hell. This is the place where souls exist at our mercy and for our pleasure." The pungent hatred and despair experienced by these souls was palpable. They swirled around her madly, begging for release. "These are the souls who have given themselves to us. These, you may think of as your own. Satisfy yourself with them however you desire," Haden told her. Her sense of their desperation and agony faded away, and in its place, she felt an all-consuming, burning need to experience their darkness, feed upon it.

"Come to me," she whispered. Her words, her voice, her presence pulled the souls to her. They were helpless to resist her. Already, she could feel their darkness—their pain and suffering without end, as it coursed through her body. It would burgeon and grow—making her stronger. She could feel the hard surge of it, like the rush of an illegal drug. Their darkness would bring her, heretofore, unknown power. It was hers, her destiny—all she had to do was accept it.

Then through the cloud of suffering and hopelessness that surrounded her, she heard a faint voice. The voice called to her. It called again and again without giving up. "Persey." Although it was only one word, it was enough. Her humanity recognized it. She knew that voice. It belonged to someone kind and good. "Persey, Persey, Persey," it called.

She remembered his most terrible secret was his desire to keep her safe from harm. It was Aaron. Throughout his life and into this dark Underworld, he was still her protector, her champion. Despite all evidence to the contrary, he still believed she was worth saving.

"PERSEY," he called to her again. His voice gave strength to all that was good inside of her.

"Aaron," she responded. "It's Aaron," she said as a feeling of light flooded over her. The light fed her humanity—made it strong again. She pushed her monster deep down into that place where it had always existed. "Aaron, he's here," she said. All the goodness that was Aaron Strait surrounded her. He held her, loved her, and believed in her.

The full import of Aaron's presence dawned on her and she turned to Haden. "Is he here?" she demanded. "Is he one of these souls in Hell?"

Haden looked at her but made no response. He made one last frantic attempt to shut her out. She felt him try to force her back to the surface of his mind where he could keep things hidden. But it was too late. He had kissed her. He had opened himself to her and allowed her to come to this place where darkness had almost overtaken her.

"Tell me Haden," she demanded, moving closer to him. "Tell me the truth."

"He does not belong to us," Haden whispered. His voice was small—almost defeated.

"He has been judged and you have no power over him?" she asked.

"Yes," he said after a moment's hesitation.

"And what about me, Haden" she asked. "Do I belong to you?" This time she didn't wait for an answer. She already knew it. She held his secrets. They were part of her—inescapable. She couldn't change the past but the future was hers. She let go and felt her body straining toward the light as though she were swimming up through endless murky waters.

She opened her eyes and pulled away from Haden, severing their bond. "You lied to me," she said. Her eyes burned into his. "You let me believe his death was my fault. I thought I owed you my soul." She took another step away from him. She could feel her body shaking as the true magnitude of her words sunk in. "I don't owe you anything. I never did."

"Persephone, wait," he said. He grabbed her roughly by one wrist and pulled her closer to him. "You've seen my kingdom. You lie to yourself if you think you don't belong there. After all, it is you who brought us to the darkest part of my realm."

"No!" she cried, shaking her head. "I don't belong there. You can't keep me because I've seen your secrets. I know I don't belong to you. I never did."

Haden caught her other wrist and pulled her closer up against him so that her body pressed against his. "I may not have anything left to hide," he whispered. "But don't forget I know your secrets too. I've seen your essence and I've felt your hunger. It is strong and someday it will resurface. When it does, I will be waiting."

Persey clamped her eyes closed. It was the only way to escape his eyes. They contained the swirling reflection of her inner monster—her terrible darkness. Their minds were conjoined. She knew his secrets and he knew her weakness. Slowly, his hands released their vice grip on her wrists. He walked across the room and she heard the door click softly behind him. Still, she remained frozen where she was with her eyes squeezed shut. Tears made their way out from underneath her eyelids and down her cheeks. She was crying with relief and with sadness. Haden was gone. She had won the battle but it had not been without cost.

When she opened her eyes, the first thing she saw was her own face. It was reflected back at her by the large mirror hanging on the wall across the room. She walked over to it, entranced by her own image. The face that looked back at her was beautiful. There was no doubt about it. The deep blue eyes, the perfectly molded mouth, the flawless skin framed by soft waves of hair. Even the most casual observer would be unable to find a fault.

Persey knew better. She understood what was hidden inside of her. The beautiful face she saw in the mirror was just a shell—a trick of the eyes designed to hide the darkness within her soul. She'd been to hell and back. She'd seen the monster that waited for her there. Her beauty was lost—even if she was the only one who could see the difference. Unable to meet her own eyes any longer, she turned her back on the mirror and headed toward the door. The elevator dropped her down to the main floor where she passed one last time through the lobby of the hotel and out into the welcoming night. She was headed towards Daniel—towards home. She had her freedom. In the end—beauty wasn't such a high price to pay.

Chapter Sixty-Six

It was early morning but Persey was already awake. She was thinking about all the things she needed to do. Since coming back to New York, she'd taken up residence in Daniel's spare bedroom. She loved him. She knew she did. But she also knew she couldn't move on until she'd made amends. Hence, the to-do list in her head. She sighed and shifted, making the bed springs creak. Outside the door, there was a soft knock.

"You awake?" Daniel asked, easing the door open an inch.

"Yes," she whispered, curling her legs up underneath her and sitting up in bed. He came in carrying a tray. "You don't need to bring me breakfast in bed every morning," she said with a smile.

He set it down on the nightstand and then sat down on her bed. "I have my own selfish reasons for coming into your bedroom every morning," he said, tucking a stray curl behind her ear.

"Really, like what?"

"Like this," he said as he kissed her. "And, maybe this." He moved closer to her—the breakfast tray forgotten as his kisses became more urgent. Persey wanted to let him stay, let him into the warmth of her bed but she couldn't. She couldn't start her new life until she'd said a proper good-bye to the old one.

"Daniel," she admonished, pulling back from him.

"I know, I know," he said relenting. "Are you sure you don't want me to go with you?" It was the same question he'd asked her every day since they'd been back in New York.

"Do you mean, have I changed my mind since yesterday?"

"I just want to be there—in case you need me."

"I do need you," she said, allowing her eyes to meet his. "And you were there for me when I needed you most. But this is something I have to do on my own."

She took a taxi to LaGuardia and boarded her flight to Des Moines, equipped with head phones and mindless reading; prophylactic measures against other people's confessions. In Des Moines, she located the airport rental car agency, and it wasn't long before she was speeding down I-35 towards her destination.

She was going to Clear Lake. Even if it no longer felt like home, it was still part of her. Its small town streets and surrounding fields held her memories and her past. The sun over Western Iowa was warm and strong—a late April gift to the residents of the state. She took the second exit off the freeway for Clear Lake and turned the car towards the center of town. Passing the Fareway grocery store where her mother used to shop, she noticed the "r" in the sign was faded, just as it had been when she was a kid. As she drove down Main Street and turned onto Second Avenue, she had the ridiculous feeling that nothing had changed—or ever would change—in Clear Lake. It was almost as if the town itself had been granted a special gift of immortality.

She parked the rental car in the small parking lot across the street from the Clear Lake Cemetery. The gate creaked when she opened it—just the way it had when she was a girl. Without hesitation, she made her way towards the oldest section of the cemetery, where the shade trees and overgrown rhododendrons protected the resident's eternal slumber.

The Campbell's were one of the first families in Clear Lake and, fittingly, their family plot was located in the oldest section of the cemetery. Persey wound her way through familiar gravestones—her grandmother and grandfather, great-uncles and aunts. Every surname in this part of the cemetery was the same. She'd visited this cemetery throughout her childhood, playing underneath the trees while her mother sat beside her father's grave. Later on, they'd brought flowers for her grandfather and then her grandmother—as those members of the family took their rightful places in the Campbell plot.

The headstone that sat next to her father's had to wait twenty years. But it was no longer blank. Two years ago, Persey had written the words that were etched into its cold, smooth surface. Two years ago, she'd watched as her mother was lowered into the ground. She sank down in front of the two headstones and traced the words on the cold marble with the tip of her finger. Demeter Ellen Campbell was in her final resting spot beside Michael James Campbell.

Persey had cared for her mother throughout her fatal battle with cancer. She'd been at her side and prayed for her survival—although, even as she whispered them—Persey understood the selfish nature of her prayers. Without her mother, she would be alone. The thought was terrifying. "Please, God, let her get better," were the words she murmured in the hospital chapel. What she really meant was, "Please God, don't leave me here all alone." Her prayers hadn't been enough. Now she understood they hadn't even been heard. The cancer progressed rapidly, ravaging and laying waste to its victim. It left Persey alone—frightened and numb.

She made the necessary arrangements for her mother's burial then fled Clear Lake, as though it was the site of a disaster. It was too painful to think about those last days. She'd locked the memories away, but here—in the cool grass next to her mother's grave—the memories came flooding back.

There was her mother—once so beautiful—but now frail and wasted in her sterile hospital bed, slipping in and out of consciousness. Persey knew she was dying but she couldn't—wouldn't admit it. During the last few moments of her mother's life, she seemed to regain her clarity.

"Persey," she whispered. "I need to tell you something."

"I'm here Mom." She took her mother's frail paper-thin hand in her own.

"Your father watches over you," her mother said. Demi met her daughter's eyes as though searching for confirmation that she was understood. "He has always has. He's always watched over you."

"What do you mean?" Persey asked, clutching at her mother's hand. The words had the feel of a secret. There was something more, something unexplained.

One time—and one time only—Persey had screwed up the courage to ask her mother about the discrepancies on her birth certificate and the strange certificate of adoption. "Persephone Campbell," her mother said, snatching the papers out of her hands.

"I don't know what kind of nonsense you have in your head or where you found those papers but I'll tell you one thing for certain. They don't belong in your room. They belong in my safe with all the other important papers. Michael Campbell was your father. Now I don't want to hear another word about this ever again. Do you understand?"

Persey understood. She'd never brought the subject up again, but here on her mother's death bed, a surge of irrational hope shot through her. She clutched her mother's frail hand in her own and said, "Who was my father? Mom, is he still alive?"

It was only then she realized the hand she held had ceased to exert any pressure. "Mom," Persey cried. "Mom, don't go." The rest of the memory was a jumble. There was the high-pitched static beep of the monitor. Then the nurses and doctors rushed in, crowding Persey away from her mother's bedside. Whatever measures of resuscitation they performed, it wasn't enough. Like everything else, it hadn't been enough. It was the ultimate irony. Demi Campbell joined her beloved husband and took her secrets with her. The girl, who heard everyone's secrets, was left to wonder whether her mother's last words were a confession or a metaphor.

The one thing Persey knew for certain is she'd been to the place where her parents' souls now resided. She hoped they were together. It made her feel less alone to think about them somewhere light, safe from the darkness that had threatened to consume her.

Haden had assured her there were places of safety and happiness in his Underworld. "There are beautiful places," he told her. "The souls who inhabit those places have lived lives entitling them to an eternity of peace and absence from suffering. Once you become my queen, you will begin to understand that each of them 'reaps what they sow'."

Persey opened the bag she was carrying and pulled out the bouquet of flowers she'd stopped to purchase at the airport florist. She separated two white roses from the other flowers and placed one on each of her parent's graves.

"May your harvest be peaceful and free from the torment of darkness," she whispered into the stillness of the late afternoon.

She retraced her steps away from her parent's final resting place, meandering through the familiar headstones. She was reluctant to leave this part of the cemetery but she still had one good-bye left to make. The trees and shrubs were smaller, more immature, in the modern section of the cemetery. The headstones were set in rigid, military lines with small holders containing plastic flowers. Everything looked new and shiny—like an antidote to the disease and ill-fate that had overtaken the bodies beneath the ground.

She found what she was looking for unexpectedly. The name engraved on the shiny black granite headstone brought her to a sudden stop and took her breath away.

Aaron Mathew Strait

1978-2010

Beloved Son, Brother and Husband

She stared at the words unable to move closer. Tears swam in her eyes. She wiped them away, knelt down and placed the rest of her white roses at the base of Aaron's headstone. She read the inscription on the cold granite again and swallowed hard. She had no right to be memorialized here. She hadn't come to Aaron's funeral. She hadn't grieved with his family. Her only contribution to his funeral had been to add insult to injury by not attending. And yet, in Aaron's place of eternal rest, he was remembered as a husband. Instead of living up to her responsibilities, she had hidden from her pain in the arms of another man. She had shirked her duty. Then Haden had come and it was too late to make things right.

Until this moment, she'd harbored no hope Aaron's family would ever understand or pardon her absence. But as she looked at the headstone and touched the word "Husband" she suddenly had hope.

"He was a good boy. I take it you knew him?" said a voice from behind her. The voice startled her and made her turn around quickly. A small elderly woman leaning heavily on a cane was making her way across the grass.

"Yes," said Persey, wiping away her tears as she glanced back at the headstone.

"Always sad when they pass so young," observed the woman in the tone of voice of one who has seen much suffering.

Persey nodded in silent agreement and together they contemplated the dates on Aaron's headstone. She glanced at the woman again. Something about her seemed familiar. Persey was struck with a rush of sudden anxiety. Could this be someone she knew? Was it one of Aaron's relatives, a great-aunt or a cousin she'd met long ago and since forgotten? She wanted this woman—whoever she was—to stop imposing herself, to leave her alone. This was her moment of private grief.

She knelt back down beside Aaron's grave. Instead of departing, the woman rested her knobby hand upon Persey's shoulder.

"How did you know him?" she asked.

Persey was silent for a moment. Then, without taking her eyes from Aaron's headstone, she said, "He helped me when I needed it most."

The woman bent down stiffly and picked up one of the roses Persey had laid on Aaron's grave. She held it in her hand for a moment, as if inspecting it, before plucking a discolored petal from its recesses. "Even things of beauty contain imperfection," said the woman, letting the brown petal drop to the ground. "Of course—no one understands that better than you."

Persey looked up at the old woman with a flash of annoyance. Her clear blue eyes met the rheumy brown ones, and she felt the horrible shock of recognition. She jumped to her feet. "No," she cried. "I don't owe you anything."

"You belong to me," insisted the old woman, advancing toward her.

"I don't," said Persey. "I never did and I never will." Her voice sounded hollow and unconvincing, even to her own ears.

"Give this to Daniel for me," said the old woman, thrusting the damaged rose back into Persey's hand. "He and this flower share a common fate. Death awaits them both. When it happens, I will be waiting. You can never escape me Persephone because I know what lives inside you. I am your destiny."

Persey ran. She ran away through the fading light of the cemetery. She knew death and darkness could follow her but for the moment she was safe. All she had was the future. She was determined not to waste it. The End.

A special preview of
Losing Hope
By Johanna Garth

And

Fantasy Island Book Publishing

Coming Fall 2012

Losing Hope

"Yet what difference does it make whether the women rule or the rulers are ruled by women? The result is the same."
Aristotle

Chapter One

Persey Campbell was in New York. No, she mentally corrected herself. She was home. New York was home because that's where Daniel was. That was the realization she'd had during her last night in Bangkok when she wasn't sure if she would ever see Daniel again. Home is where you love and are loved in return. Daniel loved her. And she loved him back. She was home.

It was almost evening, not quite dark yet. Together they threaded their way through the stalls and hordes of people in lower Manhattan's Chinatown.

"The restaurant doesn't look like much but the food is amazing," Daniel said as they sidestepped a family of tourists, followed closely by another family of second generation Chinese-Americans clutching their offspring tightly by the hand. A short burst of staccato syllables came from across the street. The shopkeeper closest to them leaned on her broom as her eyes swept over them in quiet assessment. She shouted something back across the street in incomprehensible Chinese.

Except, Persey thought as a cold chill ran down her spine, it wouldn't have been incomprehensible to Haden. Language wasn't a barrier to the lord of the Underworld. He spoke every language, and in the end, everyone spoke the language of death.

Her grip on Daniel's hand must have tightened because he stopped and glanced down at her. "You okay?" he asked.

"Yes." She nodded, letting her deep blue eyes meet the warm brown of his. "I'm fine."

And she was. She was fine. Haden could follow her but he couldn't claim her. He'd tricked her into believing she owed him something. He'd allowed her to believe he could harm the ones she loved (or rather had loved) because Haden's powers were strongest over those who were already in his kingdom of the dead.

But all along, he'd been lying. Persey understood that now. Everything he'd ever told her was lies and half truths. The only reason she knew this is because, as surely as Haden spoke the language of death, she spoke the language of secrets. His secrets were hers. Even though sometimes, when she woke in the night, her heart pounding and the dark piercing hunger swelling inside her like a beast that refused to be contained, she wished they weren't.

Except without the knowledge of his secrets she would have been lost. She would never have had the strength to find her way out of his dark clutches. Knowledge of Haden's secrets was a necessary evil, she reminded herself. The part of her hidden deep within—stowed away like some kind of alien invader—stirred at her recollection of evil. It was almost as though someone had mentioned it by name.

"The restaurant's just another two blocks," said Daniel, putting one arm protectively around her waist and pulling her closer.

Persey smiled up at him and leaned into the crook of his arm, relishing his warmth. She knew, almost without looking, that people were watching them as they passed. She also knew it was likely the shopkeeper's earlier comment had been about them. People always stopped to look at her, glancing furtively in her direction while she ate dinner in a restaurant, turning their heads to keep her in their line of sight a moment longer when she passed them on the street. It wasn't the attention that was new. It was the quality of the attention.

When she was with Daniel, people did more than stare. They smiled. It was as though something about the sight of Persey and Daniel together warmed people's hearts.

"Love is a beautiful thing, ain't it," said the cab driver who brought them home last night. His eyes met Daniel's knowingly in the rearview mirror. It was as though they were surrounded by some shining aura which announced them as public property— public property to all those who knew what it meant to be in love. Persey glanced up at Daniel again and unsuccessfully tried to hide a little smile.

"What?" he asked.

"Nothing, nothing at all. Are we almost there?"

"Almost," Daniel promised.

The first time Persey met Daniel Hartnett she had been a recent graduate from law school. She still remembered the way he'd looked a little bit like a movie star cast in the role of successful corporate lawyer. Even though he wasn't famous, there was something about the amused quirk of his mouth and his intelligent eyes that gave Persey the definite impression he'd spent most of his life getting exactly what he wanted. Some of that arrogance had diminished since she first sat across the desk from him answering his interview questions.

Although his manner was still casually charming, he had a few more wrinkles around the corners of his eyes. His smile wasn't quite as carefree. He'd experienced a year of loss and despair. If you looked deep enough you could still see the shadows of it in his eyes.

Not that Persey minded. In fact, at this point in her life it would have been impossible to trust anyone who hadn't experienced some kind of pain. She'd been to hell and she'd returned. Chances were slim she would be able to relate to anyone who didn't have a bit of darkness hidden within. The shadow in his smile and wrinkles around his eyes made him look like someone she could trust. And she did trust Daniel. She trusted him with her life. That being said, she was beginning to not trust that he knew where he was going.

"Hold on a sec," she said, stopping for a moment. She bent down and pulled up the strap of her sandal that kept slipping off her heel. "These aren't the best shoes for walking," she added, straightening back up.

He looked down at her with an amused smile. "Just around the corner, I promise."

Persey laughed. "I think you said that five minutes ago." She leaned in closer to him and tilted her face up towards his. Daniel quickly responded to the unspoken invitation. Neither one of them noticed the old woman with the curved spine who hobbled out of the doorway of a nearby building. Persey felt Daniel's lips as they brushed against hers. She closed her eyes and returned the pressure. His hand grabbed hers with a grip that was surprisingly firm. There was a moment where her brain registered the strange, rough texture of the hand that held hers before she felt the searing pain.

Persey whirled around. Her hand was held tightly by an old woman whose gray hair floated thickly around her wizened brown face. The eyes, boring into Persey's own, were like twin black holes. Persey jerked her hand hard but the old woman's grasp was strong and unyielding. The sudden movement only served to increase the throbbing pain until it radiated up her entire arm causing her to gasp out loud. A cold shiver of fear ran through her body and she was aware of gulping for air as though the woman had siphoned every bit of oxygen from the surrounding atmosphere.

In retrospect, she knew it all happened quickly. The whole encounter couldn't have lasted more than ten seconds. But in the moment before Persey forced herself to look deeply into the woman's eyes it seemed like an eternity passed. Persey's eyes met the woman's and, with a dizzying rush of relief, Persey understood the lord of the Underworld had not come to reclaim her.

"I know your secret," the woman whispered. Her speech was heavily accented with the tones of Eastern Europe. Instead of searching for an escape from the deep blue truth serum of Persey's eyes or spouting her darkest secrets, as most people did, the woman met her gaze. Her dark brown eyes bored into Persey's, as though she was searching for something.

"My secret?"

"You have secret. You think to hide, but I see it." The woman pulled Persey's hand closer to the breast of the shabby black dress she wore and bowed her head in a gesture of supplication. "Your secret is your destiny."

Persey felt the woman's grip on her hand tighten. As it did the searing sensation deepened, became almost unbearable. "Let go of me," Persey screamed trying to shake her off. The tangled head of grey hair reared back and an unearthly hiss emitted from her lips. Before either Daniel or Persey could react, the old woman pulled Persey's hand to her mouth and spit into its center. Pain, more intense than anything she'd felt before filled her body, followed by blood. It coursed down her arm pooling at her feet. Persey heard herself let out a little involuntary whimper as her knees buckled beneath her.

"Remember," hissed the woman as she leaned closer. The withered lips brushed Persey's ear as a word was whispered, soft and sibilant, and then there was only the pain. Strong arms caught her before she hit the ground. Persey felt her eyes flutter shut for a moment but she couldn't let go. It was too important that she remember. She turned her head, seeking the source of her pain, but the woman was gone. She had already slipped away into the crowded streets and the whispered word was gone too, as though it had been carried away in the folds of her dark dress.

Johanna Garth is a lawyer turned writer. She lives with her husband and two young children in Portland, Oregon. This is her first novel.

Her Web site is **www.johannagarth.com**.

Check out all of Fantasy Island Book Publishing's great books at your favorite retailer or: **www.fantasyislandbookpublishing.com**

CPSIA information can be obtained at www.ICGtesting.com
Printed in the USA
LVOW12s1526201113

362109LV00002B/236/P